ROYAL INSTITUTE OF MAGIC

The Shadowseeker

VICTOR KLOSS

An Original Publication From Victor Kloss

Royal Institute of Magic Elizabeth's Legacy
Written and published by Victor Kloss
Cover by Andrew Gaia
Formatted by Frostbite Publishing
Copyright © 2015 by Victor Kloss
All rights reserved.

www.RoyalInstituteofMagic.com

— CHAPTER ONE —

A New Commander

Date: *29th March 1603*

"Spellshooters are not permitted in Prince Henry's throne room."

The guard felt the full force of Michael James Greenwood's and Charlotte Rowe's stares. To his credit, he didn't flinch. Much.

Michael extended his hands, palms up. "Eric, how many times have you let me in fully armed when I was summoned by our last commander?"

Eric remained resolute. "The Queen is dead, Director. The prince has new rules."

Eric's crass remark almost earned him a black eye, but Michael swallowed his anger. The truth was, Eric, like everyone else at the Institute, was still reeling from the Queen's death.

Everyone except the Queen's son.

It had been only five days since she passed away, and Michael still half-expected Elizabeth to return from the dead. She had done it before.

"I'm sorry, Director Rowe, but your forreck is not allowed in either," Eric said. He had gone quite pale and was looking fearfully at the animal standing next to Charlotte. It was the size of a large tiger, with jet black fur, except for a white stripe that zigzagged down its back and covered its tail. The forreck's eyes were like two brilliant sapphires, and they stared right at Eric with the sort of zen-like calm that reminded Michael of a cat.

Charlotte raised an eyebrow. Though she was petite and almost doll-like in appearance with flawless skin and soft features, the steely determination in her large brown eyes and the five yellow diamonds floating above her shoulder made people stand up and take notice of the Director of Trade. Her hand stroked the forreck's forehead, which came up to Charlotte's shoulders.

"You wish to stop George from entering? That would not be wise. He may become angry if I leave him."

Michael almost felt sorry for Eric. If he let the forreck in, he would face the wrath of Prince Henry. If he didn't, he might face an angry forreck. As unpleasant as Prince Henry's wrath was, Michael knew there was only ever going to be one outcome.

4

"You may pass," Eric said, stepping aside, eyes still trained on the forreck.

"You're too kind," Michael said graciously, handing over his spellshooter with a mock bow.

Michael put his hand on the door but didn't open it immediately. His good humour was momentarily replaced with a frown, and he turned towards Charlotte. "Be careful what you say when we go in. We could be in danger, especially if Prince Henry talks about you know what."

"I will be on my guard," Charlotte said.

Michael opened the door; Charlotte and George followed him in.

Prince Henry sat on a gilded chair in the centre of a spacious, exquisitely furnished room. The last time Michael had been in here, Queen Elizabeth had sat in the chair. It didn't seem to suit the prince as well as it had the Queen; he sat awkwardly, his back so straight it was almost arched. Michael was again struck by how alike and yet different Henry was to his mother. He had the same curly auburn hair, hooked nose and peculiar gold tint in his eyes, but the calm, regal aura Elizabeth had was missing. Instead, his eyes seemed constantly narrowed, as if he suspected everyone and everything.

"Welcome, directors," Henry said. His eyes went straight to the forreck and Michael saw the prince fail to mask a flicker of fear. "It seems I need a new guard, one that will obey my orders and not allow dangerous animals in my vicinity."

"It is not Eric's fault, Your Highness," Charlotte said, with a small, but perfect curtsey. "It is safer for my forreck to remain with me."

"I see." The prince continued to regard the forreck, his lips pursed, fingers tapping the chair. "I believe it will soon be time to do something about forrecks. They are simply too dangerous to be roaming around."

"They helped us win wars," Charlotte said.

"Any animal that can best a dragon should be strictly controlled," Henry continued, either not hearing Charlotte or simply ignoring her. "Yes, I will do something about that during my reign."

Michael could sense Charlotte struggling to keep her temper. She made to reply, but Michael nudged her in the ribs.

"You summoned us, Your Highness?" Michael said, switching subjects.

Prince Henry finally looked away from the forreck. "Yes, I did. However, I was expecting all of you. Where are the other directors?"

"They will be here presently," Michael said.

The prince nodded. "I would have called this meeting sooner, but I have been extremely busy since my mother passed away. As you know, my mother and I often had differences of opinion when it came to governing the Institute, and there were several occasions where we didn't see eye to eye. One area in particular was her method for choosing her directors, the most senior of Institute positions, which should never be taken lightly."

Prince Henry paused, and Michael knew the prince was trying to build the suspense, but, to his disappointment, neither Charlotte nor Michael reacted.

"With that in mind, I will be conducting a thorough review to establish whether you are still the most suitable choices as directors of the Institute."

Michael had been expecting this and he remained impassive, though it didn't make it any easier to take. Charlotte made a small choking sound, but to her credit managed to stay calm.

"Queen Elizabeth promoted me to Director of Trade ten years ago and I have never let her down," Charlotte said. "I have opened up trade agreements with countless Unseen Kingdoms, which has helped the Institute flourish."

Prince Henry gave a curt nod before Charlotte had finished speaking, and Michael suspected he wasn't even listening.

"You two are the perfect example of my mother's poor decision making," the prince said, giving them a disapproving frown. "Your breeding, Michael, leaves much to be desired, coming from a poor baker family. And while you, Charlotte, are at least nobly born, I was always sceptical of having a woman in such a powerful position within the Institute. Indeed, the only director I am satisfied with is Lord Samuel."

Michael could have made several choice replies, but they would only get him in trouble. Prince Henry was just as stubborn as his mother and his mind would not be easily swayed.

"We will endeavour to prove ourselves worthy of our position," Michael said, giving a stiff bow. "Is there anything else you require of us?"

The prince nodded. "There is one other thing. My mother had an exquisitely crafted suit of armour that used to reside in this very room. Do you happen to know where it went?"

Michael feigned mild surprise. "No, I'm afraid not, Your Highness."

Prince Henry ran a hand over his chin thoughtfully. "That is most peculiar. You are sure you haven't seen it recently? I would very much like to have it. It has powerful magic that was specifically intended for my bloodline."

There was an edge to the prince's voice, and the gold flecks in his eyes seemed to glow for an instant. Michael was conscious of the guards surreptitiously putting their hands on their spellshooters, but unless they had death wishes, they wouldn't act while George was still in the room.

"I will issue a search for it immediately," Michael said.

There was a moment when the prince's narrowed eyes tried to bore holes through Michael, but the Spellsword Director met the prince's stare without flinching.

"Very well," the prince said finally. "I will expect a daily report on your progress. If it is not found within the week, I will not be pleased. You are dismissed."

Michael and Charlotte made their bows, and then left the throne room, George in tow. When Michael was sure they were out of earshot from any prying guards, he started talking, quickly and urgently.

"Find the others. I need to see them before the prince does."

"What are you going to do?" Charlotte asked.

"Each director needs to hide the piece of Elizabeth's Armour they were entrusted with. It needs to be done today, before Prince Henry can sniff them out. You can bet he has people searching for the Armour already."

"I have somewhere in mind," Charlotte said. She scowled suddenly and clenched her fists. "I've never wanted to hit a member of royalty before, until today. I can't believe how he insulted us."

"I'll deal with the prince," Michael said, his expression darkening. "We can't worry about that now. The Armour is far more important. It needs to stay safely hidden until Suktar's return."

They stopped by the double doors that led to the open gallery and the spiral staircase.

"I can't believe we will have to face Suktar again. When do you think he will resurface?"

Michael shrugged. "It could be months, years or it could be centuries. Should that happen, it will be up to our descendants to re-unite the Armour to stop Suktar."

Charlotte tugged her braid. "Centuries? The Institute may not even exist then, especially if we have many more Prince Henrys in command."

"The Institute will survive. It has to."

"What about our descendants?" Charlotte said. "We are asking a great deal of them. If they have to wait centuries, they may not even know about the Institute anymore."

"We have to make sure that doesn't happen," Michael said. He gave a sudden grin, his eyes sparkling. "As for our descendants, we Greenwoods have a long history of getting things done. Whether it's one year or five hundred, I'm confident my family will be able to re-unite the Armour and topple Suktar once and for all."

"I wish I shared your optimism," Charlotte said.

Michael put a friendly arm around Charlotte's shoulder. "We Greenwoods are also optimists. You should try it sometime; it makes life a lot easier. Come, let's get back to work. We have much to do."

— CHAPTER TWO —
The Wait is Over

Present Day

A sharp rapping on Ben Greenwood's door woke him with a start.

"Ben Greenwood!" His step-grandmother Anne's voice was even shriller than usual. "I don't know what you think you're playing at, but it's 7:36am and there's no milk in the house. You know how much I enjoy my tea while I watch the morning news. Is this some sort of cruel joke?"

Ben thought about trying to drown his grandma out by putting a pillow over his head, but her voice could penetrate a three-foot-thick steel vault. He sat up and yawned.

"There was milk last night when I checked," Ben said, his voice croaky from sleep.

"That was barely enough for my Coco Pops this morning. How many times have I told you to keep at least two cartons in the fridge?"

"None," Ben said softly to himself. Then in a louder voice he said, "I'll go get some, Grandma."

"I need it in the next ten minutes, so get a move on." She gave another rap on his door. "And stop calling me Grandma. Do you ever listen to me?"

"I try not to," Ben said, making no attempt to keep his voice down.

There was a huff from the other side of the door and then some muttering – Ben heard the words "ungrateful" and "selfish" mentioned – before Anne headed back downstairs.

Normally Ben would go straight back to bed – after all, it was the start of the summer holidays and no self-respecting teenager would be up before 8am. But today was different. Today was special. Today was his first day as an apprentice at the Royal Institute of Magic.

Ben sprang out of bed, heady with excitement. It had only been a couple of weeks since his adventures at the Institute, but when he had been told he would have to wait until the end of July to start the apprenticeship, it had seemed a lifetime away. Each day seemed to contain twice as many hours and he and Charlie had exhausted every possible subject on the Institute until there was nothing left to do but wait patiently. Patience was not one of Ben's strengths.

Suppressing another yawn – he had trouble getting to sleep last night – Ben threw on a pair of his newer jeans and a plain white t-shirt. He spent a moment in the bathroom taming his wavy blond hair. His deep blue eyes were full of life and showed no sign of his poor night's sleep.

Ben hurried downstairs. The kitchen was a mess again, filled with dirty dishes. The fridge was left ajar – probably from Anne's search for milk – and from it came an unpleasant smell. Ignoring the urge to clean up, Ben headed out to the corner store to get some milk.

It was 8:15am by the time Ben had returned and downed some breakfast. He went back to his room, preferring to keep his distance from his grandma and the blaring TV she had on. Charlie was due over in fifteen minutes and together they would set off to the Institute. Ben found himself checking the time every thirty seconds.

Ben couldn't decide what he was most looking forward to: the apprenticeship programme; the Unseen Kingdoms; the magic; the ridiculously cool dragon transport system; or the Institute itself. More significantly, he would have the chance to keep looking for his parents. They were out there somewhere. He was sure he had seen them during the final battle at the Floating Prison. Why they hadn't come back for him was still a mystery that constantly played on his mind, and he was determined to find out.

His thoughts were disrupted by a buzzing in his pocket. He pulled his mobile out and saw a text from Charlie.

"I'm outside. Can you come out? I'd rather not have another encounter with the devil (carefully disguised as your grandma)."

Ben grinned, grabbed the backpack he had packed last night and bounded down the stairs three at a time.

"I'm going out for the day," Ben told his grandma. She was facing the TV with her back to him, but turned around slowly in her swivel recliner.

"I hope you're going to look for a job," she said, eyeing him suspiciously. "You need to start pulling your weight around here at some point. My pension isn't designed for two."

"I've got a job," Ben said firmly. "In fact, that's where I'm going now." He gave her a friendly wave and his most impudent grin. "I'll be back late, so don't wait up."

He left before she could respond with another barbed comment and found Charlie outside, standing by a large tree in front of the neighbour's house.

"I needed the tree to hide behind in case your grandmother stepped outside," Charlie explained, as they started down the road together. "I swear she can sense when I'm around; it's uncanny and, frankly, quite scary."

Almost as scary as his grandma, in Ben's opinion, were the clothes Charlie was wearing. He had a blue and white chequered shirt with beige trousers – both looked like they'd been ironed to within an inch of their lives. His black leather shoes shone as if he'd spent the last hour buffing them and he wore a large backpack with both straps over his shoulders. It was clearly heavy because he was hunched over while carrying it, making him look even smaller than usual. There was even a gleam of sweat on his forehead.

"I want to make a good impression," Charlie said, when Ben questioned his choice of clothes. "I know you'll breeze through the apprenticeship programme, but it's not going to be easy for me."

"I doubt that," Ben replied. "Anyway, there will be plenty of studying to do, which you're great at. We have a whole new world to learn about. You'll be fine, trust me."

Charlie brightened a little, and started to show some of the excitement that was threatening to burst at Ben's seams.

"I can't believe we're finally going," Charlie said. "I had to make up the most terrible lie to fool my parents. I told them I'd been accepted for an apprenticeship programme at a respectable web design firm. They took it rather well, but I have a feeling Wren had one of her Spellswords do some sort of magic to help them buy it."

"Wouldn't surprise me," Ben said. "Anyway, your parents work all hours of the week, right? And you'll be home on the weekends."

"Yeah," Charlie said, lapping up the support. "They won't miss me. So, what do you think our first day will be like? I've gone over it in my head a hundred times and each one is different."

They talked with growing excitement for the next twenty minutes through the dull housing estate to the town centre. The weather was perfect, with blue skies and a bright sun beaming down on them, adding to their good moods.

"Did you hear that?" Charlie asked suddenly, raising a chubby finger. He rolled his eyes, indicating that the sound came from behind.

Ben glanced casually backwards and saw two men in suits walking behind them, deep in conversation. Ben perked his ears up to listen.

"...I've seen four Wardens already," the taller of the two was saying. "I've never seen so much security around the Croydon headquarters before."

Ben couldn't believe they were talking so openly about the Institute on such a busy street. There were people constantly walking alongside and past them. Strangely, nobody seemed interested in what the two men were saying. Was everyone completely lost in their own worlds or was there something more to it?

"I've seen five Wardens," the smaller man was saying. "You didn't see the one at the corner just now. Slim fella, easy to miss. There are probably half a dozen others we missed. The good ones are impossible to spot. You think this is all because of the dark elves?"

"Course it is," the taller one said. His voice was deep and gruff, even for his size. "The Institute has been on alert for the last couple of weeks. Haven't you heard the rumours about the invasion on Fiorgan?"

"I heard the dark elves were threatening to attack, but they haven't done anything yet."

The tall man gave a humph. "Could happen any moment. I heard there have been plenty of troop movements – and that's *not* rumour. Let's not forget how tactically important Fiorgan is. It's the gateway to Europe."

"I know how important it is; I'm not an idiot," the small man said, resentment in his voice. "But why would they post so many Wardens here?"

"Because the dark elves are masters at creating havoc. It wouldn't surprise me if they sent all manner of creatures here to raise hell and distract the Institute."

"That's true," the small man conceded. He paused for a moment and then, in a lighter tone of voice, said, "What did you think of United's performance yesterday? I can't believe they let in two goals right at the end."

Ben stopped listening and turned to Charlie; his eyes were wide, his sizeable cheeks flushed.

"That was interesting," Ben said. He gave a quick look round, but could see no sign of anyone who looked like a Warden.

"I wonder if the Wardens are here for another reason," Charlie said.

"What do you mean?"

Charlie gave a surreptitious look around, before leaning into Ben. "What if they are here to protect you from the dark elves?"

Ben scoffed at the idea. "Me? I don't think so. I'm not that important."

Charlie wagged a chubby finger at him. "No, you're not. But you're the link to your parents, remember? And the dark elves still want them. What's to say they won't make another move for you to try to get to your parents again?"

"Possibly," Ben said. "I just can't believe the Institute would go through all that trouble to protect me. After all, they don't even know *why* the dark elves want my parents."

This time both he and Charlie looked around, to make sure nobody was close by.

"I've been thinking about Elizabeth's Armour," Charlie said, his voice now a whisper. "How much do the dark elves know?

Are they aware that it's split up into different families? If so, are they also hunting the other families?"

Ben had spent countless hours thinking the same thing. "It's impossible to know. But if they are, then it's going to be twice as hard for my parents, trying to avoid the dark elves and get to the other descendants before the dark elves do."

Charlie tapped his chin thoughtfully, but any reply he might have made was drowned out by a succession of beeping cars. They had entered the heart of the town and the roads were jammed as everyone rushed to work. The pavement was equally busy, with men and women on phones, listening to their iPods or just lost in their own worlds. A few people filtered into coffee shops, but most hurried past the high street, with the single intention of getting to their offices before the clock struck nine.

Ben knew the Institute's Croydon headquarters were difficult to spot, despite knowing the exact location. Sure enough, his eyes wandered past the O2 mobile store to the Starbucks coffee shop several times before he spotted the building in the middle. It was small, squeezed in between the two, and purposefully unassuming. Above the revolving door and frosted windows, inlaid into the brickwork, was the R.I.M. logo, cast in bronze and overlaying a royal coat of arms. In front of the door was the same bulky bodyguard they had encountered when they first entered.

Ben felt a thrill of excitement from his back down to his toes. Just beyond those innocent-looking revolving doors had been an adventure that had changed their lives just two weeks ago.

"Look at that guy," Charlie said. He was pointing to a slim man dressed in casual clothes, standing outside Starbucks holding a hot drink. Ben noted the way he was looking closely at everyone who entered the Institute.

"You think he's another Warden?" Ben said.

"I think so. I wonder how many more there are around?"

"Several probably," Ben said. He drew out his brand new ID card. It was made of silver and was heavy enough to feel valuable. Next to the embossed logo on the card the name "Ben Greenwood" was etched.

"Shall we go in?" Ben asked Charlie, with a grin.

— CHAPTER THREE —
Unexpected Trouble

The inside of the headquarters was just as Ben remembered. There was one long room, with a high ceiling and a pristine white marble floor. To the right was a reception desk, with several busy secretaries typing away, dealing with enquiries in person or on the phone. At the back of the room, perfectly camouflaged against the wall, was the lift that had plummeted them deep underground like a roller-coaster a few weeks earlier.

Last time the reception had been almost empty, but now there were plenty of people about, many milling by the lift; Ben supposed it was because everyone was heading to work.

"I hope there is a variable speed setting," Charlie said, putting a hand on his little pot belly as they walked to the lift. "I don't know about you, but I had a big breakfast that I'd like to keep down."

They joined a small line that had formed to get into the lift. Charlie waited patiently, Ben less so, but the line was not moving very fast. In fact, Ben realised after a couple of minutes, it wasn't moving at all.

"What's going on?" a fuzzy-haired lady asked, standing directly in front of them. "I have to be at the Institute by 9:30 or Mr. Ludwig is going to have a fit."

She wasn't alone in voicing her frustration. There was a growing murmur of discontent. The lift was stuck on the bottom floor and wasn't coming back up.

"Not the best start to our first day," Charlie commented.

"Does the lift break down often?" Ben asked the fuzzy-haired lady.

"It can't break; it's operated by magic. Some idiot is purposefully holding it at the bottom."

"Why would they do that?"

"I have no idea; it's never happened before. But they're going to be in deep trouble, making everyone late for work." The lady turned back around and joined the complaints that had now grown from a murmur to something more vocal.

Ben felt his stomach lurch, as if he had begun his descent down the lift. "Something's not right."

Charlie groaned. "I hate it when you say that."

"There are Wardens everywhere watching for something - and now the lift gets stuck?"

"You think something bad is happening down there?"

"I could be mistaken," Ben admitted. "I'm sure they have extensive security to stop the wrong people leaving the Unseen Kingdoms."

Charlie shook his head a little too vigorously. "Your sixth sense is better than Spiderman's." He pulled a handkerchief from his pocket and dabbed his gleaming forehead. "Should we tell someone?"

"I don't think they have as much faith in my sixth sense as you do."

Charlie looked around anxiously. There were now several people lined up behind them. "Do you think we should step out of line? Maybe get a little closer to the exit, just in case?"

"Absolutely not," Ben said. "You're overreacting, as usual."

A sudden cheer drowned out Charlie's reply. The lift was moving again. Ben could hear a faint humming as it ascended from deep underground. The line in front shuffled forwards a bit, eager to get in; at the same time Charlie shuffled backwards, apologising profusely to the young man he bumped into from behind.

There was a ding as the lift arrived. The doors opened.

Silence. Then a collective gasp.

An explosion almost burst Ben's eardrums and sent several Institute members closest to the lift flying. An alarm sounded, loud enough to drown out the screams and shouts of surprise and horror.

Some of the Institute members fled as fast as they could, but others came forwards, grim-faced, drawing their spellshooters.

"Defensive line!" a deep voice sounded from behind.

Ben felt a tug on his sleeve. He turned and saw a white-faced Charlie screaming at him.

"Let's get out of here!"

But Ben didn't move. Many of those in front of him had fled or been blasted away, and he could almost see inside the lift.

Spells of every colour and shape were now being fired. Ben couldn't believe anything could survive such an onslaught, but it was clear that the enemy was still fighting. A woman went down in front of him and suddenly the path was clear to the lift and the enemy within – the unmistakable form of a dark elf sat on top of a huge panther.

Unlike the shoulder-length hair of most dark elves Ben had seen, this one was completely bald, with gold piercings in his nose, slanted ears and both eyebrows. In one hand he held a sword, and in the other a purple ball of energy.

With a blank, almost bored expression, he rode out of the lift, hacked down the nearest Institute member, and blasted another against the wall. The dark elf dodged and swayed the incoming spells with an inhuman dexterity, and the panther's snapping jaws consumed any that came its way with only the faintest repercussions.

"Earth and air!" someone shouted.

The shape and form of the spells changed and the dark elf took a hit on the shoulder, stopping him in his tracks. Slowly the Institute closed in on the elf and his steed. In response, the elf raised his head so that he was staring at the ceiling. With a hideous choking sound, he opened his mouth and out came a dozen large purple-winged moths. They soared upwards and evolved, growing arms, legs, and faces that reminded Ben of hungry piranhas. There was a moment of stunned silence as the moths transformed into spear-wielding pixies; then came the sound of a dozen high-pitched war cries and the spears were hurled down. Ben ducked as one soared over his head. Spellshooters rose and blasts of ice shot into the air. Several pixies went down in a frozen heap. Having expended their spears, the remaining pixies dived down, their claw-like hands extended and gnashing teeth bared.

The attack on the dark elf had momentarily stalled as the Institute took on their new adversary, allowing the dark elf, still mounted on the panther, to step forwards. Blood seeped from the dark elf's shoulder, but he showed little sign of pain.

He was heading in Ben's direction, but it was impossible to tell if Ben was the intended target or if he was just in the elf's way.

"Ben!"

Ben turned so quickly his neck cracked. Charlie lay on the ground in a ferocious wrestling match with one of the pixies. Their hands were locked together and the pixie's sharp teeth were closing in on Charlie's neck. Ben dived onto the pixie, knocking him off Charlie and they landed heavily on the floor. The pixie flew back onto his feet, but Ben was ready, and when the pixie came at him, snarling and snapping, Ben launched a right hook into his jaw. The pixie reeled. A second hook and the pixie went down in a heap.

"Can we go now?" Charlie asked, getting to his feet, his eyes darting this way and that, looking for the next pixie that might dive bomb him. The gleeful shouts from the pixies were turning into howls of anger as they were taken down by the Institute. Ben picked up one of the spears littered on the floor and turned back to the dark elf. The panther and its rider were now less than ten feet away and closing with every step, despite the spells that came their way. Was it coming for him or just trying to get outside? Ben knew he just had to step aside to find out, but he didn't. He couldn't just let the dark elf escape without doing something. A rational part of him knew that any effort he made to stop it would be futile, but rationality was buried deep beneath a raw, almost suicidal, determination to act.

He stood firm, spear in hand, ignoring Charlie tugging at his arm, until the dark elf's sword was almost in reach. He tensed himself; he had one chance with the spear, but he had to get the timing exactly right. The dark elf flicked his blade forwards with inhuman speed and, before Ben could blink, he saw the hilt of the sword flying towards his temple.

A streak of silver lightning hammered into the dark elf's chest, followed by a glowing black cannon ball that struck the panther directly on the head, producing a sickening crunch. The dark elf flew back and crashed against the wall in a crumpled heap. The remaining pixies vanished with a pop. There was a stunned silence, broken only by heavy breathing and several groans of pain. It took Ben a moment to realise that a spark had deflected the elf's sword coming at him. Hen turned to the source of the spells.

Two men had entered the room side by side, both holding spellshooters. They stood out as the only ones walking, while the rest stood and stared. One was short and stout, with heavy eyebrows, a scruffy beard and a scar that ran along his chin. The other wore a Jedi-styled, blue, hooded cloak, and in his spare hand was a Starbucks that he sipped as he walked. He had bright eyes, wavy hair and lips that seemed creased in a permanent little smile. Both had five diamonds floating above their shoulders – the short one's were red; the cloaked one's, yellow.

Ben's emotions couldn't have contrasted greater as he looked at the two men. Draven, the stocky one, seemed to have a personal vendetta against his family and had been responsible for labelling his parents as traitors to the Institute. Alex, on the other hand, was a close friend of his parents and was one of the few Institute directors to stand up for them.

"Nice shot, Draven," Alex said, taking another sip of his Starbucks.

"Nice?" Draven scoffed. "I just took out a deema in one shot. Do you know how tough they are?"

Alex gave a gentle roll of his eyes. "Let's not get cocky. The deema is but a distant relative of the forreck."

"Anything related to the forreck is deadly," Draven grunted. They had made it to the deema and Draven gave it a kick in the head and chest. The animal didn't move.

"What spell grade did you use?"

"Five," Draven said, still looking at the beast. "You?"

"Five as well, just to be sure. That spell cost me a week's wages."

They moved to the dark elf. This time Alex bent down to inspect, lifting the elf's head with rather more delicacy than Draven had done to the deema. When he got back up, Ben saw a flash of rare concern cross his face.

"Looks like a Shadowseeker," Alex said, in a soft voice that Ben could only just hear. "I haven't seen one of them in a while."

Draven's face was grim. "We'll have to summon the council."

Alex stood up and Draven turned to face everyone; most were still staring at them.

"Alright, listen up!" Draven said. Ben had forgotten how deep and powerful his voice was. "I want all expert Spellswords and Wardens and any master Traders, Scholars or Diplomats with me. We're going to clean up this mess. The rest of you, get out – you'll just get in the way. We'll call you when the lift is back in service. I have half a dozen medics on their way for those who need help."

Immediately diamonds started appearing over people's shoulders and members either gathered around Draven or left – some hobbling – through the revolving doors. Ben and Charlie made to go, but Alex caught their eyes.

"Morning, guys," he said, looking at them both in turn. "Are you both okay?"

"Yeah."

"Other than nearly being ripped to shreds by demon pixies," Charlie said. "Is this normal for a morning commute to the Institute?"

Alex smiled. "It's not normally this exciting, but we've been having a bit of trouble with the dark elves lately." His eyes lingered on Ben, but he added nothing further.

"What is a Shadowseeker?" Ben asked.

The same flash of concern Ben had seen moments earlier resurfaced. "Now isn't the time for a lesson in the dark elf special forces units. I'll explain when you get into the Institute, I promise." He gave them both a friendly slap on the shoulder. "It's going to be an uncommonly interesting Monday morning, so I'd better be going. I'll see you both later."

They watched him leave, and then Charlie turned to Ben.

"What shall we do while we wait?"

"Starbucks," Ben said.

"I was hoping you'd say that."

— CHAPTER FOUR —

Journey to the Institute

An hour passed before it was safe to travel. They left Starbucks and found a crowd of Institute members waiting for the lift. The dark elf attack was the topic on everyone's lips and both Ben and Charlie listened intently as they waited in line. Most seemed to agree that the dark elf was here to create havoc as part of their plan to distract the Institute while they continued their planned invasion on Fiorgan. Ben's ears perked up whenever he heard the word "Shadowseeker", but short of being some sort of special dark elf, nobody seemed to know much about them.

Charlie groaned when they reached the front of the line and the lift opened before them. Ben felt a tinge of excitement as they stepped into the large cubicle. Facing them were rows of black leather seats, complete with arm- and headrests. Each seat had a padded bar that you could pull down over your chest and, once more, Ben was reminded of a roller-coaster ride.

"I hope this thing doesn't go as fast as last time," Charlie said, as they picked two chairs in the centre and buckled up. The majority of the people kept talking as though the lift's speed was insignificant, though Ben did notice a few pale faces.

The lift closed and they started a slow descent. Ben gripped the armrests, waiting with growing anticipation for the sudden drop.

"It's a slow count to ten," a gentleman to Ben's left said. "Once you know when it's going to happen, it's not so bad."

"What are we on now?" Ben asked.

"Eight. Nine."

"Oh god!" Charlie said, in a soft squeal.

"Ten."

The lift plummeted and Ben gasped, his momentary alarm quickly turning into exhilaration. He just about resisted the urge to fling his arms into the air and whoop with delight – that might have looked slightly childish.

Unlike most roller-coasters, which last just seconds, the lift kept on dropping. Ben was almost getting used to the sensation and even Charlie had stopped groaning when the lift finally slowed and came to a gentle stop. The door opened with a soft ding.

A stone corridor greeted them, lit by torches hanging from the walls. Ben found himself grinning, remembering their astonishment the last time they had been here. Ben and Charlie joined the small throng of people walking two abreast along the passage.

They walked until they reached the small security chamber, where a small line had formed. When it was Ben's turn to enter, his eyes immediately went to the small sign that had so astonished him on his first visit.

"Warning:

"Electronics at serious risk of spontaneous combustion beyond this point. Please dispense with all such items before proceeding through the arch.

"Maximum penalty for smuggling science: £10,000 and three years in prison."

A large lady beckoned him forwards and Ben approached the stone wall on the left. He quickly spotted the tiny slot between the stones that had so baffled him last time. He inserted his ID card and watched in fascination as the stone in front of him faded away, revealing a small empty cubicle within the wall. He put his phone in, removed the card, and the stone faded back into existence. Then it was through the archway embedded with the large green eye, which watched Ben closely as he passed underneath.

"You know what I can't understand?" Charlie asked, glancing back at the arch before they continued on their way. "How did the dark elf get through all this to make it to the lift? How did it even get onto the Dragonway? It's not like it was hard to spot – it was riding a huge panther thing."

"I was wondering the same thing," Ben said. "Do you remember Alex's reaction when he identified the dark elf?"

"As a Shadowseeker," Charlie said, nodding. "I've never seen him that concerned, and we've seen him facing a few tight spots."

"Maybe Natalie will know what a Shadowseeker is."

"She doesn't."

"What do you mean?" Ben asked, slowing down in surprise. "You've asked her?"

Charlie's sizeable cheeks reddened. "I emailed her when we were in Starbucks."

"You have her email address?"

Charlie's words came out in a sudden rush. "She gave it to me before we left. I knew how difficult the apprenticeship was going to be, so I wanted to pick her brains and learn as much as possible. I know I should have told you, but somehow it never came up."

Charlie was fiddling with one of his shirt buttons, his brow furrowed.

"That's great, Charlie," Ben said, with a reassuring smile. "It makes sense to learn as much as possible."

"You're not upset?"

"Of course not."

Charlie's eyes narrowed. "Did she give you her email address too?"

"No, she didn't," Ben said. He looked ahead, suddenly hoping to see the Croydon Dragonway station.

"So you haven't been in touch with her these last couple of weeks?"

Ben sighed. "We've texted each other a few times."

"What?" Charlie's voice rose an octave. It echoed down the tunnel and several people looked round. Then in only a slightly softer voice, he said, "How did you get her number?"

"I asked her for it," Ben said. "It's not a big deal. I don't have a fancy phone with email and my internet connection at home is useless, so I got her number instead."

As he feared, Charlie suddenly looked like a deflated balloon.

It was time to play the white lie card.

"We only spoke once or twice," Ben said. "Talking to her about the Institute just made me miss the place more."

That seemed to do the trick. Charlie's face relaxed and he even managed an embarrassed smile. But whatever he was about to say was cut short by a sudden gust of wind. The London

Underground symbol was hanging from the ceiling in front of them – a red circle with a blue horizontal bar, which had the word "Croydon" written on it.

Thoughts of Natalie vanished. They grinned at each other and rounded the corner.

"All aboard! Nonstop to Taecia. Hop to, ladies and gents, she's not going to hang around."

The cry came from a pot-bellied goblin, who was waving people onto the Dragonway. Despite the warning of departure, Ben found it impossible not to stop and stare. A long dragon with scaly skin and stubby leathery wings sat on all fours, attached to a dozen bright red carriages. The half-doors were open, with passengers of all shapes and sizes getting on. Ben was reminded of the trams at theme parks, which took you from the car park to the entrance. Just like last time, there were three elves saddled on the back of the dragon's neck, each holding a harness.

"There – two empty seats," Ben said, pointing to a carriage near the back. He was forced to cut in front of a couple of elderly men to claim the seats he had spotted. They crammed in, Ben giving the angry men an apologetic wave.

The goblin whistled and, with a gentle jerk, the carriages started to trundle along, into the blackness of the tunnel.

Ben only relaxed once the dragon had accelerated to cruising speed, flying just below the tunnel's ceiling, and the invisible barrier had blocked out the screaming wind. He shared a relieved smile with Charlie, and settled down.

Ben's mind drifted to the Institute and the apprenticeship programme. He had absolutely no idea what it would entail. He had asked Natalie, but she had told him it was confidential. Ben was confident in his own abilities, but it was hard not to be slightly unnerved by the unknown. They had only spent a few days in the Unseen Kingdoms and at the Institute; they knew almost nothing about it. How much of a disadvantage would that be?

Beside him, Charlie wore an anxious frown, no doubt wondering the same thing, but perhaps for different reasons. The study – if there was much to be done – would hold no fear for Charlie, but what about the practical exercises? Ben smiled. Between the two of them they could produce the perfect apprentice.

The conductor's voice brought him out of his revere. "Ladies and gentlemen, we are approaching Taecia. We will be coming out of Dragon Flight momentarily. Have a pleasant day."

The dragon slowed, and Ben's stomach squashed against the metal seat belt. The carriage wheels screeched as they touched the ground. There was a loud bang and the invisible barrier vanished, letting in the rushing air. Soon the dragon was cantering no faster than a horse. The tunnel started heading upwards and they exited into bright sunlight. The dragon came to a gentle halt at the station of Taecia, steam and tendrils of fire hissing from its nostrils.

They stepped out of the carriage onto the platform. It had only been two weeks since they were last here, but Ben felt dazzled all over again. The station itself didn't look too different from those at home, barring the dragons pulling the carriages and the obvious lack of anything electrical. There were a dozen platforms, with stairs on each of them leading to an overhead walkway and the station's exit. It was the people at the station that made Taecia so different. Ben saw pixies flying just above head height, squat dwarves with beards that swept the ground, and a few seven-feet trolls carved from rock.

Ben and Charlie were so busy looking at everyone that by the time they reached the station's exit, those who had joined them on the Dragonway were long gone.

"I guess nobody's meeting us here," Charlie said.

Ben inhaled deeply, taking in the incredible sights and sounds. There were rows of timber-framed houses with lead windows, reminding him of the really old streets back home. The road was cobbled and filled with horses and other animals only found in fairy tales and video games.

"You were expecting an escort?" Ben asked, as they set off up the great hill that led to the Institute.

Charlie looked a little disappointed and mumbled something under his breath; Ben was fairly sure he heard the name Natalie but let it slide.

They made their way through a hodgepodge of winding lanes and crooked intersections, always taking the turn that would continue their course up the hill. Occasionally they had to watch out for horses and open-top antique cars, often driven erratically by dwarves that Ben suspected had a little too much to drink. The buildings got bigger and the roads, such as they were, became wider as they neared the Institute at the crest of the hill. Trees and torch-lit lampposts started lining the cobbled path and they soon had a clear view of the stone wall that surrounded the Institute. The only way in was through a large open gate, guarded by two armed Institute members. Ben thought they might have to produce their ID cards, but the guards nodded at them when they approached and let them through, into an open courtyard consisting of manicured gardens, trimmed hedges and an elaborate water fountain.

Ben's excitement had been steadily building, but instead of rushing to the entrance, both Ben and Charlie stopped to admire the magnificent building before them. The Institute was a mansion as grand as any of the great historic houses in England. The white façade was criss-crossed with timber panels and leaded windows. Dozens of gables and balconies spanned the building, giving the building a majestic, yet cosy feel. A pair of mighty wooden doors stood at the entrance. Above them the words "Royal Institute of Magic" were etched and seemed to pulse with a warm, silver glow.

"You ready?" Ben asked, glancing over at Charlie.

Charlie was staring up at the Institute, looking a little daunted. "Kind of. I'm feeling nervous and excited at the same time. Is that possible?"

"Course it is," Ben said, giving Charlie a friendly slap on the shoulder.

"What do we do once we get in? I mean, are we expected? What if nobody is there to help us?"

Ben grinned. "Let's find out, shall we?"

Together, they walked up to the doors of the Institute, pulled the grand iron door knob, and entered.

— CHAPTER FIVE —

Master of Apprentices

The sky-lit atrium looked every bit as magnificent as Ben remembered. There were exposed wooden beams everywhere. An old-fashioned staircase snaked its way up the building, leading to the open galleries above. In the centre of the lobby stood a magnificent statue of Queen Elizabeth.

"In or out? You can't just stand there," an impatient voice said from behind.

Ben realised they were blocking the entrance. With an apology, they shuffled forwards into the lobby. As soon as Ben took his eyes off the magnificent architecture, he noticed something very different to his last visit. The place was buzzing. Institute members, adorned with diamonds of varying colours, went to and fro, up and down the stairs, and even into doors Ben had never noticed before, within the lobby itself.

"Now what?" Charlie asked, watching an elderly gentleman with three white diamonds talk animatedly to a couple of colleagues.

"We ask someone," Ben said.

Charlie made a face. "Who? Everyone is walking a million miles an hour. I feel like we'd get our heads chopped off for stopping any of these people."

"I'll do the asking," Ben said, his eyes narrowing on a younger fellow with only one red star.

"Mr. Greenwood. Mr. Hornberger."

Ben turned and saw a small, round figure marching towards them. It took Ben a moment to realise that it was a woman. She walked like a drill sergeant and even had a peculiar baton tucked under an arm. Her feet were so large they reminded him of a clown and they pounded the stone floor. Her only concessions to femininity were her ponytail that went all the way down her back and her long eyelashes, which looked out of place in a face so angular it could have been carved from rock. Above her shoulder were four white diamonds, marking her as a Scholar.

"Oh god, it's a female Mr. Bullins," Charlie said anxiously, referring to their army-like sports teacher.

"Relax, Charlie."

Ben took a step forwards to meet the lady. She barely came up to his shoulder, but there was an air of authority about her, from her posture to the slightly raised chin, making her size irrelevant.

"My name is Dagmar Borovich," she said, thrusting a small hand out, which Ben took. Her grip threatened to stop the flow of blood to his fingers. Charlie winced and fervently massaged his hand back to life after his handshake.

"I am the Master of Apprentices. Welcome to the Institute. Please follow me," she said. Her voice was serious but not unkind. She gave them both searching looks as she spoke, and Ben could tell he was being assessed. He matched her gaze, and was quietly pleased that Charlie did too. Dagmar gave a little nod and turned around, heading for the stairs.

"Walk by my side, please; I prefer to see my apprentices' faces when I speak to them," Dagmar said, without turning round. There was no anger in her voice, but her no-nonsense tone reminded Ben of a number of school teachers.

Ben and Charlie exchanged looks, before joining Dagmar on either side.

"Where are we going?" Ben asked.

"To the Department of Apprentices," Dagmar replied. Ben was pleased to note he wasn't reprimanded for asking questions. "We are going to drop your bags off and then head straight to the Initiation Test."

Charlie made a noise. "I'm sorry – the what?"

"You are to be tested," Dagmar said, matter-of-factly. "Before you start the apprenticeship programme, we need to establish if you are suitable."

Ben noticed Charlie's face getting redder by the second, and not just from the exertion of climbing the stairs.

"What sort of test is it?" Ben asked, with forced nonchalance.

"Confidential," Dagmar said.

Charlie gave Ben an anxious, almost panicky look. His eyes were wide and his mouth open, as if he'd seen a ghost.

"Dagmar, we—"

"Please call me Ms. Borovich."

"Sorry. Ms. Borovich, we did not grow up knowing the Institute and the Unseen Kingdoms," Charlie said. "Won't that put us at a considerable disadvantage?"

"The test is confidential," Dagmar repeated evenly. "I cannot tell you anything about it. Please ask no more questions."

Charlie mouthed something frantically to Ben. It was hard to make out, but he was pretty sure it was a string of curses someone like Dagmar would probably not appreciate.

They left the staircase upon reaching the first gallery and turned towards a set of double doors that read "Department of Apprentices", engraved with a symbol of a tree. Dagmar pushed open both doors, despite their size and obvious weight, like a cowboy, minus the style and flair. They entered a corridor that, if Ben remembered correctly, ran all the way round the building, with doors popping up left and right along the way. The hallway was too narrow to walk comfortably three abreast, so Ben and Charlie lagged slightly behind. Dagmar stopped by a door, her leading foot giving a little stomp to emphasise the halt. The sign on the door said "Cloakroom". Dagmar turned the handle and opened the door.

Ben stepped in cautiously. He had learnt from his last trip that you never knew what was behind each door no matter how innocent the sign.

This door was no exception.

The room was entirely constructed of stone, and Ben almost felt like he was back underground. Giant lanterns hung from the ceiling, illuminating an area not much wider than the tunnels they travelled in. Running left and right were lockers, constructed from single huge slabs of stone, with no visible handles. On each locker was a single green eye, as big as a watermelon, staring straight ahead without blinking.

"That's just creepy," Charlie said softly.

"Mr. Greenwood, you go first," Dagmar said. "Walk slowly down the room. When one of the eyes winks at you, stop and stand next to that locker."

Ben took a deep breath and started walking. Immediately the green eyes came to life and focused on him. Having scores of giant eyes watching you was unnerving, despite the fact that they clearly weren't going anywhere. Ben was almost at the end of the room when one of the eyes winked at him. Ben stopped and turned. The eye was looking right at him; the others reverted back to their blank stares. Ben walked towards the eye cautiously. What was going on inside that huge green iris? Ben couldn't shake the thought that he was being inspected.

"Your turn, Mr. Hornberger," Dagmar said, her voice echoing down the room.

Charlie toddled forwards even slower than Ben had. He stared at each eye with a mixture of anxiety and wonder, his mouth half open. Ben watched the eyes, waiting for the wink. There! Charlie had ended up at the adjacent locker to Ben.

"These eyes clearly have good taste," Ben said.

"Or bad judgement. What do we do now?"

Charlie's question was answered by Dagmar, who marched down the room, her large shoes stomping the ground, making Ben's ears ring. She stopped right in front of Ben's locker and motioned him to join her. Then she spoke directly to the green eye.

"Phyliss, this is Mr. Ben Greenwood." Dagmar switched her gaze to Ben. "Mr. Greenwood, this is Phyliss."

The green eye gave another wink. Ben was clearly unable to shake hands. Should he reciprocate the blink? But Dagmar was already talking again.

"Phyliss is one of the lazier lockers, and naps three times a day, at 10am, 1pm and 3:30pm, normally for about an hour. So make sure you don't need anything then. If you do, I suggest trying to bribe her with candy, especially anything strawberry-flavoured. On the plus side, she is the strongest locker here; most lower-grade spells won't affect her, and certainly none that any apprentice could perform. So your bag is certainly safe with her. Any questions?"

Ben had plenty. "How do you know she is a girl?"

"Men have a blue eye. Now, I want you to ask Phyliss to open her door. Speak with authority, but make sure you are not too aggressive. Phyliss is one of the harder lockers to open."

"Is there no password or phrase I should be saying?"

"She's not some secret door in a children's story," Dagmar said.

Ben cleared his throat, which suddenly felt constricted. He had a fleeting thought: *what if this is some sort of preliminary test?* It would be highly embarrassing to fail before the actual test had even begun. Ben cast the thought aside and focused on the big green eye.

"Please open your door, Phyliss."

The eyelid lowered slowly until it looked like Phyliss was again inspecting him. The green pigment swirled within its huge iris and the colour shifted slightly. Ben met the green-eyed stare without batting an eyelid.

The mighty stone door creaked and swung open slowly. The space inside was at least ten feet high, but only just deep enough to put his backpack in. Had he anything else he would have had to stack it on top.

"Your locker space increases with your position in the Institute," Dagmar said, seeing Ben's look.

Ben placed his bag inside and then stepped back. "How do I shut the door?"

"By using your hands."

"Fair enough." He sized up the door; it looked as though it would need three men to move it. But when pushed, he found it surprisingly light and shut with a soft click. The green eye was now closed.

"It must be 10am," Dagmar noted. "She has gone to sleep. We got here just in time."

Dagmar turned to Charlie, who was looking a little pale, and introduced him to Ayla. Upon describing her character, Charlie's pale face turned red and, when she had finished, he had only one question.

"Can I have someone – anyone – else?"

"No, you may not. You were chosen by Ayla," Dagmar said, in that mildly reproachful tone that Ben was starting to find extremely effective.

Charlie's shoulders sagged. He faced up to Ayla and in a timid voice ordered the door to open. Nothing happened.

Charlie stood there awkwardly, before turning to Dagmar.

"Don't break eye contact," she said sharply. Her voice was like a whip and Charlie span back to face the locker.

"I don't think she likes me," Charlie said.

"Ask again, and give your voice more authority. You sounded like a mouse."

Charlie's second attempt was far better, but it still took a good twenty seconds before the door finally creaked open. Charlie sighed and placed his bag inside. He shut the door as hastily as possible and jumped back, out of harm's way.

They left the cloakroom considerably lighter and continued their way round the hallway.

"Can I store my stuff with you?" Charlie whispered, leaning into Ben.

"What's wrong with yours?" Ben asked, with a little smile.

"Are you serious? Didn't you hear what Ayla is like? I don't want to fear for my life every time I try to go to store my bag."

"Sharing lockers is not allowed for apprentices," Dagmar said from ahead. Her ears were as sharp as her voice.

Charlie's eyes narrowed and shot daggers at Dagmar's back, but he said nothing. His anger was quickly replaced with anxiety the moment he spotted the door they were approaching.

The Initiation Test.

The wooden door with its panelled sign looked just like all the others, but this one made Ben's heart motor. They had absolutely no clue what lay inside the door. Would the test require physical exertion? Ben was now wishing he'd eaten a bit more for breakfast in case he needed the energy.

"So if we fail this, we're out?" Charlie asked.

"Technically you were never in," Dagmar replied, without looking round.

The three of them stopped by the door. Dagmar turned to them. Her face, which had been serious so far, looked more so now.

"The only information I can tell you is that blood will be spilled," she said, giving them both extended looks.

Both Ben and Charlie waited, in the hope that she would keep talking.

"That's it?" Charlie asked, his voice rising. "You want us to take a test we know nothing about, except that we could potentially face some sort of blood bath?" He started breathing very quickly and took his handkerchief out, dabbing his cheeks and forehead.

"You can choose not to take the test. You will then be escorted out of the Institute and onto the Dragonway, back home," Dagmar said.

"No," Ben said immediately. "I'm ready."

Charlie gave a wistful look down the hallway, the way they had come, and sighed, his shoulders sagging. "I'm not even close to ready, but I'll do it. I just hope you have some first aid spells in your spellshooter, because I'm sure I'll need them."

"Who will go first?" Dagmar asked.

Ben raised a hand. "I will."

— CHAPTER SIX —
The Apprenticeship Test

Ben opened the door slowly, his body tense. He was half-expecting to face a flaming fireball or some axe-wielding maniac, but to his surprise and relief, the room was almost empty. It was small, and dimly lit by a chandelier that floated just below the ceiling. There were no windows or doors except the one he came through. An ornate table and a single chair were placed in the middle of the room. On top of the table was a large hardback book and a plaque that stood upright.

There was something strangely familiar about the room and its set-up that tickled Ben's memory. Perhaps it reminded him of some movie? He discarded the thought and spent another moment making sure the room was completely safe, before approaching the table. The book that lay on it was a work of art. The outside was leather of the deepest red, titled with the words *Royal Institute of Magic* in a flowing yellow script. Beneath that, cast in silver and fastened to the centre of the book, was the Institute's coat of arms. It was shaped like a shield and cut into four quarters. Each quarter alternated between a picture of a lion and a peculiar flower.

Ben opened the book. Or at least he tried to. The cover wouldn't move. Ben frowned. Was it glued together? He tried picking it up, but it was stuck to the table. He couldn't open or move it at all.

Ben stepped back, hands on hips. It was then he noticed the plaque again. Now that he was this close, he could see a message scrawled on it.

"Dear applicant,

"Congratulations on making it this far. Should you wish to proceed with the Initiation Test, place your right thumb on the centre of book, in the centre of the coat of arms.

"I wish you the best of luck.

"Elizabeth."

Ben sat down on the chair and rested his arms on the table, either side of the book. He was beginning to think this was not going to be a physical test. Ben placed a thumb on the coat of arms, right in the middle of the four small quarters.

Nothing happened. Ben pressed a little harder, until his thumb went red. Still nothing. Was he doing it wrong?

Something sharp pricked the underside of his thumb.

"Ow!" Ben exclaimed, instinctively pulling his thumb away.

A trickle of blood started flowing down the coat of arms. Instead of dripping off the book, the blood flowed around the small coat of arms, until the small trickle surrounded it.

The coat of arms started to glow, as if the blood had connected a circuit. Ben leaned down, placing his hands on the book, to inspect it closer. His hands began to tingle, so Ben quickly removed them – or tried to. His hands wouldn't come off the book. He tried harder, but they wouldn't budge. They were stuck to the book, just as the book was stuck to the table.

Ben cursed. Now what? He stood up and tried moving the table, but it was too heavy, or perhaps stuck to the floor. After several tugs, he leant against the table, panting. If the test involved getting out the room, he was in trouble.

His deflation lasted only seconds. There *had* to be something he could do. He sat down, wracking his brain, examining every inch of the room.

Suddenly, the temperature dropped. Ben was so busy trying to concoct a plan he only noticed when he spotted the hairs on his arms standing up. The temperature kept dropping and he shivered. His breath was starting to mist up.

The lantern above flickered and then went out.

Darkness, total and complete. Had he been able to wave a hand in front of his face he wouldn't have seen it.

The Initiation Test must be about to start, but Ben was still stuck to the book. For the first time, anxiety crept in; not from the test, but of the possibility of failure. How could he possibly do anything while stuck to the book? His plans to make a career at the Institute, and more importantly find his parents, would disintegrate before they had even begun.

A breeze in the room disrupted his thoughts. A white mist began to form just behind the table. From within Ben saw a shape appear. At first it was nothing more than a white blob, but as the mist continued to solidify, a female ethereal figure took shape. She had auburn hair and a strong nose. Her posture and dress oozed regality. Her long-fingered hands rested on the hilt of a magnificent sword.

Ben stared into the dark brown eyes of Queen Elizabeth and saw an intelligence and determination that took his breath away. Was this some powerful spell or could it be a ghost?

"Your Majesty," Ben said, bowing his head.

The Queen did not respond. Was he supposed to ask something? If she *was* a ghost, would she know about his ancestor, Michael James Greenwood? The thought made his heart jump. What about the Armour and the dark elf king, Suktar? Ben was busy trying to work out what to say when the Queen broke the silence.

"Greenwood," she said. Her voice was a whisper but spoken with such intention that a deaf man would have heard her.

Ben managed a subtle nod; he didn't trust his voice.

"Do you deem yourself worthy of the Royal Institute of Magic?"

"I do," Ben replied, pleased at the calmness of his voice.

"Very well," Elizabeth said. "Let us find out if that is true."

The Queen's eyes started to glow, becoming two white orbs. Ben steadied himself and widened his stance, in preparation for whatever was about to happen.

A beam of energy from Elizabeth's eyes speared right into Ben's forehead, connecting the two of them. The beam penetrated his skin and he screamed.

A picture flashed before his eyes: his mother, wearing a blue gown, holding him in her arms and smiling lovingly. There were white lights everywhere and loud beeping noises. It was the hospital, moments after his birth, Ben realised. The picture vanished and another appeared where he was still a baby, but now able to crawl. He could see the legs of his father.

The Queen was sifting through his memories, from birth to present time. Ben watched helplessly as memories came, were inspected and then discarded. Months, and then years, passed in a heartbeat. Ben soon realised what she was looking for: memories that defined character. There were plenty of moments of courage, loyalty and overcoming the odds. But there were times of recklessness and anger. How much would they count against him?

A recent memory flashed up. Unlike most of the others, which came and went in a flash, this one received an extended appraisal. Ben took one look at it and cursed. He and Charlie were reading the note Wren had left to his parents, urging them to seek refuge at the Institute. It was the letter that had sparked their first adventure to the Institute.

The queen now went more slowly through the memories, following their journey to the Dragonway and the Institute. Ben felt something unpleasant move in the pit of his stomach. The Queen was going to discover their plan to find his parents and the Armour. In excruciating slow motion, all of Ben's intentions were laid bare.

When the memories finally reached present time, the energy beam retracted and the Queen's eyes stopped glowing. Ben met the Queen's thoughtful gaze with defiance. His insides were churning and his legs felt like jelly, but he managed to stay calm. The desire – the need – to join was almost overwhelming. Was he good enough for the Institute? Or would he pay for the secrets he was keeping?

The staring contest seemed to last an age and Ben's eyes were beginning to water, when Elizabeth finally nodded.

"Another Guardian," she said, and gave Ben what he could have sworn was a relieved smile. "I have been waiting some time. Welcome to the Institute."

The Queen faded back into the white mist and, in a puff of smoke, vanished.

The lantern above flickered to life.

Ben stood there, panting, a trickle of sweat running down his forehead. He relaxed his shoulders, only then realising how tense they were. He felt a warmth beneath his hands. The binding spell that held them to the book vanished and he let go. Underneath the book's title, the words "Ben Greenwood" were now written into the leather cover.

A flicker of light appeared at the corner of his vision and he turned. Floating above his right shoulder was a small colourless diamond.

He'd made it. He was in! He gave a fist pump, but his delight was tempered by the Queen's final words, and her hauntingly penetrating voice still rang in his ears. *Another Guardian.* What did that mean? Ben was sure it was significant, but right now he could think about only one thing: he had qualified for the Royal Institute of Magic. A wonderful warmth started at his chest and went all the way down to his toes.

Ben picked up the book that now had his name on it and tucked it under his arm. He exited the room and saw two very different sets of eyes looking his way. Charlie was inspecting him, clearly looking for signs of injury. Dagmar's impassive stare went straight to the colourless diamond above Ben's shoulder, and she gave a rare smile, a subtle upturning of the lips.

"Congratulations. Welcome to the Institute," Dagmar said, extending her hand. Ben took it with a smile, matching her vice-like grip with one of his own.

"So the colourless diamond means you're now an apprentice, right?" Charlie asked.

"That and also the book," Dagmar said. "You cannot take it unless you have passed."

Charlie wiped his brow. "It's not protected by a dragon or something, is it? Because if I have to fight my way to anything, I can tell you right now it's not going to happen."

Dagmar would have been a fantastic poker player, Ben thought – her expression didn't change a jot.

"Your turn, Mr. Hornberger," she said.

Charlie shuffled reluctantly towards the door, giving Ben an imploring look.

"You'll be fine," Ben said, with a reassuring smile, which he managed to maintain until Charlie had disappeared through the door.

The wait to see if Charlie passed was almost worse than the test. He had no control over the outcome and felt powerless. For all Charlie's complaining, his integrity and loyalty were unquestionable and, when needed, so was his courage. Would the ghost/spell of Queen Elizabeth see past his dramatics, anxiety and pessimism?

Time ticked by slowly. Dagmar stood, back to the wall, in a manner reminiscent of the guards at Buckingham Palace. Ben knew asking her anything would be pointless.

Five minutes passed. Ten. Ben started tapping his foot anxiously. How long had the test taken him? It hadn't seemed long, but time had lost all meaning once inside. What would he do if Charlie didn't make it? Ben would stay, but it would be a mighty blow not to have his best friend with him.

A creak from the door interrupted his thoughts, and Ben whipped his head round.

Charlie emerged, looking as though he had just fought a dragon. His chequered shirt was damp with sweat, his hair a mess, and there was a cut on his lip. But it was the single colourless diamond above his shoulder and the book under his arm that made Ben grin ear to ear.

"Congratulations, Mr. Hornberger," Dagmar said. Ben caught a flicker of surprise in her eyes. "I did not expect you to pass."

Charlie extended his hand and smiled. "Nor did I. Can we go and get a cup of tea? I'm about to collapse."

— CHAPTER SEVEN —
Old Friends and Enemies

Charlie got his wish for once.

"Lunchtime is at 12pm," Dagmar said, marching in front of them along the hallway. "Muster is at 1pm, after which you will begin your apprenticeships. Do not be late."

"How can we tell the time?" Charlie asked, his voice slightly timid. It was hard not to be intimidated by the tiny Dagmar.

"You will need to buy watches in town. I would do that today if I were you. My other apprentices will tell you how much I dislike slack punctuality."

Dagmar's warning did nothing to dampen Ben's feeling of elation. His feet had barely touched the floor since he left the testing room. He kept glancing above his right shoulder at the floating colourless diamond. Charlie looked like a weight had been lifted, and Ben spotted his friend smiling to himself on more than one occasion. Charlie even managed to deal with

Ayla, his locker, when they stopped to drop off their books. It was only when they heard voices coming from the lunch room ahead that Charlie's anxiety returned.

"I will leave you here," Dagmar said, turning to face them. Ben wondered again how someone so small could exude such authority. "I will see you in fifty-eight minutes time."

She marched back down the hallway, her over-sized feet clomping on the wooden floor. She was almost out of sight when her voice floated down the hallway. "Try the veal."

"Shall do!"

"What a peculiar lady," Charlie said, when he was sure Dagmar was out of earshot.

"She's interesting, isn't she?" Ben said. He pushed open the double doors and they entered the lunch hall.

Warmth and the pleasant smell of chicken hit their senses. Laughter and chatter filled the air. Two long tables, flanked either side by wooden benches, ran down the centre of the room. Most of the spaces were taken by boys and girls. Ben guessed most to be about sixteen to twenty, though he spotted a few adults old enough to be his parent. Ben and Charlie surveyed the scene and received a few curious glances.

"I feel like this is my first day at school," Charlie whispered. "And not in a good way."

"Relax," Ben said. "Let's get some food. I'm hungry."

They made their way to a set of trolleys at the end of the room and Ben piled his plate full of veal, potatoes and a couple of obligatory vegetables. He found a few empty spaces at the end of one of the tables.

"Did you notice that many people have more than one diamond?" Charlie said, sitting down opposite Ben. "They must have a ranking system for apprentices just like the main departments of the Institute."

Charlie was right. Many of the older kids had several colourless diamonds above their right shoulders. It took some willpower to focus on eating rather than staring at everyone. Ben was mid tucking into a juicy potato when he heard a familiar voice from across the room.

"Ben! Charlie!"

Natalie was waving at them. She was mingling with a group of friends and appeared very much the centre of attention, which didn't surprise Ben, as most of her friends were boys. As soon as she spotted them she detached herself, to the disappointment of her suitors, and came running over.

Ben had almost forgotten how attractive she was. Her dark brown hair fell in curls over her shoulder, and there was something exotic about her almond-shaped green eyes. She was slim, but shapely; even her slightly pointed ears, due to her tenuous elf heritage, added to her looks.

Ben stood up as she approached, hastily wiping his mouth, and Natalie flung her arms around him.

"You made it!" she said. "You passed the test!"

Natalie turned to Charlie and he stood up awkwardly. He received a hug that was just as enthusiastic, though perhaps slightly gentler.

"Don't stop eating," Natalie said, motioning at both of them to sit, and then doing so herself, sitting down next to Charlie. "The Initiation Test leaves you starving. I'm really sorry I couldn't tell you anything about it. The rules are very strict. I knew you'd both pass of course, but I was still nervous. Have you been chosen by a locker yet?"

"Funny way of putting it, but, yes," Ben said. He couldn't help smiling at Natalie's effusiveness. Charlie appeared momentarily flustered by it, but that could just have been his re-adjustment period to having a close friendship with someone as pretty as Natalie.

"We have so much to catch up on, I hardly know where to start," Natalie continued.

"You have two diamonds now," Charlie said. His voice sounded a little squeaky, but he pressed on. "Did you graduate or something?"

Ben hadn't noticed the extra diamond floating above her shoulder, but he did so now.

"I passed the first grade exam last week," Natalie said. "It wasn't too bad. My Spellsword work isn't great and I only just scraped past that part of the exam. But enough about me, I want to hear about you guys. How was your trip here?"

Together Ben and Charlie recounted their morning, from the attack at the Croydon headquarters to the Initiation Test. When Ben mentioned the ghost of Elizabeth labelling him as a Guardian, both Charlie and Natalie interrupted him at the same time.

"What does that mean?" Charlie asked. Both he and Ben turned to Natalie expectantly.

"I've never heard of it before," she said. "But it sounds important. She said 'another' Guardian? Who else is there?"

"My parents, maybe," Ben said.

They debated the matter in hushed tones for the next several minutes, but as none of them had any real insight to add, they were soon going round in circles and decided to move on. By the time they'd finished, Ben had cleaned his plate and was eyeing up seconds.

"I can't believe that attack on Croydon," Natalie said, her locks falling over her forehead as she shook her head. "The security on the Dragonway is really tight. There are very few breaches."

"So you've no idea what a Shadowseeker is?" Ben asked.

"No, but I bet we can find out in the library. I would also like to know what animal he was riding."

"Do you think the attack had anything to do with Ben, or was it just a coincidence that he happened to be there?" Charlie asked. The topic of mystery solving had quickly melted his lingering shyness.

"It's hard to say, isn't it?" Natalie replied. She looked around to make sure nobody was eavesdropping, then leaned onto the table – Ben and Charlie did likewise. "We know the dark elves wanted Ben to get to his parents. But it also looks like they're trying to start a war, which they've been threatening for a long time. The Shadowseeker could easily be trying to create havoc and distract the Institute. It might have nothing to do with Ben at all."

Ben glanced up to make sure nobody had started listening. There were a few older kids watching them at a distance. Ben recognised one of them. He was tall, with expensively styled blond hair and teeth so white Ben could have sworn they were glowing. The sleeves of his dark blue shirt were rolled to his elbows, and his trousers and shoes looked like something Ben could only dream of affording. He stood in the middle of a small group, surrounded by a few girls and boys.

Joshua whispered something to one of his friends and they started approaching.

"We're about to meet an old friend," Ben said, watching them near. Their first and only previous meeting with Joshua hadn't been a pleasant one – especially for Joshua, and Ben knew there might be trouble.

"Oh dear," Charlie said. "I swear, I've got some sort of bully magnet."

"Nobody's going to get bullied," Ben said, shifting his chair back a fraction to make room for manoeuvre.

"Let me handle this," Natalie said. "I'm friends with them."

"Is there anyone you're not friends with?" Charlie muttered to himself.

Ben had seen that type of smirk a hundred times before, normally on the faces of idiots who would try to have a go at Charlie. There weren't normally five of them, though, and they weren't normally a good two years older than him. On top of which, his reputation at school didn't exist here. But how much damage would they do in the middle of the lunch room?

A collective gasp from the lunch room and a sudden turn of heads made Joshua and his crew stop in their tracks. People were twisting in their seats and voices suddenly lowered to hushed whispers. Everyone was looking towards the entrance. Ben turned to see what the fuss was about.

Wren Walker was making her way serenely through the lunch hall towards them. She looked just as Ben remembered, with long silvery hair elegantly piled on her head. She had that agelessness that made Ben wonder how old she could be. Her eyes were a sparkling grey and her ears were slightly pointed. Floating above her right shoulder were five green diamonds and they were attracting a good deal of attention.

"Good afternoon," Wren said, smiling at them. "Welcome back. Congratulations to you both for passing the Initiation Test. I had no doubt you would."

As nice as Wren was, she was also one of the most powerful members of the Institute, and Ben didn't believe she had just come down here to congratulate them.

"Is the Queen a spell or some sort of ghost?" Charlie asked.

"That is a very good question," Wren said. "The test was put in place by Queen Elizabeth herself many centuries ago. Nobody quite knows, but my feeling is that it's a very old, powerful spell, combined with a tiny remnant of the Queen's consciousness." She clearly saw the look on Ben's face, for she added, "We are not privy to what happens in the Initiation Test, so your secrets are safe."

Ben tried to conceal his sigh of relief.

"I have a request," Wren continued. "I'm sorry to break up your reunion but would you mind coming with me, Ben? There is an important meeting I would like you to be part of."

"Sure," Ben said, standing up. If there was one Institute member he trusted above all others, it was Wren. It was her letter to his parents that had triggered their initial adventure. As

Director of Spellswords, she was Ben's parents' boss and had been open from the beginning about how much she liked and admired them. Wren had been a rock of stability amongst the confusion of their last visit to the Institute.

"We shouldn't be more than thirty minutes," Wren said. "I will bring you back down when we are done."

As Ben followed Wren out of the lunch room, he glanced at Joshua and his crew watching him. He hoped they didn't turn their attention to Charlie and Natalie, but he couldn't worry about that now. His mind was buzzing with questions. Where was Wren taking him?

— CHAPTER EIGHT —
An Ignored Warning

Ben wasn't surprised when Wren led him up to the executive floor at the very top of the Institute. They passed through the double doors and entered a lavish hallway, impeccably decorated with gold leafing and ornate panels. The torch lights seemed to shine lighter here, and the ceiling was a fraction taller, creating a feeling of space. Ben refrained from asking questions. If Wren wasn't talking, there was nothing she wanted him to know. Any questions would just result in tactful deflections.

"Here we are," Wren said.

They had stopped by a door that said "Meeting Room Two".

Wren turned to Ben and gave him a reassuring smile, which was almost magical in its ability to help relax.

"It goes without saying that you're not in any sort of trouble. We just wanted to have an informal chat with you, as certain things need to be said. We shouldn't be long. Are you ready?"

"Sure," Ben said, wondering who "we" constituted.

The room inside was typically lavish, and contained an expansive wooden table, surrounded by intricately carved wooden chairs. Standing in front of the table were two men Ben recognised immediately. Draven he had seen earlier that day, and looked much the same, though perhaps his beard was slightly less scruffy. Ben wondered, not for the first time, if Draven had dwarf blood in him. His heavy eyebrows exaggerated a grumpy-looking scowl. Colin, by contrast, looked like a bank manager. His hair glinted in the light, hinting at liberal amounts of grease to achieve the perfect parting. His posture was so straight it looked as though he had a broom thrust up the back of his suit. His clothes were ironed to within an inch of their lives and his black shoes gleamed. Both men had five diamonds above their shoulders – Draven's were the Wardens' red; Colin's the Diplomacy's blue.

"Mr. Greenwood," Colin said. Every syllable was attenuated perfectly, reminding Ben of royalty.

"Ben," Draven said, with a curt nod.

It was clear nobody was going to sit down, which gave Ben hope that the meeting might indeed be short. He stood facing

Colin and Draven and was pleased when Wren chose to stand by his side.

"Right, let's not draw this out," Draven said, his voice gruff. "We're all busy at the moment, especially me."

"Eloquently put," Colin said. "First of all, Mr. Greenwood, myself and Draven would like to clear the air. We were, quite frankly, catastrophically wrong to entertain any notion of allying with the dark elf Elessar. We were trying to avoid conflict with the dark elves until we could work out where your parents were and why their king wanted them so badly."

"You thought they had murdered his son, didn't you?"

"That was the line we were fed," Colin said, unflustered by Ben's open resentment. "We went with it because your parents were not present to disprove the king's accusation, and it gave us time to find your parents and establish the real reason Suktar wanted them. However, nothing worked as planned and we put your life in danger, for which there can be no excuse. Draven and I apologise unreservedly. It will not happen again."

Ben was beginning to see why Colin was the Director of Diplomacy. He never thought he would forgive Draven and Colin so easily for plotting to hand him over to the dark elves, but Colin's sincere apology and frank explanation eased a good deal of Ben's ill will. He glanced over at Draven, who shifted a little uncomfortably. Colin gave him a little nudge.

72

"There's more to it than that," Draven said, "but there were a few things we did, because we were desperate, that weren't right. Of course, all of this could have been avoided if your parents had showed up."

"Draven," Colin said politely, turning to his peer. "I think you're deviating from the point I'm trying to make."

Draven looked as though he was sucking a lemon. He scowled at Colin, and then turned to Ben. "I'm sorry for how things turned out," he said, sounding like he was being strangled.

Ben grinned, enjoying the moment. "Apology accepted."

"Good, now let's move on," Wren said. "We are here to give Ben an update on what is going on with the dark elves and how it might involve him, in order to warn and protect him from any potential danger while on his apprenticeship."

"An excellent idea," Colin chimed in.

Draven looked ready to retaliate to Ben's impudent grin, but he took a deep breath and seemed to put the matter aside. "We have known that Suktar has been building his army for the last fifty years, despite his insistence that it was only to defend his borders. The Department of Diplomacy did a pretty good job maintaining any sort of relationship with Suktar. But being the evil, power-hungry dark elf king that he is, war was inevitable sooner or later. Now it looks like sooner. We have reports that he is moving his army and targeting Fiorgan, a small but tactically important country about five hundred miles west of Spain."

Ben was enraptured by the revelation, but it didn't answer his most basic question. "What does that have to do with me?"

"I'm getting there," Draven said. "Part of Suktar's strategy when preparing an invasion is to try to distract us. So the Shadowseeker who caused havoc in our Croydon headquarters could easily have been Suktar's attempt to do just that. I hope, for your sake, that it was."

Ben didn't like the way Draven finished that sentence. "Why? What is a Shadowseeker? And what else would he be doing?"

"Shadowseekers are Suktar's personal assassins," Wren said, taking over. "They can move almost undetected and can penetrate enemy lines like nothing else I know. Normally they are sent to eliminate a specific target. Now it's only speculation, and I personally feel it unlikely, but there is a chance the Shadowseeker was looking for you."

Ben's throat suddenly felt dry. "Why me?"

"The same reason as before," Draven said. "He wants to get to your parents. The real question is – why does he want them so badly?"

Draven, Colin and even Wren were now looking at him expectantly. Ben managed to keep a straight face and said nothing.

"Obviously we cannot let the dark elves use you as bait again," Draven continued. "So I would like to have one of my Wardens watch over you. Additionally, I don't want – I mean I would prefer it if you did not leave Taecia until your parents have returned."

"What?" Ben said, his voice rising. "Is that an order?"

"No, it is not," Wren said, before Draven could reply, her voice soft and soothing. "It is simply a request we feel would help you and make your time here safer."

"If the Shadowseeker is after you, then you could be in considerable danger, even within the safety of the Institute," Colin said.

"They could infiltrate the Institute?"

"Possibly," Colin said.

"But if I had one of my Wardens watching you, it's unlikely they would reveal themselves. And even if they did, my best Wardens are more than a match for them."

If they were trying to scare him, it was working. Ben felt sick at the thought that a Shadowseeker could be lurking round the corner, waiting to take him out. But having a Warden watching him would scupper all his plans, and give Draven the perfect excuse to have someone spying on him the whole time.

"I'll be fine on my own," Ben said.

"Fine?" Draven said, his face going red and his bushy eyebrows soaring upwards. Ben prepared himself for the inevitable tirade, but Wren raised a slender hand, and Draven's voice seemed to stick in his throat.

"You are perfectly entitled to decline," Wren said. "It is extremely unlikely a Shadowseeker would ever penetrate the Institute. We have powerful wards at every entrance point and even within the building."

"What about the incident with Prince Robert?" Draven said.

"That was a long time ago," Wren said, giving Draven a stern look. "A lot of things went wrong that have been rectified since then."

"It's still possible," Draven said stubbornly.

"I would definitely recommend the security," Colin said. "Draven's Wardens are very good; you will barely notice them. However, as Wren says, the choice is yours."

"Good. I'll pass, thanks," Ben said, giving Draven a meaningful stare.

Draven clenched his fist, and gave Ben a nasty smile. "You think this is all some joke, don't you, Ben? Well, I'm going to be watching your progress closely. The apprenticeship success rate for those new to the Unseen Kingdoms is less than one in ten, and if you think you're a special case because of your parents, then you're horribly mistaken. The passing mark for you is the same as for everyone else."

"That's enough, Draven," Wren said.

But Draven wasn't listening. He pointed a stubby finger at Ben, ready to launch another tirade. A sharp knocking on the door cut him short.

"Who is it?" Draven asked sharply, staring daggers at the door.

The door opened and in stepped Dagmar, calmly surveying the scene.

"What do you think you're doing? Can't you see we're in a meeting?"

Draven's fury was lost on Dagmar.

"You have my apprentice," she said calmly. "It is 12:53pm and I would hate for him to be late for his first muster."

"My goodness, you're right," Wren said, glancing at her watch. "Off you go, Ben. And good luck."

Ben didn't need telling twice. He turned and headed for the door, enjoying Draven's look of pure frustration.

"I'm going to speak to your director about you, Dagmar. Your behaviour is unacceptable."

"As you wish," Dagmar said. She gave a formal nod to Wren and Colin, before exiting the room, Ben hot on her heels.

— CHAPTER NINE —
A Surprise in the Library

Ben hurried down to the dining hall, where Charlie and Natalie were waiting impatiently. Everyone else had left already, and Ben barely had time to give them an update before Natalie was leading them to the muster room.

"Draven really doesn't like you, does he?" Charlie commented, as they hurried down the hallway, along with a dozen other apprentices. It was clear nobody wanted to be late.

"We're definitely not best friends," Ben said. "What I don't get is how Dagmar was able to interrupt the directors and take me away."

"When it comes to the apprentices, she has total authority, and nobody, not even the prince, will cross Dagmar when it comes to that."

They entered the muster room with only a couple of minutes to spare. The apprentices were already lining up, and Ben noticed they each stood on a coloured square. The floor resembled a chess board, with alternating shades of wood. At the front of the room stood Dagmar, hands behind her back, rod under her arm.

"Highest to lowest rank, from the front right corner to the back left corner," Natalie said.

Ben saw what she meant. Those with the most colourless diamonds were towards the front. There were a couple of boys and a girl with five colourless diamonds occupying the front right squares. Ben spotted Josh, with three diamonds, near the middle. Natalie, with only two, was nearer the rear. Ben and Charlie went right to the very back. They got a few nods and smiles from apprentices who had spotted them for the first time.

"Jimmy Stroud," said a cheerful-looking boy thrusting his hand out. He wasn't much taller than Charlie, with a serious case of acne. "You're new, right?"

"First day," Ben said.

"Ooh, fun," Jimmy said, giving him a goofy smile. His front two teeth reminded Ben of a rabbit.

A loud dong came from somewhere at the front of the room and the soft chatter stopped immediately.

"Muster," Dagmar said. Ben couldn't see her at the front of the room, but her voice carried effortlessly.

The name of each apprentice was rattled off and promptly answered. Nobody was absent.

"Very good," Dagmar said. "I have two announcements to make. First, we have two new apprentices in our ranks: Ben Greenwood and Charlie Hornberger. Please welcome them."

The apprentices turned and gave them a chorus of greetings. Ben acknowledged them with a smile and a nod; Charlie did the same, with an air of embarrassment.

"I'm sure you all remember how difficult your first days as apprentices were," Dagmar continued. "It is unlike anything you have done before and fifty percent of those who fail do so within the first week. So please assist Mr. Greenwood and Mr. Hornberger in any way you can."

Ben heard Charlie shuffle beside him. Those figures were alarming. *What's so difficult about the first week?* Ben wondered, with a mixture of anxiety and excitement.

Dagmar continued. "I have been getting reports that certain Twos have been falling behind in Diplomacy. I shall not name names, but you know who you are. This is your first and only warning. I suggest you put more time into that department before it's too late."

Ben had almost no idea what Dagmar was talking about, but he noticed a few people with two diamonds in the rows ahead shuffle uncomfortably.

There was a sharp clapping noise, which Ben guessed was Dagmar slapping her rod into an open hand.

"Apprentices dismissed. Mr. Greenwood and Mr. Hornberger, please stay behind for your orientation briefing."

Everyone filed out, with a haste that was probably due to wanting to put distance between themselves and Dagmar.

"Good luck!" Natalie said, squeezing through the departing apprentices to reach them. "You'll do fine. I'll see you in a couple of hours. Meet me by the Institute's entrance at 3pm."

Ben and Charlie were soon standing alone with Dagmar, who somehow made the room seem small.

"Go and retrieve the red books from your lockers and come straight back. Do not open them," Dagmar said.

They left the room and headed down the hallway to the locker room.

"Does she realise telling us not to open the red books only makes it more likely that I will?" Ben said.

"I wouldn't. I bet she'll know if you do. Then she'll turn you into a pig or something."

"I think you're getting a bit carried away."

But her order, combined with Charlie's ridiculous warning, was enough to put Ben off the idea.

Ben wasn't surprised to see that Dagmar hadn't moved at all when they returned.

"Hold them out," Dagmar said.

Ben did so, staring at the dark red leather and the yellow flowing script. His desire to open it grew with every moment, but Dagmar was a sufficient deterrent.

"The apprenticeship is, on average, a two-year course. Those who make it through and become full Institute members amount to approximately thirty-six percent. There are five grades, represented by the diamonds on your shoulder. At the moment, you are first-grade apprentices. Each grade takes progressively longer. Those who pass grade one normally do so within fifty days. The fifth grade takes closer to nine months. During the final two grades, you will choose just two departments to focus on. If you fail to graduate within two years, you will not become a member of the Institute. Is that clear?"

They both nodded.

Dagmar took the rod from under her arm and pointed it at their red books.

"Those books will take you through the apprenticeship. They are all called *Institute Handbooks*. In there you will find a checklist containing a series of steps you must do, for each department. Once you finish the checklist, you will face a final examination in order to graduate to the next grade. The checklist is split into theory and practical. Theory involves studying books and then answering questions to prove your understanding. In practical you put theory into practice. For the theory, you can study in the common room, the library or a classroom. I do not care which, as long as you are progressing. If you have any problems, you come to me, nobody else. All clear?"

Two more nods.

"The apprenticeship runs from 9am until 3pm. That gives you one hour forty-seven minutes left for today. I suggest you get going; you have a lot to do."

Dagmar took a step back. Charlie and Ben took the hint. They quickly left the room, handbooks under their arms.

"Where shall we go?" Charlie said, as they wandered down the hallway.

"The common room," Ben said at once. "Isn't that obvious, when the other options are a classroom or the library?"

"I was going to suggest the library actually," Charlie said. "I bet the common room will be too distracting, and the classroom might be too strict." Charlie gave him a meaningful look. "Plus, if we're in the library, we can use it for other purposes."

"Such as what?" Ben asked.

"Well, wouldn't you like to know what a Guardian is? I bet we could find some answers in the library. I would also like to see if I can find any information on Shadowseekers."

Ben had become so enthralled with the apprenticeship programme, he had almost forgotten about Elizabeth's words during the examination. He had even forgotten about his parents and their mission to find Elizabeth's Armour. Ben felt a little stab of guilt.

"The library it is," he said, with a firm nod.

Such was their desire to get to the library that Charlie matched Ben's pace and they took the stairs two at a time. It was a strangely satisfying feeling having the diamond floating above his shoulder. He had only had it for less than an hour but already he felt like he belonged here. He had been so engrossed in joining the Institute to find his parents that he hadn't had time to consider how much being part of it would mean.

"Here we are," Charlie said. They had arrived at a set of double doors, decorated with a picture of a large scroll.

Ben had forgotten how musty the Scholar corridor was; it smelled of old books. Shelves lined the corridor, sometimes on both sides, making walking a bit of a squeeze.

The door to the library was large and well used, and creaked as it opened. They entered a vast open room that reminded Ben of the old museums in London. There was a huge globe floating in the centre of the room, circling slowly, with all the countries mapped out, including the Unseen Kingdoms. Running along the walls were colourful illustrations detailing a timeline of the Institute's history. Then there were dozens of exhibition stands showing things like the evolution of spellshooters, various animals and foods found in the Unseen Kingdoms, and charts showing every type of spell with its composition element and strength.

"Over here," Charlie said, tugging on Ben's sleeve.

He led them to an adjoining room that was filled with benches and tables with small lamps. Ben spotted many apprentices in groups of twos and threes – friends choosing to study together. Not everyone was an apprentice and Ben spotted diamonds of various colours. There was a quiet, calm feel about the place that reminded Ben of the few libraries he'd ventured into.

"Guys! Over here!"

A high-pitched, cheerful voice cut through the quiet concentration and several people looked up angrily, making hushing noises. The perpetrator was Jimmy Stroud, the goofy boy they'd seen at muster. He seemed oblivious to the dark looks, waving enthusiastically at them.

"Should we pretend we can't see him?" Charlie whispered.

"Don't be so harsh," Ben said, with a smile.

Jimmy was one of the few apprentices studying alone, and his face lit up when Ben and Charlie sat down opposite him.

"Hey, guys!" Jimmy said, with such enthusiasm that a trace of spittle left his mouth and hit Charlie right on the forehead. "Welcome to the newbie table. This is where all the new chaps sit. Zach and Raphy should be here. They've gone to the toilet and are taking an unusually long time to get back."

"When did they leave?" Charlie asked.

Jimmy glanced at his watch. "Oh, about twenty minutes ago. But I'm saving these seats for when they return." He patted the bench next to him. "It can be really hard finding space here sometimes."

The angry glances continued, and a couple of older boys looked as though they were going to come over.

"Could you lower your voice a bit?" Charlie said. "I think people prefer it quiet in a library."

"Oh right, sorry," Jimmy said, in quite possibly the loudest whisper outside of Ogre-ville. "You're not the first person to tell me that, actually."

Ben had met a few geeks in his time, but Jimmy was up there with the best of them. He made Charlie look cool.

"Listen, me and Charlie are going to study for a bit. We're new here, so it would be great if you could let us concentrate for a while. Is that okay?"

"Yeah, okay, sure," Jimmy said, his thin, straggly hair bobbing up and down as he nodded. "Hey, if you need anything, just ask. I've only been here a month, but I know quite a lot already."

Jimmy turned back to his book. He seemed to have a runny nose and resorted to sniffing a lot. Charlie looked up once or twice in irritation, but the moment he placed his handbook on the table he forgot Jimmy existed.

Ben opened the hardback cover. On the first page, in large letters, were the words *First Grade Checklist*. Below that each department was listed with their corresponding colour. On the right edge of the page were tabs guiding you to the departments' relevant sections.

"How do we know where to start? I guess we have to pick a subject?" Charlie asked. He was already thumbing through the book.

"I know where I'm starting," Ben replied. He turned straight to the tab marked in green, and went to the first page.

"Department of Spellswords: First Grade."

There was a list of numbered actions; each one was titled "theory" or "practical". The theory steps pointed to different sections of books to read. The titles sounded far more interesting than your average science book – "Introduction to Spellswords", "How a Spellshooter Works" and "The Basics of Combat" to name just a few. The practical steps were even more interesting, but they were always paired with a theory step that had to be completed first.

"I suggest we do three steps of each department, before switching to the next. That way we never fall behind on any one area," Charlie said.

"Good idea," Ben said, and got to his feet to find the first book.

"You guys need a hand?" Jimmy asked, rising with them.

"No, we're okay, thanks," Ben said, putting a hand on Jimmy's shoulder and easing him back down. "Save the seats for us, though, okay? We'll be back in a minute."

They headed to the book shelves. They were packed tight and went all the way up to the ceiling. Occasionally a ladder lay resting against the books, to help the reader reach the top shelves.

Ben glanced at a huge brown book titled *A Brief History of the Troll Wars*, sandwiched between two other equally interesting titles. "Any idea where we should start looking? You spend a lot of time in libraries. How do they work?"

"It's pretty simple," Charlie said. "Each section is cross-referenced by subject and then placed in alphabetical order. So we just need to find the Spellsword section and then look for the letter 'I'."

Charlie led them deeper into the library, turning left and right until Ben was completely lost. The light was poor and the occasional ray highlighted the dust particles coming off some of the older books that probably hadn't been touched in years. The soft footsteps and rustle of pages faded away as they worked themselves deeper into the library.

"Are you sure this is the right way?" Ben said.

Charlie's eyes were scanning each shelf. "We should be coming up to it."

"Maybe we should have recruited Jimmy's help after all," Ben said.

"You don't mean that – ah, here it is!"

Charlie bent down and picked up two copies of a thin green book titled *An Introduction to Spellswords.*

"Well done," Ben said. "Now it's just the simple matter of getting out of here. Any ideas?"

"I made sure I remembered each turn we took. Now I just have to reverse that. Where would you be without me?"

"Completely lost," Ben admitted. "Let's get— what was that?"

Something moved, right on the edge of Ben's peripheral vision. He would have missed it if not for the tiny ray of light peeking through the books; there was a small gap between two shelves just ahead of him.

"What is it?"

"I thought I saw someone," Ben said.

He walked over to the gap, but there was nobody there. Ben frowned. He was sure he had seen somebody, yet there was nowhere to hide. It was as if the person had just disappeared.

"I don't like that look on your face," Charlie said. "What is it?"

"Nothing," Ben said, shaking his head.

The lie came easily. He didn't want to scare Charlie when he didn't have any proof, but when Ben replayed the moment in his mind, he could have sworn he saw the glimmer of steel.

The sudden sound of quick, heavy footsteps made them both jump. They were coming from just round the corner.

"Mr. Greenwood and Mr. Hornberger," Dagmar said, as she came into view. Under her arm were several dusty books, as well as her rod.

"Ms. Borovich!" Charlie said.

Ben thought he caught a flicker of surprise in Dagmar's eyes, but if so, it was gone in an instant. "What brings you to this section of the library?" she asked.

"Looking for our first book," Ben said, and Charlie held them up helpfully.

"I see." A subtle furrowing of the brow was the only indication of her displeasure. "You do realise there is a section for first-grade books near the front, right next to the study room?"

"Ah. We didn't know that," Charlie said, scratching his head.

"Please stick to that in future," Dagmar said. "You are nearing the restricted section of the library, which is out of bounds for apprentices."

"We'll do that," Ben assured her.

Dagmar gave them both a nod and then strode on by. Charlie and even Ben felt compelled to step back and give her plenty of space as she passed. She stopped, right at the gap in the shelf where Ben thought he'd seen something. She frowned and gave a sniff, her eyes widening for a fraction of a second. Then she tapped her rod thoughtfully and disappeared amongst the shelves.

— CHAPTER TEN —
Professor Rafakat

"Should we tell someone?" Charlie asked.

Ben waited until they were back in the pleasant atmosphere of the main library before revealing to Charlie what he'd really seen.

Ben shook his head. "Definitely not. They'd have someone watching over me in an instant, and then our chances of searching for my parents would vanish."

"That's true," Charlie admitted. "Do you think that glimpse of steel you saw could have been from the Shadowseeker?"

"I don't think so," Ben said, with a certainty that was mainly for Charlie's benefit. "It could have been anything."

The calm, peaceful ambience of members reading helped Ben take his mind off the Shadowseeker and he soon spotted Jimmy waving at them with great enthusiasm.

"I saved your seats, like you asked," Jimmy said, with a surprised smile. Ben suspected that Jimmy hadn't expected them to return.

"Oh, crap," Charlie said, as they sat down.

"What?"

Charlie, mindful of Jimmy sitting next to them, spoke carefully. "We forgot to search for the other things."

Guardians and Shadowseekers, Ben realised. How could they have forgotten? He consoled himself with the knowledge that there would be ample opportunity to research them in the future.

Ben glanced down at the book, *Introduction to Spellswords*, in front of him, and he was gripped with a rare eagerness to start reading. He opened the book and flicked to the first page.

"Spellsword was the first department to be established by Queen Elizabeth, only months after she discovered the Unseen Kingdoms. Initially they were soldiers, skilled in both spellshooting and weaponry, but their role quickly expanded, thanks largely to Michael James, the first Spellsword Director, whose contribution to the department remains unparalleled. Today they are senior and superior to the armed forces of most Unseen Kingdoms. Many battles can be avoided simply by their presence. However, should force be required, it is common knowledge that one Spellsword is the equivalent to a fully armed military squad."

Ben paused, trying to digest what he'd just read. He was learning about his ancestor in the founding years of the Institute. It was crazy. How many times would Michael be mentioned during their studies? Ben had to resist the urge to see what else he could find, and continued reading. The rest of the chapter read like an enthralling fantasy novel. When Ben finished, he looked up, eager to discuss the chapter with Charlie.

But Charlie had disappeared.

"He's gone back into the library to search for another book. He seemed pretty excited about it," Jimmy said, seeing Ben's confusion.

Ben had been so engrossed in the book he hadn't heard Charlie leave.

"Your friend is a really fast student," Jimmy said. "He completed all the questions and left about ten minutes ago."

"Questions?"

"You know, the questions you answer after studying the theory."

Ben referred back to his handbook and to the Spellsword checklist. Jimmy was right; beneath the step detailing what to read was a set of questions to answer. It took Ben another twenty minutes to answer everything, occasionally having to refer back to the chapter he read. By the time he had finished, Charlie had returned and was watching Ben intently, his chubby fingers tapping against each other.

"Finally," Charlie said, with an air of impatience.

"Where have you been?"

"Researching," Charlie said, a smile creasing his face. He made a subtle nod towards Jimmy. "I'll explain on the way. Let's go."

By the time they left the library, Charlie was bubbling with excitement. "I finished about thirty minutes ago. I didn't want to keep going as I thought it would be better if we were at the same point on the checklist."

"How did you finish so fast?"

"I'm a quick reader," Charlie said, waving a dismissive hand. "Anyway, while you were finishing, I thought I'd try to find what I could about Guardians and Shadowseekers."

Suddenly, he had Ben's undivided attention. "What did you find?"

Charlie raised a chubby finger. "I know this is going to sound annoying, but I want to wait until we meet up with Natalie because I really don't like explaining things twice."

Ben ran a hand through his hair. "That is annoying. When are we going to see her?"

"By the entrance at 3pm, remember? That's less than ten minutes away. I suggest we drop our handbooks off with the examiner and head over."

"The examiner?"

"Oh yeah, Jimmy told me about him while you were glued to the book," Charlie said, with a smile. "He's the guy who checks our answers. Look."

Charlie was pointing to a door they had stopped by. *Examiner's Room. Knock Before Entering.*

"Maybe I should double-check what I wrote," Ben said, looking at his handbook with concern. His face lit up hopefully. "Could I compare my answers with yours?"

"Absolutely not," Charlie said. "I'm sure you did fine."

Ben knew better than to argue the point. There were some rules Charlie would never break.

With a little sigh, Ben knocked on the door.

"Come in, come in. By that I mean both of you."

Ben exchanged a surprised look with Charlie.

"How did he know there are two of us?" Charlie asked.

"I don't know, but I have a feeling this could be interesting."

Ben opened the door into a small office, dominated by one big desk in the middle. On the left side of the desk was a basket, piled halfway to the ceiling with Institute Handbooks. On the right was another basket with a smaller collection of handbooks. In the middle was a man, for lack of a better word, sitting on a chair. He was so small the table came up to his chin and his legs were too short to dangle off the chair. He had a long grey beard, which trailed down to the floor, tied together by a bunch of colourful elastic bands. His face was wrinkled and his arched eyebrows were accented by the bald head. In his long bony fingers was an expensive-looking pen. Three white diamonds hovered above his right shoulder.

Ben and Charlie stopped a respectable distance from the desk and watched with curiosity.

"Just a moment, please," the man said. He mumbled something to himself, then shut the book and threw it with a flick of the wrist, sending it spinning upwards. It landed perfectly on top of the smaller pile of books.

He finally looked up, and Ben realised then that he definitely wasn't human. He had a long chin and a nose that would have rivalled your stereotypical witch.

"Ah, new blood! My name is Professor Rafakat. You can call me Professor, Rafakat, Professor Rafakat, Raf, or even Prof. I've been called them all and have no preference. What are your names?"

His voice was high-pitched and croaky, unsurprising given he was probably less than three feet tall.

"Greenwood, eh?" Rafakat said, after they had introduced themselves. He gave his beard a stroke. "An interesting family, with considerable history." Rafakat turned to Charlie. "Hornberger? First generation to the Institute. Good luck to you."

"You know about my family?" Ben asked.

"I know many people," Rafakat said. When he smiled he revealed a set of yellow teeth. "I was friends with your parents. Your mum I especially liked. A fine-looking woman. Fantastic legs."

Charlie made a choking noise and even Ben struggled to keep a straight face. His mum's legs were bigger than Rafakat's entire body.

"I'd love you to stay and chat, but as you can see, I'm snowed under for a change," Rafakat said, nodding towards the huge pile of books. "Leave your books on my desk. They will be marked by tomorrow morning."

Ben wanted to ask more about his parents, but knew it might not be a good idea to press the matter, especially if he wanted to pick the professor's brains at a later date. He and Charlie placed their handbooks on the desk. Rafakat took them and threw them into the air. The left pile must have been ten feet tall, but the books flew up and landed at the top with such deftness that Ben suspected magic was involved. Rafakat then pulled the bottom handbook from the pile with such speed that the remaining ones didn't even sway when they dropped down.

Ben and Charlie left the room, feeling in awe of the little man.

The Institute wasn't as busy as in the morning, but there were still plenty of people coming up and down the spiral staircase, creating an energetic atmosphere that Ben warmed to.

"There she is," Charlie said, waving vigorously.

The three of them left the Institute and stepped out into the courtyard, which was bathed in pleasant sunshine.

"I know a great little café not far from here," Natalie said. "For an extra five pounds they give you a silencer spell, so we can talk without being overheard. They also do fantastic cakes."

"I'm sold. Let's go," Ben said.

They passed the Institute's manicured garden, with its water fountain, and through the open gate. Soon they were heading down the hill along the cobbled path that was lined either side by trees and torch lamps. Halfway down, Ben caught a smell that made his mouth water. He turned instinctively and saw the most incredible cakes lining the front of a small café, with the words "Fuddleswell Tea Room" above the door.

"This is the place," Natalie said.

Inside was busy – not surprising given the food on offer. Cakes, scones with cream and jam, and all sorts of teas and coffees created a feast for the eyes and nose. Small circular tables surrounded by chairs were laid out haphazardly across the room. By sheer luck, they managed to snag a table by the window.

A young girl dressed all in white with a black apron came over, took their order and gave Natalie a small white pellet. She loaded it into her spellshooter and, after the food had arrived, fired it above their heads. A shimmering field surrounded them and the external noise receded to an inaudible mumble.

"Privacy at last," Natalie said, with a smile. "We can talk freely. The spell isn't that strong, but I can detect if someone penetrates the field. If that happens, I will slap the table lightly and we must stop talking at once."

Ben and Charlie took turns bringing Natalie up to speed. When Ben recalled the incident in the library, her eyes widened.

"How certain are you of what you saw?"

"Not certain at all. I have no idea if I really saw a flash of steel, and even if I did, there could be a dozen possible explanations for it."

"I'm not so sure," Charlie said.

"Whatever. I'm not going to freak out about it," Ben said. "And I'm certainly not going to tell the directors what I may or may not have seen. That would kill any chance we have of looking for my parents."

"That's true," Natalie said. She looked worried, but Ben was pleasantly surprised that she showed more understanding than Charlie had. "I wonder what Dagmar was doing," she continued. "It was lucky she happened to be there, in case anything did happen. I know she's only a Scholar, and she might be rather small, but she is really good with a spellshooter. Wren wanted her to join the Department of Spellswords. I bet she could handle a Shadowseeker."

"Speaking of Shadowseekers," Ben said, turning to Charlie. "Can you let us know what you found out about them?"

"You managed to find something in the library?" she asked, sitting up a little straighter.

Charlie revelled in her disbelief, and his cheeks went a little rosy. "It wasn't that hard. You would have found it just as easily as me."

"Moving on from the ego-massaging... what did you find?" Ben asked.

"I couldn't find much on Shadowseekers beyond the fact that they are a special forces unit that serve Suktar directly."

"Draven said they were assassins," Natalie said.

"Not always. I read an article where one was sent in to rescue a prominent dark elf captain from a heavily barricaded dwarf stronghold. That was basically all I could find. There were references to other books, but I have a feeling we don't have access to them."

"Fair enough," Ben said. "What about Guardians?"

Charlie smiled. "I made better progress with that. I found a book, by an author called Frederick Von Lipzig."

"A nice, traditional English name."

"Quite," Charlie said. "I wanted to look him up, but I didn't have the time. Anyway, the book is called *Truths, Myths and Legends of the Royal Institute of Magic*. He discusses many different historical topics, and debates whether there is any truth in them or whether they are myth or legend."

"So what did he say about Guardians?"

Charlie paused to heighten the tension. Ben almost felt like slapping him.

"A Guardian is a living descendant of an original director," Charlie said. "Which makes sense, as we know one of your ancestors is Michael James Greenwood, the original Spellsword Director."

"It makes sense, but we already knew that."

"I'm not done yet," Charlie said, looking affronted. "Frederick Von Lipzig writes that the Guardians have unparalleled access to the very heart of the Institute."

"What does that mean?" Natalie asked.

"He doesn't say exactly. But he does say that the original directors were involved in the design and architecture of the building. *Only a Guardian truly knows the secrets of the fabled Royal Institute of Magic building.* Lipzig's words, not mine."

Nobody spoke for a minute.

"That is interesting," Ben said, eventually breaking the silence. "The question is – did Lipzig say whether it was a truth, a myth or a legend?"

"He says it's most likely a bit of all three," Charlie said. "Which isn't that helpful, I know."

"Well, it's a lot more than we knew before," Natalie said. "I think we should research this Frederick Von Lipzig fellow, and also see if we can find some early drawings of the Institute to see if it holds any secrets."

"Good idea," Charlie said, nodding a little too vigorously.

Ben didn't respond. Natalie had triggered an idea that made his heart leap. He slapped the table, making Charlie and Natalie jump, and leaned forwards, nearly spilling his tea.

"What if Lipzig is right? What if Guardians can access the building's secrets? What if there are areas that only they can get to?"

"That's a big 'if', but go on," Charlie said.

"My parents," Ben said. "Nobody can find them, right? What if all this time they have been hiding in the Institute?"

— CHAPTER ELEVEN —

Unusual Chores

Nobody spoke for a full minute. Charlie broke the silence, dabbing his cheeks with his napkin. "It's a long shot, but if true, then – wow. How would we find these hidden architectural nooks and crannies?"

"With Ben," Natalie said, a smile playing across her pretty face. "He's also a Guardian. If there are any secrets in the Institute, Ben should have access to them."

Ben's excitement didn't quite match Charlie's and Natalie's. "How would I do that? I hardly know my way round the Institute."

Neither Charlie nor Natalie had an answer.

A sudden popping sound made them all jump, and the noise of the café rushed back into their little table.

"The spell has expired. I guess that's meeting adjourned," Natalie said.

Ben was tempted to ask for another silencer spell, but they were getting several dirty looks from other customers waiting for their table.

"I need to get back home," Charlie said, glancing out the window. "My parents will suspect something if I'm not home by five."

"I'll come with you," Ben said, and Charlie gave a grateful smile. Ben had a feeling his friend might feel envious if he stayed to hang out with Natalie at the Institute. "My grandma will be expecting some more milk."

As they said their goodbyes, Natalie ran a critical eye over their clothes. "Charlie, though I love your colourful fashion, make sure you're wearing something a little more casual tomorrow."

"What does that mean?"

Natalie smiled. "Wear something you don't mind getting dirty."

Charlie gave a worried frown as they left and headed down the hill towards the Dragonway. "Why did she have to leave us with a warning like that? Now I'm going to be worrying all night."

"Relax," Ben said, slapping his shoulder. "We're probably just going to be doing something that's going to wreck our clothes a bit."

"That's supposed to relax me?" Charlie asked, giving him an incredulous look. "That would mean we're going to be doing something that involves physical exercise, which isn't exactly my strong suit."

Ben stopped listening to Charlie's worrying, and he barely noticed when they arrived at the Dragonway, or when they boarded their dragon home. His mind played over his first day as an apprentice, with a mixture of pride and excitement. So much had happened, from the Shadowseeker attack in Croydon to the Initiation Test, to the peculiar incident in the library. It was enough to fill a week, let alone a day. The thrill of starting the apprenticeship combined with the possibility that a dark elf assassin could be hunting him produced a peculiar set of contrasting emotions. To complicate matters further, there was his parents. Could they really have hidden at the Institute? Could they still be there? The thought was thrilling but frustrating, that they could be so close and yet remain out of reach.

"Well, that day was interesting," Charlie said. "Same time tomorrow?"

Ben blinked. They were standing outside the Croydon headquarters on a pavement congested with commuters and shoppers. Ben had been so lost in his own world he could only vaguely recall the journey. The smell of petrol and exhaust fumes brought him back to the world he was used to.

Sleep that night did not come easy and his plan to go to bed early in the hope that tomorrow would arrive sooner backfired.

He lay in bed, unable to drift off; his body was tired, but his mind was wide awake, wondering what tomorrow would bring.

Despite the poor night's sleep, Ben was up early, dressed and out the house at 7:30am the following morning, with only the minimum of sparring with his grandma. When he spotted Charlie coming down the road, Ben couldn't help laughing.

"What on earth is that?" he asked.

Charlie was wearing a pair of blue tracksuit bottoms and a white collared t-shirt. His backpack was smaller today, but he still had it strapped round both shoulders.

"This is my sports gear," Charlie said. "They are the only clothes I have that I don't mind getting dirty. I realise I may not look as fashionable as usual." He gave Ben a lookover. "I see that you still manage to look good despite wearing clothes I wouldn't give to a homeless man."

Ben was wearing a black paint-splattered t-shirt and loose-fitting jeans that were torn at the knees.

"Do you have a good set of clothes as spare?" Ben asked.

Charlie patted his bag. "I'm hoping we'll be able to change out of these at some point. The sooner the better."

Both Ben and Charlie were slightly anxious when they entered Croydon headquarters twenty minutes later, but unlike yesterday, the lift opened smoothly and their journey to Taecia proved uneventful. They talked almost nonstop throughout their trip and only stopped when they arrived at the gates of the Royal Institute of Magic.

"I reckon it's about ten minutes to nine," Charlie said, as they entered the courtyard. "We should buy watches today, as I really don't want to be late for one of Ms. Borovich's musters."

Charlie's time estimation proved spot on. They entered the Institute, stopping for a second to admire the magnificent entrance, then headed up one flight of stairs to the Department of Apprentices, where they joined a group of boys and girls filing into the muster room. Ben was glad to see many other apprentices dressed in rough clothes, and they all had fewer than four diamonds above their shoulders.

They spotted Natalie near the centre of the room, talking to a couple of older boys. She waved at them, but there was no time to talk, as Dagmar came striding in. The room quietened down and everyone found their square in double-quick time.

"Good morning," Dagmar said, with a face that clearly didn't care if the morning was good or not. Muster was rattled off quickly with military precision.

"Announcements," Dagmar said, putting her hands behind her back. "For this morning's chores, you will be working up top. For those of you not informed, everyone except the senior apprentices helps keep the Institute clean. Each day you are assigned a different task. Tuesday is animal care. Mr. Greenwood and Mr. Hornberger, if you stick with your fellow one star apprentices, or Ones, as you will now be called, you will be told what to do. Dismissed."

Everyone except the Fours and Fives made their way along the hallway and up the stairs. Ben counted about a dozen apprentices with only one diamond, them included. Natalie was a little way ahead, with her group of Twos, and the staircase was too busy to barge their way past.

Charlie was fidgeting nervously as they climbed. "Did you notice the subtle groans the other Ones made when Dagmar made the announcement?" He was staring at the other apprentices, oblivious to the looks he was getting. Charlie did have a point. Many of the Ones wore resigned expressions.

"This can't be good," Charlie said.

"We'll soon find out."

Ben's curiosity increased with every flight of stairs they climbed, until they reached the top gallery. Looking over the railing, Ben could just make out the Queen Elizabeth statue far below. Ben and Charlie followed the crowd through the door that led out to the roof.

"Oh man, I forgot about the smell."

Charlie had one hand squeezing his nose and the other making a futile attempt at wafting away the smell of manure. But Ben barely noticed the smell. Surrounding the glass pyramid that towered over them was a series of paddocks, filled with animals that made Ben's body tingle. There were huge eagles, pegasi, griffins, wyverns and even small dragons. Between them they created a cacophony of roars, squawks and growls. Ben spotted apprentices already hard at work. Some were cleaning the beasts; others were attempting to feed them with varying degrees of success. The lucky ones got to relax while the animals they were charged with dozed in the morning sun.

"This way, gang."

The voice came from an older boy near the front of the group. He led them round the corner and into a small paddock that was empty except for a large, shallow storage tank. From it came a smell that almost made Ben gag. The tank was filled with pooh.

"Alright, people, it's time for everyone's favourite chore. Let's grab a shovel and get started. Remember, those who slack off make it harder for the rest of us. Yes, I'm talking to you, Billy and Hans. If I catch you sword fighting with your shovels again, I'm going to report your arses."

There was some laughter, mainly aimed at two small, skinny boys who looked ready to sulk. They, along with the rest, picked shovels resting next to the storage tank, and headed off in different directions. Ben and Charlie watched, uncertain what they were supposed to be doing.

"Guys, over here."

It was the boy who had given the orders. He looked considerably older than them; Ben guessed around eighteen. He was well built, with biceps indicating regular gym work. His head was shaved and he had small studs in each ear.

"My name is William – or Will," he said, offering his hand. Will gave them a friendly smile and Ben found himself warming to the boy. "I am the Chief One; the title is less impressive than it sounds. I get lumped with things like getting people to work, making sure nobody bunks off, and occasionally helping if I can. I'm guessing you're wondering what on earth you've gotten yourselves into?"

"Not at all."

"I am," Charlie said. "Shovels, and pooh? I really hope it's not what I think."

"Are you thinking that it's shovelling shit?"

"Yes."

"Bingo," William said, with a grin. He went over and picked up three shovels and three sets of gloves, lying next to them.

"It sounds worse than it is," William said. Seeing Charlie's cringing look as he stared at the latex gloves, William added, "I'd put them on if I were you. You don't want the pooh going on your hands, and not just because of the smell. Dragon's pooh is red hot and the wyvern's burns like acid."

"And yet you said it sounds worse than it is?"

"Yeah, it grows on you," William said, giving Charlie another smile. "Plus, it works the body, especially the arms. You'll put some muscle on."

"This just gets worse and worse," Charlie said, as he fumbled with the gloves.

"You'll get used to it. Come on, I'll show you the ropes."

William swung the shovel over his shoulder. Ben did likewise, while Charlie dragged his along, and they followed

William onto one of the small dirt paths that ran between the paddocks. Ben supposed the animals must be confined by magic, because the wooden paddocks would surely be futile by themselves. They passed several winged animals, plus something that looked like a two-headed ostrich, before finally coming to a halt.

"There she blows," William said, pointing proudly. "Your first job."

Charlie dropped his shovel. "Please tell me you're joking."

In a small enclosure sat two large chimpanzees. They looked ordinary enough, except for the bat-like wings protruding from their backs. They were staring at Ben, Charlie and William with an intelligent curiosity inherent in most apes. Ben's eyes went to the pooh; it was scattered across the enclosure, in some places mounds of it a foot high.

"As you can see, they have healthy bowel movements," William said, leaning easily on his shovel.

"Why the climbing frame?" Charlie asked. He was referring to the wooden construction that spanned the paddock. "And what stops them flying away?"

"There are spells round each of the paddocks. Each spell is different, depending on the animal within. As for the climbing frame – they are still chimpanzees; they like to climb."

As William spoke, one of the chimpanzees took off and flew towards them, landing right at the front of the paddock just a couple of feet away. The chimpanzee screeched and slapped his head so violently that Charlie fell over trying to backpedal. Ben was marginally less alarmed, but only showed it with a widening of the eyes.

"Relax," William said, giving Charlie a hand and helping him up. "That's just their way of saying hi. They always get a bit excited when somebody new shows up. They're really quite friendly."

"I'm not sure I'd count slapping my skull and screaming as friendly," Charlie said. He glanced at an adjacent paddock. A large cat-like animal slept peacefully.

"Can't we start off with that cat over there?" Charlie asked. "I think I could handle that. It's even piled all its pooh up nicely in the corner."

"That's a baby deema," William said, his friendly face turning momentarily serious. "If you wake it up, it will most likely kill you."

"A deema?" Ben had heard that word before. "That's the animal the dark elf was riding when he attacked the Croydon headquarters."

William nodded. "So I heard, though that one was fully grown. The dark elves like to ride them. They're a right pain to train, and not at all loyal. But if you can handle them, they're extremely useful. Fast, powerful, and they can run forever."

"I guess it's back to the chimpanzees, then," Charlie said reluctantly.

"Good idea. There are only a couple of things to look out for. Don't get any of the pooh on your skin, as it's acidic. And try not to look them in the eye. They will think you're trying to engage them, and they may try to play with you."

"Play with us?" Charlie said. "How do they 'play'? I'm guessing they're not about to whip out a chess set."

"No, they're not into chess," William said, with another smile. Ben got the idea that he was enjoying Charlie's sense of humour. "They look at us as toy things. So they will most likely poke and prod you."

"Does it hurt?" Charlie asked, subconsciously wrapping his arms around his body.

"It's not too bad. The throwing can hurt a bit, though."

Even Ben reacted to this. "Throwing?"

"Yes. One of their games is to grab you by your arms or legs and throw you across the paddock. Sometimes they even like to play catch, with you as the ball."

"That's a joke, right? Tell me you're joking."

"Afraid not," William said. "Right, I think you're ready. Let's get cracking. I'll help for a bit, until you get the hang of things."

William picked up his shovel, opened the gate, and went straight into the paddock. He walked past the chimpanzee without making eye contact and then stopped and turned around, beckoning to them.

"She's not interested in me, so it was easy to get past," William said. "It may be a bit trickier for you. Just walk confidently and act disinterested. And don't be afraid. They can smell fear and it excites them."

"I must reek, then," Charlie said.

Ben put a hand on Charlie's shoulder. "Let's go together. Come on, no use drawing it out."

He hauled his shovel over his shoulder. Charlie sighed and dragged his own shovel along.

Despite the folly of it, Ben was still tempted to look at the chimpanzee as they walked by. He could feel its eyes on them and couldn't help cringing a little, imagining those long hairy arms reaching out to touch him. He thought he caught a flicker of movement from the corner of his eye, but with three quick steps, they were past, and walking hurriedly to William in the middle of the paddock. Next to him was a small wooden cart with two wheels and a pair of handles.

"Good job," William said. "Now, let's work from right to left. Concentrate on the darker pooh, if you can. That stuff has been sitting there longer. Transport it to this cart and we'll wheel it out when it gets full."

"Shovel the dark pooh. Got it," Ben said.

Aside from the horrible smell, Ben found it was a strangely satisfying experience. Sometimes the most basic manual chores with easily observable results can be quite fulfilling. The hardest part was keeping an eye on the chimpanzees, to make sure they kept their distance. William tackled the pooh closest to the animals. Ben felt a pleasant soreness in his arms as he worked, picking up the pooh and transporting it into the cart. Charlie could only lift a fraction of what Ben did, but there was a grim determination in his face as he worked.

They got into a nice rhythm, and Ben was just getting into his groove when William cursed.

"Charlie," William said. His voice contained a note of caution.

Charlie stopped mid-shovel and looked round. "What— oh dear."

Both chimpanzees were making their way over to him.

"Help! What should I do? Should I run?"

"No," William said immediately. "Running is a very bad idea. Just keep working and ignore them. Make sure you don't look them in the eye."

Charlie went back to shovelling, though Ben could see his spade shaking a little. The chimpanzees came right up to him, stepping in the pooh Charlie was trying to dig. With forced nonchalance, Charlie attempted to turn and find another pile to clear up.

The taller of the two chimpanzees reached out and grabbed Charlie's t-shirt. With surprising ease, he lifted Charlie up and placed him directly between him and his fellow chimpanzee. Charlie managed to remain quiet until they started pushing him back and forth.

"Help!" Charlie said.

Ben looked imploringly to William, who was now watching the scene, and looking around the paddock, as if searching for something.

"Prepare yourself, Charlie," William shouted. He ran a little to the left, then adjusted his position. "Ben, stand ten feet to my right."

"Prepare myself for what?" Charlie shouted back, with increasing panic.

The answer came before William could reply.

The chimpanzees began a tug-of-war with Charlie's body. The taller one was victorious. He grabbed Charlie's wrists and then, like a professional athlete, spun him around and around, releasing him at maximum velocity.

"Here he comes!" William shouted. Ben watched in astonishment as Charlie sailed through the air. The impact would have been horrible, but William was ready. He took a couple of steps back and clenched his teeth as Charlie crashed into him. They both hit the grass hard in a mass of arms and legs.

Ben ran over to help them up. "Are you guys okay?"

"I'm alright," William said, getting to his feet. Charlie looked dazed, but managed to stumble to his feet with William's help.

"I've just been thrown fifty feet by a flying chimpanzee. I've felt better," Charlie said, rubbing his backside.

"Something to tell your future kids about," Ben said, with a grin.

"We're done here," William said. He was looking at the chimpanzees again. They were chatting away to each other, and pointing their lanky arms in their direction. "They'll come over in a minute. The other chimpanzee will want to see if he can throw you further. It's a little competition they have going."

The three of them ran to the cart, now laden with pooh and started pushing it to the gate. As soon as the chimpanzees saw them leaving, they bellowed their chests and took to the air.

"Faster," William grunted, his biceps bulging.

Ben didn't need encouraging. Between the three of them, the cart almost flew across the paddock. They crossed the gate and made it out just in time. Ben, Charlie and even Will lay on their backs, panting.

"Is it always like that?" Ben asked, eventually finding his breath and sitting up.

"It's not normally that exciting," William admitted, getting to his feet. "I'll give you guys a well-earned ten-minute break. Then come and find me and we'll tackle the next animal."

"You want us to do that again?" Charlie asked incredulously.

"The next one will be easier, I promise." He gave them a salute and started walking. "Enjoy your rest."

— CHAPTER TWELVE —
Prince Robert

"I'm thinking of quitting," Charlie said.

"Oh, shut up."

There was no comfortable place to rest, as getting away from the screeches and roars was impossible, but they found a little spot next to the glass gable and sat down on the grass.

Charlie's clothes reflected his mood. They had been stretched and even ripped in places thanks to the chimpanzees, but he did brighten a little when Natalie appeared, waving at them.

"Oh my, Charlie, you look terrible!" Natalie said, wrinkling her nose. "What happened?"

"I had an incident with a chimpanzee," Charlie said.

Natalie couldn't help laughing after hearing the story. "You're not the first, I promise," she said. "And you've got a great story to tell people."

"So I've been told," Charlie muttered, but Ben saw that Natalie's amusement was melting Charlie's foul mood.

"What are you up to? Not shovelling pooh, well, I hope?" Ben asked.

"No, that job is just for Ones. Twos are responsible for feeding the beasts, which is sometimes fun and easy, and other times makes Charlie's chimpanzee ride look pleasant. Today we got to feed some baby schvolts, which was really nice."

Ben was about to ask what a schvolt was when he heard a whistling noise and saw something flying right at him. A flash of brown. He ducked instinctively.

The pooh missile skimmed his hair and splattered right into Charlie's already filthy chest.

Coming towards them was Joshua, surrounded by the same five apprentices he seen in the lunch room. Joshua threw his head back and laughed, his white teeth gleaming in the sun. Unlike nearly everyone else, Joshua was still wearing fine clothes and they looked untouched.

Joshua cupped his hands round his mouth. "You shouldn't have ducked," he said; his voice had a nasal tint to it and only just carried over the animals' noise. "You let your little friend take the hit."

Ben saw a spellshooter in Joshua's hand – none of the others had one. He pointed at another piece of pooh on the floor and fired. The pooh elevated and formed into a round ball, the size of a tennis ball. Ben watched it closely.

"Now, be a man and don't let your friend take this one for you," Joshua said. He flicked his spellshooter and the ball of pooh came hurtling towards them. Ben dived to his left. A fraction of the ball of pooh caught his arm, leaving a small mark, but the rest whistled harmlessly by.

Joshua's smile was momentarily wiped from his face and replaced by a flash of anger. "Would you stop moving?" He brought his spellshooter forwards, searching for another piece of pooh to hurl. There now was only a few feet between them. Ben marched right up to Joshua, so they were almost nose to nose. Joshua had a good few inches on him, but Ben's steely gaze and complete lack of intimidation seemed to unsettle Joshua.

"What's your problem?" Ben asked, just about keeping a rein on his temper.

Joshua, despite being taller, took a small step backwards. He shrugged and smiled. His friends smiled too. "Relax, Ben. We're just having a bit of fun. It's normal to mess around with the new apprentices."

"Really? Well, if you mess around with us again, I'm going to take one of the many piles of pooh lying around, and shove it down your throat. Got it?"

Joshua raised both hands in mock defence. "Are you threatening me?" His friends started chuckling and making baiting noises. One of the boys gave Ben a little push.

"Joshua, what are you doing?"

Natalie stepped into the fray, attempting to get between Joshua and Ben. She tried to push Joshua back. He appeared unwilling to use any force against her, but a tall spindly girl next to Joshua intervened, and shoved Natalie away.

"Get lost, Natalie," she said.

"Oi!" Charlie stepped in, despite being several inches smaller than everyone else; his soft face was creased with anger and he raised a chubby finger at the skinny girl. "Don't push her."

"You going to stop me, midget?" the girl said, with a cruel laugh.

There was only one way this was going to end, Ben realised. He clenched his fists into balls. If he could take Joshua out quickly, they might have a chance, but the girls – especially the tall one – looked like they could fight.

A horn blasted, so loud it made Ben's body vibrate. Everyone turned, the potential melee momentarily forgotten. From the door that cut into the glass gable came a girl – or woman to be more precise; she looked at least eighteen and had five colourless diamonds on her shoulder. In her hand was a curved horn.

"Positions, apprentices!" she shouted. "The prince is on his way up. Look lively!"

There was a murmur of surprise, which quickly turned to alarm. Joshua's friends ran, and Joshua followed, with one last calculating look at Ben.

"I've got to run," Natalie said, looking anxiously towards the door the prince would come out of.

"What are we supposed to do?" Ben asked.

"Just look busy," Natalie said, giving them both a smile. "I'll be back as soon as the prince has gone."

And with that, she too darted off.

Ben looked helplessly about. Everyone seemed to start working at twice their original pace.

"Get your shovel," Ben said, picking his up. "Let's go find William."

The paddocks were large, and with the sloping glass roof in the middle, it was impossible to see more than one side at a time.

"Follow the smell of pooh," Ben said, his eyes scanning the area.

"I'm covered in it. I think it's overwhelmed my senses. I can no longer smell anything," Charlie said, sniffing. "I can't see William anywhere. Should we just stop and pretend to be working? That might look less conspicuous."

"Good idea."

But the moment they started genuinely wanting to shovel pooh, there was none to be had. They had obviously entered an area where their fellow Ones had already cleaned. Ben started getting anxious; the prince would be turning up any moment.

"Psst – over here!"

The call came from a couple of apprentices whose paddock they were just passing. They were standing near a gate, loading the final bits of pooh onto their cart. The animal was nowhere to be seen.

Ben and Charlie hurried over, entered the paddock and, with grateful smiles, started helping with the shovelling. They made it just in time. A quick glance up revealed three figures walking down the muddy path parallel to the glass gable. Two figures walked in front of the prince, a man and a woman, both with four green diamonds over their shoulders, but it was the man behind them who Ben was drawn to. Prince Robert was tall and well built, with dark hair and peculiar gold-flecked eyes. He wore a deep red cloak emblazoned with the Royal Institute of Magic emblem. For the first time, Ben noticed the diamonds on the prince's shoulder. He had five, one of each colour representing the departments in the Institute. This was the first time Ben had seen Robert genuinely looking like a prince, and it was an impressive sight.

"Stop staring," one of the apprentices whispered in his ear.

Ben quickly lowered his eyes, but not before the prince turned and looked his way. There was a moment, no more than a second, where they locked gazes. Ben's heart jumped. Should he bow? The prince gave the most subtle of nods. It was all over in a heartbeat, as the prince and his two Spellswords passed them by and were soon out of sight.

"That was crazy!"

Ben turned to the apprentices who had saved them. It was Billy and Hans, the two scrawny boys William had chided for slacking off. Billy was the one who had spoken and was looking at him with something approaching awe.

"The prince looked at you! I've never seen him look at an apprentice before, let alone recognise that we exist."

Ben turned back to where he had last seen the prince, thoughtful. He remembered Natalie's words when she had described the prince. *"Instead of leading the Institute, he spends his time travelling to the most obscure places in the Unseen Kingdoms. It was the same with his father; in fact, the last three commanders have all died while travelling. They become obsessed with it."*

Ben hadn't thought much about Natalie's comments until he had been thrown into a memory spell left by his parents, where he saw his ancestor Michael entrusted with Elizabeth's sword and re-uniting her Armour. But that wasn't all – the Queen had issued a firm warning about her son. *"If Henry has even the slightest inkling of the Armour's whereabouts, he will go mad searching for it. Should he don the Armour, the consequences would be dire."*

Which begged the question: was Prince Robert looking for the Armour? Was that why he had been searching for Ben's parents?

— Chapter Thirteen —
Apprenticeship Training

"There are other departments besides Spellsword, Ben," Charlie said.

They had changed into their spare clothes and went straight to lunch, where they had far too much to eat. They were letting it digest by relaxing in the common room – a place full of squishy armchairs, low-lying tables, and a thick red carpet Ben longed to sink his feet into. In the corner was a snack bar, manned by an apprentice, serving hot drinks and freshly baked treats. The smell filled the room and, despite Ben's full stomach, he had to use considerable willpower not to grab a sticky bun. There were others reading, chatting, and Ben even spotted two playing Captains of Magic, the multi-tiered chess-like game Charlie had tried at the hotel a few weeks ago.

"Charlie is right, Ben," Natalie said. "I think it might be a good idea to try out each department before racing ahead in just one."

"We're not racing ahead," Ben said firmly. The three of them formed a small triangle of chairs, with a table in the middle. Charlie and Natalie had their handbooks open on their laps. "I just think we should do the practical step that accompanies the theory before moving on to a different department. That way we can practise what we learned, else we might forget it."

That certainly wouldn't be the case with Charlie, who rarely forgot anything. The Spellsword training involved the least theory and Ben hadn't found the first theory test easy. He had passed, with 88% (Charlie got 100%), but wasn't looking forward to future tests.

"Fine," Charlie said, slapping his handbook shut. "But tomorrow I'm choosing the next department to study."

"Let me guess – something boring?"

"Scholar."

"What a surprise," Ben said.

"The Department of Scholars isn't as bad as it sounds," Natalie said. "There's a lot of really interesting knowledge that will help you better understand the Unseen Kingdoms."

"Like history," Charlie said, pointing a chubby finger on the cover of his book. His eyes had lit up. "There's some incredible stuff about what really happened during the Spanish Armada. You know the Institute helped us win?"

"Really?" Ben, who hated history at school, suddenly had a feeling it would be different here. But he was determined to hold his ground. "No, we do the Spellsword training practical first."

Charlie reluctantly agreed.

"I need to get going," Natalie said, glancing at her watch. "Let's meet up again at 3pm."

As Ben climbed the stairs with a slightly downbeat Charlie, the excitement started building. Would they get their own spellshooters? Visions of loading it up with some serious spells and fighting mock battles with spell-generated bad guys filled his head all the way through the department's double doors and along the hallway to a door marked "Spell Training".

"Here we go," Ben said, rubbing his hands.

"Let's just hope I don't embarrass myself too much," Charlie said, rubbing a hand on his forehead.

The room was exactly as Ben remembered. The high ceilings gave the room a feeling of space. There was a large table, chest high, and a few apprentices were sat on stools, fiddling with their spellshooters. All the action was to their right. A series of long, narrow rooms were partitioned by glass walls so that you could see through each one. At one end of each room was a circular target, and at the other was one or two apprentices, taking turns to shoot spells at it. There were balls of fire, ice-like spears and many other spells of different elements and shapes, all bombarding the targets with varying degrees of effectiveness.

"Ahah, Ben Greenwood! I've been expecting you," a booming voice said. "And Charlie Hamburger!"

"Hornberger," Charlie said, with a resigned voice that indicated that was not the first time his name had been pronounced wrong.

James McFadden was just as imposing as Ben remembered. He must have been at least six and a half feet tall, with shoulder-length blond hair and shoulders so broad they could probably carry a small car.

"I bet you're anxious to get going, eh?" James said, slapping both of them on the shoulder; Charlie almost fell over. James led them to another door Ben hadn't noticed, on the opposite side of the room.

"Keep working, everyone! Don't think I can't see you just because I'm not in the room," James shouted at his students, as they passed through the door.

The room was a pale imitation of the one they had just left. It was far smaller, with five small targets at one end that Ben could reach with a moderate throw. At the other end was a shelf with five drawers, labelled one to five. In each one were mounds of spell pellets.

"Hi, guys!"

Jimmy's clothes were dirty, with several brown stains that looked as though they had been vigorously scrubbed without success. Clearly he had forgotten to bring spare clothes, but this did nothing to dampen his cheerful demeanour. There were two brown-haired girls next to him who were trying to stand as far away as possible and Ben spotted them waving their hands in front of their noses. When they spotted Charlie and Ben, they gave a cheerful wave and introduced themselves as Emma and Debbie. Ben felt Emma's eyes linger on him a little longer than necessary.

All three had red pellets in their hands. Jimmy closed an eye, stuck out his tongue and, with a back swing that looked like a baseball player, threw his pellet at the dartboard. It missed entirely and bounced harmlessly onto the floor.

"That was hopeless, even for you, Jimmy," James said, hands on hips. "You're distracted. Concentrate!" He said the last word so loud that Jimmy's feet left the ground.

The two girls at the end of the room fared better. They threw their pellets with swings that instantly told Ben they were both sporty. Both hit the target, and both pellets exploded in little puffs of flame.

"Good, good!" James said, nodding. "How many in a row?"

One girl held up two fingers; the other, three.

"Get to five and you can progress to the next grade. Keep going!"

Ben watched with a mixture of fascination and disappointment. There was no spellshooter in sight. Charlie, though, was looking a little brighter.

"You're not ready for them, not by a long shot," James said, with a chuckle, when Ben asked the question. "You need to master these spells first and show you have what it takes to command a spellshooter."

"What about the spells in the shop?" Ben asked. "Charlie and I both threw those."

"Pah," James said, scrunching his face and waving a gigantic dismissive hand. "Those things are designed to work for all but the weakest minds." He walked over, and pulled a small red spell from a shelf that was clearly labelled "One". It was tiny, and James' fingers looked like they would squash it any moment.

"This is your first test. There are five difficulties of spells you will need to master. When you can make the most difficult one explode, you will move on to the spellshooter."

James threw it, without even looking. It hit the middle of the target and burst into flames. James casually walked over and picked up another one.

"There are three factors to getting any spell to cast: willpower, concentration and vision, in that order of importance. You must will the spell to do as you command. You must be able to concentrate, and block out any exterior distractions – not easy when you might have a screaming, man-eating troll bearing down on you. Finally, you must be able to envision what you want the spell to do. With this little spell, you simply want it to explode into a little flame when it comes into contact with something."

Ben's disappointment at not getting hold of a spellshooter had disappeared. He was looking at the shelf of spells, itching to get his hands on one and launch it at one of the targets. But

James had other ideas and, barring a handful of times when he excused himself to check on the other room, he spent the next half an hour lecturing them on exactly what did and did not constitute willpower, concentration and vision, until Ben felt he could recite every definition of each word. When that was done, James spent another fifteen minutes telling them how to handle the spell ("Do not squash it; the magic could leak out and it would become worthless") and even how to throw it ("If you spin the spell, it could lose its potency and perform in unexpected ways").

"I think you're ready to give it a go," James said, rubbing his huge hands together. "I've only given you a basic overview, but it should be enough to get started on the first spell."

James had them stand opposite the two remaining targets, and placed a spell each in their hands, with surprising delicacy.

"Your first spell," James said, with a solemn nod. "An important moment in any apprentice's journey. The question is – will you be the first to successfully cast a spell on their first go?"

"Nobody has done it before?" Ben asked, holding the little spell up to his face.

"It takes, on average, two dozen attempts before you get one to cast," James said. He stood back and folded his arms. "I will be counting for both of you."

Ben felt a little rush of adrenaline. Jimmy had stopped throwing, and even the two girls, Emma and Debbie, had paused, to watch. James gave them a frown, but didn't tell them to return to practice.

The small pellet weighed more than he expected, enough to give Ben confidence that he could throw it a good distance. The target was no more than thirty feet away, a series of red and white concentric circles, standing just in front of the wall. Willpower. Confidence. Vision. James' booming voice kept running round his head, making it difficult to clear his mind. He could feel eyes on him and he had the sudden urge to look up. Little noises like Jimmy's annoying nasal breathing and occasional sniffs suddenly seemed difficult to ignore. What had seemed like the simple task of hitting a large dartboard with a pellet suddenly became infinitely more difficult. Concentrate! Vision. That was easy, at least. He wanted the spell to burst into flames in the middle of the target. Ben positioned himself in line with the target. He raised his arm, and threw, his whole body following through like a tennis player. The little red spell flew forwards and just missed the bull's-eye. There was a tiny flashing glow and, for just a moment, Ben thought it was going to ignite. But instead it bounced off the target and hit the floor. He stared at the pellet on the floor with a mixture of disappointment and frustration, his confidence deflating like a popped balloon.

"Very good!" James said, breaking the silence, and clapping. Jimmy joined in enthusiastically, and the two girls gave him admiring looks before turning back to continue their training.

"Really?" Ben said, lifting his head. "It looked a bit pathetic to me."

"Not at all. You achieved a minor glow on your first attempt. That's rare – very rare. Your willpower is excellent and there was nothing wrong with your vision. But your concentration needs work. Go and get another spell." James turned to Charlie. "Right, your turn. Remember, don't worry about throwing it as hard as you can. That isn't important."

Charlie narrowed his eyes, and Ben saw a steely determination that few people knew existed. He threw the pellet; it hit the outer rim and bounced harmlessly away.

Charlie smiled brightly. "I'm quite pleased with that. Did you see me hit the target?"

"I've seen worse first efforts," James said, glancing briefly at Jimmy. "Your concentration was good, but you need to work on your willpower. Believe that you can make the spell cast and it will."

Ben hurried over to pick up his spell and get back into position. He was determined to make it cast second time. *Has anyone ever managed that?* he wondered. Ben took a deep breath, to relax his body. He wound his arm back, his eyes fixed on the bull's-eye. A loud cough echoed in the small room just as Ben was swinging through. He jerked and the spell hit the target just to the right of the bull's-eye. It glowed again, brighter this time, before bouncing to the floor.

Ben turned angrily, assuming it was Jimmy. But someone else had entered the room, leaning casually against the door frame with his legs crossed.

"I'm sorry, did I distract you?" Joshua asked with a smirk. "I had something in my throat."

Ben was furious. He made a move for the door, but a huge hand clamped down on his shoulder.

"I'm coming over to inspect your snow storm spell in a minute," James said, staring hard at Joshua. "I expect to see a vast improvement."

Ben was pleased to see the smirk wiped off Joshua's face and he turned to go.

"Wait," James ordered, and Joshua turned round. "I want you to watch Ben's next attempt."

"What? Why?" Ben asked. The thought of Joshua smiling if he messed up again was not a pleasant one.

"To help you focus," James said. "The fear of failure will drive you."

Ben had no answer to that. He flashed a dirty look at Joshua, who was now watching with renewed amusement.

"No pressure," Joshua said. "I promise not to cough this time, but I've had hiccups all morning. Let's hope they don't re-surface."

Ben had several nasty responses ready, but held his tongue. Instead he turned to James. "Did my last go count? It's a bit unfair; Joshua distracted me."

"You think it's going to be nice and peaceful every time you fire a spell?" James said, his humour returning. "That would be nice, wouldn't it? No, that effort counted just as much as your first one. This is your third attempt."

Ben bit his tongue, retrieved another spell and marched back to the starting position. He swung his arm back, but before he could thrust forwards, a hand grabbed him.

"Slow down," James said, releasing Ben's arm. "I want you to count to sixty before throwing."

Ben almost ignored him and threw anyway. His count to sixty started off rushed, eager to get to the end so he could smash the spell against the target as hard as he could. But by the time he neared sixty, his breathing had slowed and he gave James a grateful nod.

"Now, concentrate," James said. "I don't mean block out all the noise, because that's impossible. Just focus on what you're doing and don't worry about external distractions."

It was a lot harder than Ben had imagined. He kept trying to block out all the noises and create a cone of silence. But as James said, that was impossible, and eventually he figured out a way to accept the external sounds and not be bothered by them. He took a deep breath, eyed up the target, and then, instead of giving everything in the follow through, launched the spell at a much more measured pace. It arced through the air and hit the target. There was a puff and a tiny flame, no bigger than a candle, before disappearing.

"Very good!" James said, clapping, his huge hands sounding like a drum. "Success at the third attempt. You join a very exclusive group."

Charlie gave him a high five and Jimmy attempted the same, but missed his hand completely. Both the girls were smiling and clapping too.

Ben grinned, and couldn't help turning to Joshua who looked like he'd swallowed a lemon. There was a look of undisguised hatred in his eyes that was so strong it sucked away some of Ben's elation. Surely that couldn't stem from the silly incident when he stole Joshua's spellshooter in the library a few weeks ago? There was something else there, Ben was sure of it. As Joshua turned to leave, Ben decided he was going to find out.

— CHAPTER FOURTEEN —
An Uninvited Guest

It took the rest of the session for Ben to cast five consecutive spells and move up to the next grade, which earned him a pat on the back from James. Charlie managed to cast his first spell on the twentieth attempt, which he was delighted about, having been worried that he was simply incapable of it at all.

To Ben's surprise, training in the other departments turned out to be just as interesting. In Diplomacy, they learnt about the different races and cultures in the Unseen Kingdoms and how to deal with them, from the Grey Dwarves in the north (always place your left fist to your chest in greeting) to the Sea Fairies (they are easy to bribe, especially with sweets). Despite Ben's dislike for Draven, the Department of Wardens was almost as cool as the Spellswords. A large part of their job was to watch the country borders and make sure no Unseens entered the ordinary world without authorisation. They sent out teams to track and capture those that did. In their first practical, Ben and

Charlie got to watch a group of three Wardens poring over a map, tracking the location of a rogue troll in Yorkshire. The Department of Trade was again completely different. The Institute had many valuable assets, and the Traders used these to bargain with the Unseens for goods and, most importantly, spells. Even the Department of Scholars proved to be fascinating. There was a lot more to it than just reading books – they were constantly investigating and researching unsolved mysteries, and often went travelling to dangerous places to solve them.

The next two weeks passed in a blur, with both Ben and Charlie so busy with cleaning in the mornings and learning in the afternoons that other than the trip into Taecia Square to buy watches, they had little time for anything else. Ben had wandered the Institute a few times in the hope that his Guardian status might trigger something, but to no avail. The Institute was huge, and he had no idea where to go or what to do. Natalie's suggestion of searching for architectural designs of the Institute had proved fruitless. Even the prospect that the Shadowseeker might still be searching for him became secondary to progressing with the apprenticeship. But that all changed at the beginning of the third week.

"What's the plan today?" Charlie asked.

They were in the locker room, picking up their handbooks. It was Monday morning and Ben and Charlie were both bubbling. They were probably two of the few people who preferred weekdays to weekends.

"We're a bit behind on Trade," Ben said, flipping through his book. "We've got a practical step where we have to successfully haggle with one of those devious gnomes in the Southern Quarter to purchase a level two spell for no more than thirty quid."

"That sounds— ow!" Charlie jumped back, shaking his wrist. "Ayla, stop it!"

Charlie's locker gave a lazy blink of her huge green eye, and then shot another spark, which crackled and hit Charlie square on the chest.

"I'm warning you!" Charlie said, pointing a finger at the eye. "I went out and bought some olive oil spray, and I'm not afraid to use it."

Charlie retrieved his handbook, and closed the locker with a last meaningful stare at Ayla, who replied with one more cheeky wink.

"Graduating from this apprenticeship will be worth it just to get another locker," Charlie said.

"You don't have any family in the Institute, do you?"

The question came from Emily. Her locker was just three away from Charlie's, and she had been watching him, combing her long brown hair.

"No, why?"

"Oh well. You're allowed to share lockers with family members," Emily said. "Olivia, my locker, is almost as bad as yours. She completely shuts down on the weekends, so sometimes I store my stuff with my older sister up in the Department of Wardens."

"So your sister's locker opens for you?" Charlie asked.

"Yeah. My sister just had to order her locker to grant family access. It's really handy."

"How long does it last for?"

"Forever, I guess, unless my sister cancels the order. It's not uncommon for families to share lockers, especially if someone ends up with a troublesome one."

Charlie was starting to look unusually interested, which Ben found peculiar, as he had no family within the Institute.

"So, if your sister left the Institute for a while, you'd still have access, right?"

"Yeah, I guess," Emily said, slightly taken aback by Charlie's intensity. "Listen, I gotta run. Good luck with your locker."

Charlie watched Emily leave the room with a thoughtful smile. He turned to Ben, tapping a finger on his chin.

Ben gave him an odd look. "What is it?"

Charlie gave a warning glance at the handful of apprentices still in the room. They quickly left and headed for the stairs. Charlie gave several surreptitious glances as they worked their way up the marble staircase, searching for anyone who might be able to overhear. They spotted Natalie, just in front of them, chatting animatedly with some friends. Ben called out to her. She immediately saw the meaningful looks on their faces and excused herself.

"What's going on?" she asked.

"Not here," Charlie said. "Let's find somewhere quiet."

The Department of Trade often had empty negotiating rooms and it didn't take them long to find one. The room had one small table and a window looking out on to the Institute courtyard, lined with heavy curtains that were half open.

Charlie double-checked the lock and made sure nobody was hiding in the curtains before he was satisfied.

"So, what's up?" Ben asked.

"Emily," Charlie replied, making Ben and especially Natalie give him confused looks. "She said her sister had granted family access to her locker. What if your parents have given each other access to their lockers? You would have access too."

The thought produced a rush of hope, but it was swallowed quickly by rationality. "Even if I had access to their lockers, wouldn't the Institute have raided them already when they were looking for my parents?"

"Not necessarily," Natalie said, with sudden interest. "The lockers for the top Institute members are extremely powerful. It wouldn't surprise me if nobody had managed to open them yet, not even the prince. And they would be the perfect storing place."

They looked at each other. None of them spoke, but the hope and excitement were impossible to miss.

"We need to take a look. How difficult is it to get into their locker room?" Ben asked.

"I've never tried," Natalie said. "It shouldn't be too hard, as long as the room isn't locked. The tricky bit is not attracting attention. Friday is the best day, as many of the Spellswords are on duty then and will not be at the Institute."

"Friday it is, then," Ben said.

"Also, it would be better if we did it late, after most members have gone home. Ideally no earlier than ten."

Ben looked to Charlie, who nodded. "I'll tell my parents I'm sleeping at yours."

"Great, we'll—"

Ben stopped mid-sentence, distracted by a small flutter of movement from the curtains.

"Did you see that?" Ben asked.

Both Charlie and Natalie nodded.

"A draught from the window?" Charlie said, raising his hand to feel for any movement in the air.

"I don't feel anything," Natalie replied, her voice suddenly quiet.

The curtains were large, easily big enough to hide in.

"I checked them, remember?" Charlie said, his voice firm.

"Some things are difficult to see," Natalie said.

They were all staring at the curtains, listening as well as looking for a sign of life. They heard nothing, except their own breathing, which somehow made it worse.

"There's an easy way to find out," Ben said, breaking the trance that had befallen them. Ignoring protests from Charlie and Natalie, he walked up to the curtain and extended a hand, reaching for one of the ripples.

Something knocked Ben to the ground.

Natalie screamed. Ben saw something bulge in the curtain and then vanish. Seconds later they heard the door click behind them. Ben yanked his neck round but saw only the door shutting softly.

Ben's first instincts were to go after it, but by the time he'd gotten to his feet, he knew whatever they had faced would be long gone.

Natalie had a hand to her mouth and Charlie was taking furtive glances everywhere, as if it might still be in the room.

"Did anyone see it?" Ben asked. His heart was pumping and his words came out raggedly.

Both Charlie and Natalie shook their heads.

"Just a blur, but nothing more," Charlie said. The look of fear had left him now they were sure it had gone.

"Was it the Shadowseeker?" Natalie asked.

Ben and Charlie exchanged glances.

"If it was, why was it spying on us? I thought it wanted to take me out."

"If it's not the Shadowseeker, what else could it be?"

Ben was wondering exactly the same thing.

— Chapter Fifteen —

Broomstick Battles

For the first time since they arrived at the Institute, the days started to drag. Both Ben and Charlie had their eyes firmly fixed on Friday, and their lack of focus elsewhere reflected in their study.

"A word, Mr. Greenwood and Mr. Hornberger," Dagmar said one morning. They had been about to file out of muster to polish the grand staircase. Instead they approached Dagmar's desk. She was sitting down for once, making her look even smaller than usual. Ben couldn't help staring at her long, tightly wound ponytail and her long eyelashes – two important features that helped clarify her gender.

They stood silently for a full minute while Dagmar finished reading. Ben resisted the urge to clear his throat, knowing it would have catastrophic consequences.

"Your progress – or lack of it – has come to my attention when reviewing your handbook," Dagmar said, finally looking up. "You were running a commendable pace until the last few days. What has happened?"

"Nothing, Ms. Borovich," Ben said. "Everything is just getting more difficult."

"I don't buy it," Dagmar replied. "Your progress has been smooth among all departments. You, Ben, have excelled in Spellsword." She turned her hawk-like eyes to Charlie. "And you, Charlie, have shown some aptitude in Scholar. But the last few days you have slowed. What changed?"

Ben cursed inwardly and prayed Charlie wouldn't give anything away. His cheeks flushed, but he shook his head, a little too vigorously, and said, "It's like Ben said. Everything is getting more difficult."

Dagmar rose an eyebrow. "Are you aware of the make–break point?"

"No," they answered in union.

"Fifty days. That is how long you have to complete the first grade of the apprenticeship if you wish to progress."

"We've only been here seventeen," Charlie said, doing the maths far quicker than Ben.

"Which means you're over a third of the way through." She took the baton from her desk and patted it idly. "Your performances are watched closely during the apprenticeship. Even if you become a member, slow progression could mean not entering the department of your choice."

Ben felt like he was back at school being lectured by the headmaster. The only difference was, this time he cared.

"We'll try harder," Ben said with conviction.

"I'm sure you will," Dagmar said. "However, in order to help you to keep up, you will now find daily targets for each department in your handbooks. Meet these, and you will be fine. Fall too far behind and you will find yourselves in trouble."

Twenty minutes later, they had retrieved their handbooks from the lockers and were perusing through them in the common room.

"This is tough," Ben said. "Look what I have to get through by Friday. I've got to talk a city goblin down by fifty percent in a trade deal and bargain for the release of a Creeten in the Kingdom of Ursla. I've no idea what a Creeten is and haven't the faintest idea where to find the Kingdom of Ursla."

"You think you've got problems. They expect me to graduate to the third grade spell pellet. I'm closer to touching the moon than I am to making one of those cast properly."

"We'll manage," Ben said. He turned a page in his handbook and smiled. "Hey, guess what we're doing this afternoon?"

Charlie rubbed his cheeks and sighed. "Darn, I was hoping you'd forgotten about that."

Ben stood up, his sudden invigoration sweeping away any lingering unpleasantness from Dagmar's conversation. "Come on, let's go."

They climbed the staircase, Ben trying to pick up the pace, Charlie trying to slow it down.

"I hope there aren't too many people in there. There's something about being publicly humiliated that I'm not very fond of," Charlie said.

They entered the Department of Spellswords and headed straight to a room marked "Sword Combat Training".

Ben rubbed his hands and grinned. "You ready?"

"No – shall we come back later?"

Ben ignored the comment and opened the door. Inside, the space was open plan, the rooms partitioned by glass, giving them a look at the whole area in one sweeping glance. The room they had entered was a small lecture hall, with a whiteboard, a desk, and several rows of seats, all currently empty. To Ben's right were four square sparring rooms. Three were empty, but in the nearest was an apprentice battling a magically created soldier. The swordplay was quick and intricate, the soldier clearly skilled. But the apprentice, who had four stars above his shoulder, was no slouch, and matched him blow for blow. There was another figure in there with them, but he was just watching, arms folded. Ben noted the two green diamonds above his shoulder.

The figure looked up and spotted them. He gave a friendly wave and promptly left the glass room, completely unconcerned at leaving the apprentice alone with the magical soldier.

"Hello, hello!" the Spellsword said, with a broad smile.

Now that he approached, Ben saw that he was an elf. Unlike most elves he had seen, the Spellsword was dark skinned, with black hair that ran just past his shoulders.

"Welcome! I'm sorry, I was dealing with a student. My name is Zadaya. What are your names?"

Zadaya was clearly not fluent in English, yet unlike most people learning the language his accent was perfect, though his grammar was not.

"So, this is your first practical lesson – yes?" Zadaya said, after introductions were made. He had a youthful exuberance about him and Ben thought he couldn't have been more than twenty, though it was always hard to tell with elves.

"Yes, this is our first lesson," Ben said.

"Good! I expect you want to get straight into the box and fight, eh?" Zadaya said, making an exaggerated sword fighting motion with his arms. "Not sit down and listen to Zadaya talk about boring things like posture, balance, and technique – am I right?"

"Yes," Ben said, just as Charlie said, "No."

"I'm perfectly happy to listen to a lecture," Charlie said.

"Pah! Lecture is boring." He motioned to them. "Come! Let us fight."

Zadaya led a delighted Ben and a horrified Charlie into one of the glass boxes. Lining the back was a rack filled with all sorts of weapons and armour. Ben couldn't believe his luck. He had expected hours of lectures and rather dull practice sessions before they let him anywhere near a real combat scenario.

"Here are your weapons," Zadaya said.

Ben's excitement took a little knock when he accepted the plain wooden sword Zadaya offered. He had been eyeing up the shiny red ones near the end of the rack.

"This is all you need," Zadaya said. "It will be enough – trust me."

"What are we facing?" Ben asked, testing the sword in his hand.

"More importantly, can we get hurt?" Charlie asked, with a look of anxiety.

"Do not worry. You will feel impact, but little pain," Zadaya said. He grinned, showing a set of clean white teeth to rival Joshua's. "Ready for fight?"

"No," Charlie said, his voice rising as panic started to set in. He was shifting left and right, looking as though he was ready to bolt. "What am I supposed to do with this?" Charlie asked, indicating the sword. "I haven't the faintest clue how to sword fight."

"Do not worry, my friend," Zadaya said. "Just do your best."

Before Charlie could reply, Zadaya lifted his spellshooter and fired a pellet into the centre of the box.

Ben had been expecting a fairly straightforward opponent for their first fight – a child goblin or a clumsy swordsman perhaps. What he didn't expect was an old-fashioned broomstick, complete with slender arms and a brush of bristles for legs. It had no face, but it did have a small wooden sword in its right hand.

"What is that?" Ben asked.

"Isn't it obvious?" Charlie replied. Some of his anxiety had dissipated on seeing their opponent. "It's a magical sword-fighting broomstick."

"Do not underestimate your enemy," Zadaya said. "Now, fight!"

He fired another spell into the broomstick and it suddenly came to life, lifting its sword and turning this way and that, until it identified its opponents.

The broomstick shuffled forwards.

"What should we do?" Charlie said, holding his sword a little unsteadily.

"Surround it," Ben said immediately.

That proved easier said than done. Every time Ben shifted to his left, the broomstick shuffled with surprising speed, managing to keep both Ben and Charlie in front of it.

It soon became clear the broomstick wasn't about to charge into them, and after a few minutes of careful dancing around the floor without a sword being swung, Ben started to lose patience.

"I'm going in," he said. "Back me up if I'm in trouble."

As soon as Ben approached, the broomstick turned his way. Ben swung his sword, aiming for the middle of the handle, hoping perhaps to snap it in half. The broomstick lifted its sword and blocked. Ben struck again, and again. Twice more the broomstick blocked, with what seemed like relative ease, though it was difficult to judge as it had no face. Ben was about to strike again when the broomstick launched a counterattack. Ben got his sword up just in time for the first two blows, but the third one rapped him on the shoulder, and he felt a dull sting. Before he knew it, he was backpedalling fast, frantically blocking and occasionally dodging.

"Charlie!"

Backup arrived just in time. Charlie came in from the side, sword swinging. The broomstick was forced to block its new attack, giving Ben a bit of breathing space. But he had no time to recover, for Charlie was instantly on the retreat, barely blocking each attack.

"A little help!" Charlie cried. "Ow!" The broomstick had caught him on the side.

Ben ran in to help, aiming for the broomstick's unprotected "back". But somehow the broomstick spun and parried.

"Together!" Ben said.

From the corner of his eye Ben could see that Charlie was exhausted, but to his credit he launched himself at the broomstick with a cry. For a moment, Ben thought they were about to win; the broomstick was on the defensive and slowly shuffling backwards. It stumbled, and Charlie went in for the kill. But it turned out to be a feint, and the broomstick deflected Charlie's sword easily. With a surprisingly graceful pirouette, given that it was a broomstick, it spun and stabbed Charlie in the stomach. Then it was on to Ben, with renewed ferocity. Ben managed to block it twice before he too was stabbed.

A spell fired into the broomstick and it vanished in a puff of wood chips.

"You are both dead!" Zadaya said.

Ben was bent over, hands on knees, panting heavily. "I can't believe we lost to a broomstick."

"Ahah! Your first mistake," Zadaya said, raising a slender finger. "I told you: never underestimate your enemy – even a broomstick."

"Good advice," Ben said, standing up straight. "So was that a test to show us how useless we are?"

"A test, yes, but not to show *you* anything. It was to show me what natural talent you have."

"Absolutely none, as I'm sure you can see," Charlie said.

"Not so!" Zadaya said. "You both have heart – that is good. Come with me."

They followed Zadaya back into the lecture hall and to the wall on the far end. On it was a large poster that went up to the ceiling, and on that poster was a chart of monsters. There were pictures of each enemy from the weakest at the bottom to the strongest at the top. Next to each enemy there were small labels, each scrawled with initials.

"Write yours here," Zadaya said, handing them each a label.

Ben scrawled "B.G." on his and then, with a rueful smile, stuck it at the very bottom, next to the broomstick. Thankfully there were a couple of other names there.

"Good!" Zadaya said, clapping his hands. "Now, let us learn how to fight properly."

Ben had a natural distaste for lectures, but he had never had one with Zadaya before. Rather than the painful drone of the teachers he was used to, Zadaya was all exuberance, often dancing around the floor demonstrating a skill or principle. Several times he had them come up and duplicate an action he was demonstrating. They studied the key basics, from stance to poise and balance. By the time they had finished, Ben felt ready to give the broomstick another go.

"That wasn't too bad, was it?" Ben asked, as they left the combat room a couple of hours later.

"No, I quite enjoyed it actually, other than the humiliating defeat to the broomstick," Charlie said.

"Yeah, that was a bit— what was that?"

Ben threw out a hand and stopped both of them in their tracks.

"What?" Charlie asked.

Ben stared at the end of the corridor for a full twenty seconds before relaxing.

"Nothing – it was nothing."

Charlie didn't believe him for a minute. "Was it another sighting?"

"Possibly."

Ben's senses were on hyper alert since the incident in the diplomacy room and he was beginning to believe someone might be following him. At first it was nothing more than a hunch, or a faint movement from the corner of his eye – something he would have discarded before the diplomacy room incident. But as the week continued, they became more noticeable: a shadow in a window; a movement in the curtain; a soft footstep when nobody was about. Both Ben and even Charlie had been buzzing from their combat training, but Ben's sighting put them back on alert for the rest of the day, until they had left the Institute and were on the Dragonway heading home.

The following afternoon Ben, Charlie and Natalie all had practicals in the Department of Wardens and set off up the stairs together.

"The one good thing about this staircase," Charlie said, breathing a little heavily as they climbed, "is that it's too busy for our spy."

"I know we said not to tell anyone, but I'm wondering if we made the wrong choice."

"Absolutely not," Ben said firmly. "The Institute are on my arse enough as it is. I don't want them freaking out about someone spying on me, especially as he's not made any move to do anything."

They made it through the Warden doors and circled round the hallway until they reached a room with the words "Rogue Goblin Control".

"This is our stop," Ben said, his worries fading as his attention turned to the upcoming practical. "We get to track a rogue goblin somewhere in Taecia. Should be fun."

"I'll see you guys at three," Natalie said, giving them a smile and a wave.

Ben made to return the wave when something brushed his shoulder. He lashed out instinctively but caught only air. Ben whipped his head round to follow the intruder's path, down the luxuriously appointed hallway. Just before the corner was a door. Ben saw it open a fraction, and then shut soundlessly.

"There!" Ben said, pointing. "Did you see that?"

Both Charlie and Natalie nodded.

"What should we do?" Natalie asked.

"We go after it," Ben said, rubbing his hands together.

Charlie gave him an incredulous look. "Are you serious? That thing could be a killing machine."

Natalie looked torn between the two. "It would be good to see what is following you, Ben," she said. "But it is risky."

"I know. Are you guys coming?"

"Of course we are," Natalie said, looking affronted. Charlie didn't look quite so eager, but he didn't complain.

They tiptoed to the door with no more alarms, until they set their eyes on the door sign.

"Warden Director."

"Draven's office," Charlie said. "That *is* interesting."

"I can hear voices, but they are too soft to make out."

Natalie was right. There were at least two people in the Warden Director's office, but he could hear no more than a murmur with occasional increases in volume.

"I doubt Draven's going to welcome you with open arms and flowers if you barge into his meeting."

"Assuming it's him," Ben said.

Natalie put an arm on Ben's shoulder. "I should go in first. He won't get as mad with me."

"No," Ben said firmly. He couldn't offer a rational explanation to back up his refusal, but the idea that he wouldn't go in first didn't sit well. He grabbed the handle and gave them both a little smile. "Be ready."

Ben held his breath, turned the handle, and poked his head through.

Draven's office was far more extravagant than Wren's. It looked more like a royal suite, with deep red furnishings and elaborate gold leaf decorations everywhere he looked. There was one large carpet on the floor, red with a huge symbol of a map on it. But Ben's eyes went straight to the two people standing on the carpet, engaged in a heated conversation that stopped the moment Ben popped his head through. Side by side, Ben hadn't realised how similar Draven and Dagmar were.

"What the hell do you think you're doing?" Draven asked, his anger temporarily masked by astonishment.

"I hope you have a very good explanation for not knocking," Dagmar said. There was a rare anger in her voice that was somehow even scarier than Draven's fury.

"I'm sorry," Ben said, feigning surprise. "I got lost and thought this was the 'Rogue Goblin Control room."

Draven raised a hand and looked ready to explode, but Dagmar beat him to it.

"Hurry along, and be quick about it."

Ben apologised again. His heart was racing, but he managed to close the door calmly, and turned to face an expectant Charlie and Natalie.

"Draven and Dagmar," Ben said, as they all hurried back down the hallway.

"Just the two of them, together?"

"Yep. I didn't have time to look further into the office to see where the intruder might be."

"Could you tell what they were saying?" Natalie asked.

"No, but it seemed like they were having a heated discussion about something. I can't imagine those two getting along that well."

"I wonder what they were talking about," Charlie mused, tapping his chin. "That is interesting."

"But not very helpful," Natalie said. "It gives us more questions than answers."

— CHAPTER SIXTEEN —

Night-time Prowling

Friday arrived overcast, the summer sun hidden behind dark, ugly clouds.

"You off to hike Mt. Everest?" Ben asked, as Charlie met up with him on their morning walk to the station. He was carrying an extra big backpack and his face had a slightly pained expression.

"I want to be prepared," Charlie replied. "Part of the size is due to a sleeping bag, in case we're forced to sleep at the Institute. Then there's food supplies, if we get stuck somewhere."

"You've thought of everything, haven't you?" Ben said.

Charlie gave him an appraising look. "What about you? You're just carrying your same bag."

Ben shrugged. "I don't see this as being a long mission. The lockers will either open or they won't."

"What if they do?" Charlie said. "And what if whatever we find leads us to some crazy adventure?"

"You can't plan for every eventuality."

Charlie pulled the straps on his back, and his whole backpack jumped up, almost knocking him over. "As I said, I like to be prepared."

The strict targets imposed by Dagmar ensured their minds didn't wander too much at the Institute during the day. After a morning of sweeping hallways, they spent an enjoyable afternoon trying to convince a pretty runaway elf girl to return to her family, who had pleaded with the Institute for help. The mission had started poorly. Ben tried using his charms, but that had only earned him a slap in the face. It was Charlie who had come to the rescue. Noticing the chess-like game called Captains of Magic on her desk, he challenged her to a game, the victor getting their stated reward. Charlie had lost, but it was close. The elf girl, as it turns out, was a regional Captains of Magic champion, and her admiration for Charlie's quick aptitude for the game convinced her to come with them back to her parents.

"That was frankly quite brilliant," Ben said, slapping Charlie's shoulder as they climbed the hill back up to the Institute. "I thought you'd lost it when you sent your two battle mages into her dragon."

"That was one of my finer moments," Charlie admitted, thrusting his chest out a little. "It's just unfortunate I didn't spot the winged assassins creeping past my entire royal guard."

"Doesn't matter; we got what we came for," Ben said, with a shrug.

By the time they had put their handbooks back into their lockers, it was almost 3pm. The day was still dreary, but Fridays were always extra busy, and the buzz around the place more than made up for the weather. Ben and Charlie had to dodge left and right going down the stairs, where they saw Natalie waiting, alone for once.

"So what's the plan?" Ben asked. To his surprise, they followed Natalie out of the Institute and into their favourite café on the hill.

"Apprentices aren't allowed to stay overnight at the Institute. They say it's too dangerous."

"How is it dangerous?" Charlie said, bits of his cake falling from his open mouth.

"I have no idea. My parents are the same, though – they are very firm in never allowing me to stay there. At 8pm they do a security check of each floor, both magical and physical. It's pretty thorough, so hiding would be pointless. I know some friends who've tried it and got in trouble."

"Promising," Ben said, munching on a biscuit. "So what's the plan?"

"There is one way to stay in. It's magic proof and impossible to find. The only problem is that it's not very nice."

When Natalie told them her plan, Charlie gave an unrestrained groan, contained only by their sound bubble spell.

Ben too wasn't happy. He put down the biscuit he was eating, suddenly finding he had no appetite.

"There has to be another way," Charlie pleaded, putting his two palms together.

"Nothing that would give us such a high chance of success."

"Anything in the 80% range? I'd take that."

"No," Ben said, slapping a hand on the table. "Charlie, stop being ridiculous. We'll do it. Just tell us what to do."

Natalie looked at her watch. "Well, our first move doesn't happen for another hour and seventeen minutes."

With time to kill, they wandered into Taecia Square. Ben perused the shops and almost lost track of time browsing the spellshooters on offer at the peculiarly named "W" shop, which offered magical goods of every type. He had plans on getting a good spellshooter, though he had no idea how he was going to afford one.

When 5pm came, the three of them headed up the hill towards the gates of the Institute.

"The guards are still there," Charlie said, noting the two sturdy-looking Spellswords standing either side of the entrance.

Natalie glanced at her watch. "Not for long."

Sure enough, both guards suddenly left their positions and headed back into the Institute.

"Okay, now! We've got less than two minutes before the new guards come out," Natalie said.

They walked quickly up the remainder of the hill and through the gate. Ben kept his eye on the front door as they passed into the courtyard, praying they wouldn't see the two replacement guards emerge. It was still five hours away from their planned excursion, but according to Natalie, now was the only time the guards left the gates open.

They made it just in time. The new guards took up their positions seconds after they entered the Institute.

"First hurdle jumped," Ben said, smiling. "Where to now?"

There were still a fair number of older apprentices, as well as Institute members at work. The Institute never truly closed.

"They do the security check at 8pm," Natalie said. "That's when we need to be in our secure hiding place. Until then, I think we should just find a nice quiet place where we won't get in anyone's way."

"The library?" Charlie suggested hopefully.

Ben rolled his eyes, but Natalie nodded. "Good idea. There are so many nooks and crannies, no one will disturb us there."

"We could even catch up with some of our studies," Charlie said, looking more enthused than he had for a while.

"You can; I'm not," Ben said.

"I might find it a bit hard to study right now," Natalie admitted. "But I don't mind trying."

The library was filled mostly with Scholars so involved in their own research they didn't even turn their heads when Ben, Charlie and Natalie entered. Likewise, the few apprentices present were in their own worlds, clearly cramming for final tests.

"Probably not a good idea to sit at the tables," Ben noted.

"No, we should work our way into the book shelves and just relax there for a while," Natalie said. "I know a good place; follow me."

They wound their way deep into the maze; Ben gave up trying to remember the way out after so many left and right turns. They ended up in a small reading room with a circular table and a couple of rickety chairs.

"I think we should stay here," Natalie said. She glanced at her watch. "It's 5:20pm now. We should make a move at 7:45pm. So that gives us around two and a half hours to kill."

"At least we won't get bored," Charlie said, rubbing his hands as he stared at the books that surrounded them.

The time passed easily, as they talked and wandered round, trying to find the most interesting books. Once or twice, they heard voices and quietened down, ready to move, but the voices always faded and they remained uninterrupted. As the time approached 7:45pm, the nerves started to set in. Even Charlie found it impossible to keep reading, and he took to pacing up and down the little open space.

"It's time. Let's get going," Natalie said.

They left the library and returned to the spiral staircase. Ben led the way, moving quickly, but keeping his footsteps soft on the marble. He could hear voices up the stairs, but few people seemed around on the lower levels. The moment he passed through the double doors leading to the Department of Apprentices, his senses heightened. It wasn't the apprentices he was scared of; it was Dagmar. If she caught them now, they would be in deep trouble.

"All clear," he said, peeking round the corner before proceeding down the hallway. In the distance on the left was their target: the locker room.

"I'm really not looking forward to this," Charlie muttered.

Ben opened the locker room door and was pleased to find they were alone. Two lines of lockers with their huge green eyes lined each wall.

Ben and Charlie walked to the end, while Natalie stopped about halfway down. Ben gave his locker a friendly wave, and the locker blinked lazily in response.

"How long do we have to do this for?" Charlie said, staring nervously at his own locker.

"The security person normally checks their floor at 8pm. It doesn't take more than fifteen minutes. I think we should come out at 8:30pm, just to be sure."

"So we're stuck inside the locker for almost half an hour? Wonderful."

Charlie's protests were silenced by a sudden noise outside. A voice, perhaps more than one.

"Quick, get in!" Ben said. He was the first to get his locker door open. Ben had to stoop to squeeze inside, and sat awkwardly on his bag with his handbook in his lap. A sudden thought occurred to him.

"How do we get the doors to shut?" Charlie said, voicing the question first.

There was no easy way to pull the doors closed from the inside, and Ben stared agonisingly at the large stone door. The voices outside became louder and Ben thought he heard someone rattle the handle. How would they explain themselves, sitting inside their own lockers when they shouldn't even be in the Institute? Ben scanned the door frantically – there was simply no way of pulling it shut, as there was no handle. There was only one thing to do.

"Phyliss, please close the locker," Ben said, in a clear voice.

The inside of the locker gave a peculiar vibration and the stones seemed to judder. Thankfully, the door started swinging shut. Ben could just make out Charlie and Natalie frantically ordering theirs shut when his door closed. Blackness and silence. He waited a full minute on edge. Had someone entered the room? Had they been seen? Ben imagined the security guard knocking on his locker, demanding him to get out. But it never happened, and Ben eventually relaxed. He shuffled his position on his bag and lay his head back, in a futile attempt to relax.

Time trickled by and it seemed an age before the little dial on his watch said 8:30pm. Finally, Ben ordered Phyliss to open the door and he stepped out, stretching his back and giving a groan of pleasure. Natalie and Charlie were in the process of doing the same.

"Even though it's late, there are still people about," Natalie warned. "The threat from the dark elves has sent most of the Institute into a work frenzy. The good news is, they should assume we have clearance to be here now that we're walking around after the security check."

"What if we run into someone who knows we shouldn't be here?" Charlie asked.

"That we need to avoid," Natalie said.

"Right." Ben clapped his hands. "Let's get going."

— Chapter Seventeen —

The Lockers' Secret

They had five floors to climb. Ben went as fast as possible, bearing in mind they didn't want to look rushed and that Charlie would have trouble running up the stairs anyway. A couple of times they ran into members passing by, but most were lost in their own worlds. Ben gave a relaxed, friendly smile to those who did look their way. It did the job; they got no suspicious looks and nobody attempted to stop them.

Ben stopped at the Spellsword gallery, just to make sure Natalie and Charlie were okay, before pushing open the double doors into the Department of Spellswords. Ben resisted the urge to quicken his pace and listened intently; the only warning of danger they might get would be voices or footsteps from around a corner. As Ben walked, he clocked every door they approached as a potential hiding place. None of them knew where exactly the Spellsword locker room was, and they almost did a complete circle of the floor before they found it.

Ben started thinking about their next problem as they approached: how would they know if anyone was inside? And what would they do if there was? He was still debating the issue when he heard a creak, and the door opened.

Ben stopped and froze. Two Spellswords emerged, both with three diamonds on their shoulders, chatting softly to each other. Thankfully, they headed away from them and disappeared round the corner.

Ben breathed again. He waited a moment to see if anyone else was going to emerge, before half walking, half running to the locker room door. The three of them crowded round it.

"Now what?" Charlie asked. "If we go in and someone's in there, we've blown it."

"We go in one by one," Ben said. "That way, if one person does get into trouble, the other two still have time to get away."

"That's a good idea," Natalie said. "You, Ben, will have to go last. If we lose you, the whole plan is ruined anyway."

Ben hated to admit it, but she was right. Neither Charlie nor Natalie would have any chance of opening his parents' lockers.

"I'll go," Charlie said.

Natalie put a hand on his shoulder. "Are you sure? I don't mind doing it myself."

"No." Charlie's voice was unusually firm. "I'll raise my voice if I get into trouble, and you guys can get away."

Charlie gripped the handle, paused only a second, and then disappeared from sight through the door.

Ben listened, waiting for any signal of trouble. Seconds later, the door re-opened and a relieved-looking Charlie popped his head through.

"All clear," he said.

There was more space in the Spellsword locker room, with enough width to have a bench that ran down the middle of the room. Each locker was at least twice as wide, and the eyes were all varying shades of blue. *Males*, Ben thought. They looked a bit sterner too, if that was possible. They were all staring directly ahead, like soldiers standing to attention.

"How do we know which ones belong to your parents?" Charlie asked, staring at all the lockers.

"I'll do what we did when we were first assigned ours," Ben said.

He positioned himself by the door, and then started walking slowly down the middle of the room, paying close attention to each locker's eye. One by one, they ignored him, and as Ben neared the end of the room, he started to fear none would look his way.

"That one!" Natalie shouted, pointing.

Ben had almost missed it. The locker to his left, four from the end, flicked his large iris Ben's way. Ben stopped immediately and went straight over to the locker. The moment Ben faced up to it, Ben saw a glimmer of recognition within that large blue eye.

"This is the one," Ben said, waving them over.

They inspected the locker. Ben noticed there were a few scuffs on the door, and a couple of places where the stone had been chipped.

"Will he respond to you?" Charlie asked. "We don't even know the locker's name."

"Let's find out," Ben said. He cleared his throat and said in a clear, firm voice, "Open the door."

Nothing happened.

"You forgot to say please," Charlie said, helpfully.

Ben tried again. Still nothing. He tried three more times, without success. It was as if the eye wasn't listening.

"You need to talk more to compensate for not using his name," Natalie said.

Ben took a deep breath and composed himself. "My name is Ben Greenwood. I am the son of Jane and Greg Greenwood. If they have given family access to their lockers, then please open the door."

The iris blinked twice. Ben suddenly felt he was being measured by something far older and more intelligent than the lockers downstairs. Ben was careful to maintain a level stare with the locker.

There was a loud click, and the edges of the locker door suddenly glowed yellow. The door swung open soundlessly.

"Oh my," Natalie said, her hand going to her mouth.

The locker was far larger than their ones in every respect, but it was the contents inside that caused Natalie to gasp. There were clothes, books and bits of food scattered across the floor. Ben stepped inside and knelt down. It was clearly his mum's locker, and it was just as clear that it had been ransacked.

"I thought you said nobody could get in," Ben said quietly, as he surveyed the damage.

"I didn't say it was impossible," Natalie replied. She had also stepped into the locker. "I just said it was protected by some very powerful spells. Few people could break it."

"Check this out, Ben," Charlie said.

He was pointing to a photograph, stuck on the back wall, that had somehow survived the carnage.

It was Ben and his parents, standing outside his house. Ben was standing in the middle and both his parents had their arms around him. He couldn't have been more than six or seven years old and barely came up to their waists. He hadn't seen that photo before, and it tugged at his heart strings. Ben stared at the photo until he realised his eyes were in danger of watering.

"Shall we tidy up?" Natalie asked, her voice gentle.

"Yeah, let's do that."

Nobody commented on his slightly croaky voice.

There were hangers for the clothes, and plenty of room to stack the books.

"Woah, look at that," Charlie said.

Hidden amongst the clothes was a spellshooter. The long twisted barrel looked slimmer than usual, as did the handle. Despite the treatment the locker had received, the spellshooter shone like new. Inside the spellshooter's orb a handful of spell pellets floated.

Ben picked up his mum's spellshooter and placed it reverently on one of the hangers so that it dangled from the handle.

They stepped out of the locker and shut it. An awkward silence had fallen between them. Both Charlie and Natalie gave Ben a little distance.

Ben forced aside memories of his parents that had suddenly resurfaced. "Let's see if we can find my dad's locker."

"Are you sure?" Natalie asked.

Ben's determination came flooding back. "Absolutely. That's what we're here for." He returned to the exact spot in the middle of the locker room where he'd spotted his mum's locker watching him and continued forwards. There wasn't much left to walk, so he took it slowly.

It took just one step. This time, it was far more obvious. A locker on his right side, right at the back, was staring at him. Ben, Charlie and Natalie hurried over.

There were even more scuffs on this locker and half a stone was missing near the base. Its eye, Ben noticed, had a red gash running across it.

"Looks like someone tried getting in this one too," Charlie commented. "Did they succeed?"

"Let's find out," Ben said.

He repeated the same command as before. There was a loud click, the edges of the locker door glowed, and the door swung slowly open. Three pairs of eyes looked eagerly into the locker as it revealed itself.

It was completely empty.

Ben stepped inside. The locker was the size of a small room. There were no clothes, no books, and no photograph.

Despite finding nothing, Ben smiled grimly. "I bet my dad got his stuff away before they could trash it."

"Good for him," Natalie said.

"Doesn't help us much, though, does it?" Charlie said.

Charlie was right. There was nothing here that could help them. Ben had to swallow his disappointment. He had known it was a long shot, but was still secretly hopeful of some sort of lead or clue. He trailed a hand along the back stone wall, feeling the coarseness beneath his fingers. Not long ago, his dad would have come here almost every day.

"We should get out of here," Charlie said. "We must have been in here twenty minutes already. Someone could come in any moment."

Ben nodded. He felt reluctant to leave. Even though the locker was completely empty, it somehow felt like his dad was close by. Maybe it was the smell. Ben gave the stones one last pat.

Click.

The stone beneath his hand suddenly retreated. A small door concealed in the far corner of the locker swung open, revealing a torch-lit passageway that descended ever downwards.

— Chapter Eighteen —
Important Discoveries

A rattling came from the entrance door to the locker room, followed by a couple of hushed voices.

"Get in, quick!"

Ben shut the locker door and they stumbled in the darkness to the secret entrance. Ben led them through and into a gently downward-sloping passageway. The torch lights on the stone walls flickered, casting dancing shadows as they walked.

"I know I shouldn't be saying this," Charlie said, "but technically this passageway isn't possible. We should be walking into the floor below right about now."

"Tut tut, Charlie," Ben said. "I would have thought by now you'd know logic doesn't apply when magic is involved."

"A magic passageway right in the middle of the Institute," Natalie said, her voice filled with wonder. "At least we know what Charlie found out about Guardians is true – you do have unparalleled access to the heart of the Institute, Ben."

"We'll soon find out if it means anything. Look ahead," Ben said, pointing.

The passageway came to an end, and they found themselves facing the faint outline of a door with a small handle protruding from the stone. Ben grabbed the handle and turned. The door opened easily, and they stepped through.

"Oh wow," Natalie breathed.

They had entered a large circular room that resembled something out of a gentleman's club. It was lit by a decorative chandelier that hung from the high ceiling, creating a warm glow through magical means. Squishy leather chairs were placed in twos and threes on a thick, gleaming golden carpet. Painted on the walls were incredible murals of what Ben assumed were famous Institute members. At one end was a long cabinet, which held all sorts of bottled drinks, but it was the centre of the room that caught their attention. There was a magnificent long table, surrounded by high-backed chairs. Behind the table was a small replica version of the statue of Queen Elizabeth wearing a full suit of armour, holding her sword aloft. Strangely, Ben noticed she was missing her boots. Next to her was a large globe, much like the one in the library, which floated in the air and spun gently on its axis.

"Ben, look!" Charlie said. He was pointing to a grand fireplace at the end of the room. Charlie hurried over, bent down, and started touching the kindling. "I knew it. Come here, quick!"

Ben exchanged puzzled looks with Natalie. He hurried over and saw Charlie digging his hands into the ash.

"Feel this," Charlie said.

Ben knelt down and touched the ash gently.

It was warm.

"Not more than two or three hours old, I'd say," Charlie said.

Ben felt his whole body tense. "My parents," he whispered, staring into the fireplace, and then at a stunned Natalie and a grinning Charlie.

"Are you absolutely sure, Charlie?" Natalie said. "How did you know the fireplace was warm from across the room?"

Charlie tapped his nose. "I've got a strong sense of smell."

"On par with a bloodhound," Ben said.

Ben got up and surveyed the room, hands on hips. It was clear this was some sort of common room for the Guardians, or anyone else able to get in.

"I wonder what they were doing here," Natalie said.

"Hiding, probably," Charlie said.

Ben nodded. It made sense. "Let's take a look around."

They found nothing further of interest until they approached the table. The boots that were missing from the statue were placed on the table, on top of a whole pile of books and documents.

Charlie scrambled up onto one of the chairs to get a better look. He started picking up documents and books, and scanning them with computer-like speed. "This is fascinating. These are all about the same thing."

To Ben's frustration, Charlie was so immersed in reading a long yellow parchment that he failed to elaborate. Ben turned his attention to the books; the moment he read a few of the titles, he knew what Charlie meant. *A History of the Forreck. Forrecks and Where to Find Them. Forrecks: Should They Be Terminated? Crystal Dragon vs. Forreck: The Ultimate Battle.* Ben saw a section highlighted in yellow by someone in the book *How to Survive a Forreck.*

"While almost immune to magic, forrecks show some vulnerability to the very strongest fire and air spells. There have also been rumours that their powers of regeneration do not extend to severed limbs, though a documented case has yet to be proven."

Ben turned his attention to another open book, titled *A History of the Forreck.* There were just two lines highlighted in different places. *"It is of interest to note that, though forrecks tolerate sunlight, they do not enjoy it. The forreck is, by nature, an underground animal."* The other piece simply said, *"Never attempt to look a forreck in the eye."*

The more Ben read, the more obvious it became: his parents were searching for ways to overcome a forreck.

"But why?" Natalie asked, when Ben voiced his conclusion.

"Listen to this!" Charlie said. He was now sitting on the table, with two or three different books balanced on his lap.

"In the early days, forrecks were used as protectors for royalty or for artefacts of the most extreme value. Contrary to belief, they can be trained by a highly skilled beastmaster, though there are known to be fewer than a dozen of such men and women capable of such a feat. When successfully trained, a forreck can protect a designated area or even an item for the duration of its life. As forrecks are second only to dragons in longevity, that is often several hundred years."

Charlie stopped reading and looked up. "What if there was a forreck protecting a piece of Elizabeth's Armour?"

A stunned silence ensued as the three of them absorbed Charlie's revelation.

"Which piece?" Natalie asked.

All eyes went to the item on the table.

"The boots would be my guess," Charlie said.

Ben and Charlie were grinning from ear to ear at the discovery, but Natalie wore a worried frown.

"I don't want to alarm you, Ben, but if your parents are trying to overcome a forreck, they could be in real danger."

"What have you heard about them?" Ben asked.

"They are famous for being the only creature to be able to take on a fully grown dragon."

Charlie whistled. "That's impressive."

"Impressive but also very scary," Natalie said. "Especially if your parents, Ben, are trying to find a way past one. I'm not sure it's even possible."

Ben's elation subsided.

Charlie, however, shook his head. "That may not be entirely true."

"What do you mean?"

Charlie pointed to a paragraph in a book he was reading. Not only had the section been highlighted, it had also been circled heavily in black.

"Listen to this. It's from a book called *Forrecks: The Truth Behind the Myths* by a bloke called Lornor Taren. It says, *'Among the many myths and legends about forrecks is that, short of a crystal dragon on your side, they are invulnerable. That, I have discovered, is not entirely true. They may have a weakness, but I am still gathering further evidence before I am willing to publish such an important revelation.'"*

Charlie closed the book and looked up. "That's all he says."

Ben swore. "If this guy is right, that could be exactly what my parents need to get past the forreck and retrieve the boots."

"Perhaps he revealed his revelation in some later book?" Natalie said.

Charlie nodded. He was already grabbing several others. "I'll keep looking."

Charlie was such a frenzy of activity on the table that Ben and Natalie realised they would just be getting in his way if they tried to help, so they decided to wander round the room to see what else they could find.

Despite the urgency of the situation, Ben felt in no rush; quite the opposite, in fact. This was where his parents hung out. The thought made his insides warm and tingly, and it felt relaxing just to be in this special place, unwatched and unknown by the Institute and even the Shadowseeker. He almost didn't want Charlie to find something so they could stay in here as long as possible. Ben inspected each book on the shelf with interest, wondering if his parents had read any of them. There was a coat rack, and Ben's heart jumped when he recognised one of his mum's jackets. His eyes drifted to a glass display cabinet, with strange and wonderful items that seemed too precious for even Ben's curious hands to touch.

Until he saw the pouch.

It was a deep red, embossed with the letters G.G. in an elegant gold font. It sat there quite innocently, sitting in between a peculiar leather boot and a glass orb. It was filled with spell pellets. Ben's hands suddenly felt sweaty. He glanced around and saw Charlie still busy dissecting the books on the table, and Natalie busy looking at some diagram on the wall. Ben turned back to the cabinet and eased open the glass door. He poked his head in, until his nose was almost touching the pouch. It looked really valuable, a far cry from the ones they had bought a few weeks ago. What sort of spells would be in there? Powerful ones, no doubt. Ben reached in and picked it up. It was soft, but sturdy, and heavier than he expected. Ben stared at the pouch until his eyes started to water. He started to put it back, but hesitated, and gave Charlie and Natalie another look. Both were still busy. With a sudden unexplainable impulse, Ben slipped the pouch into his pocket. Quickly he shut the cabinet and stepped away before either of them might notice.

Ben found he was breathing heavily, and knew without inspecting that his face was flushed. He took several deep breaths and with some effort put on an air of nonchalance, resuming his inspection of the room as if nothing had happened.

"Ben!"

Natalie's voice echoed around the room and made Ben jump. He turned, his face guilty, but to his relief saw Natalie still staring at the same diagram.

"Check this out!" she said, waving vigorously to him, her eyes never leaving the diagram.

Ben checked his pocket to make sure the pouch wasn't creating an obvious bulge before joining her.

The diagram Natalie was looking at turned out to be a family tree. Names were scrawled on the paper, with lines branching out to other names that had similar surnames. Beside each name was a date. Ben spotted the name at the top of the family tree and promptly forgot all about the pouch he'd taken.

Charlotte Rowe.

"It looks like your parents are looking for Charlotte Rowe's ancestor," Natalie said. "Look how far they got."

The family tree extended down to the 19th century before the names ran out, with the last name being "Craypole", still two hundred years short of present time.

"Each original director got a piece of the Armour, right?" Natalie said. She sounded breathless and Ben was surprised to see how excited she looked, until he remembered her admiration for Charlotte Rowe. "I bet Charlotte Rowe was entrusted with the boots!"

It made sense, Ben admitted. If they were searching for the boots, which seemed likely, given their position on the table, then this family tree made it a good bet they were entrusted to Charlotte.

"Looks like they had a ways to go," Ben said, inspecting the chart once more.

"I bet I could continue it," Natalie said. She was already walking over to the table to grab a piece of paper and a pen. "Finding this person could be just as important as searching for the boots. They might know a way past the forreck – they might even still have the boots themselves!"

"Well, that sounds more promising than anything I've found since that initial blitz," Charlie said. He jumped down from the table and sank into one of the squishy leather chairs, which nearly engulfed him. "I found a few more books by Lornor Taren, who seems to be the leading authority on forrecks, but I couldn't find anything to help us."

Ben joined Charlie, taking a chair opposite him, and Natalie did the same.

"Why don't we start with what we know," Ben said. "My parents are..." He trailed off because Charlie was shaking his head. "What?"

"We don't know for sure that it's your parents," Charlie said.

"Who else would it be?"

"I don't know. But it's only an assumption until we have concrete evidence that it is your parents."

"It seems quite likely, though, you have to admit, Charlie," Natalie said. "After all, we know they are looking for Elizabeth's Armour and the passageway was linked directly to Ben's dad's locker."

Charlie nodded. "I agree. It is extremely likely – I'm just saying we don't know for sure."

"Fine," Ben said, suppressing a slight irritation at Charlie's pedantic mind. "Someone, *possibly* my parents, is looking for a way to defeat this crazy powerful creature called a forreck, because we *think* it could be guarding a piece of Elizabeth's Armour, most likely to be her boots, which have probably been handed down to a descendant of Charlotte Rowe's. How does that sound?"

"You nailed it," Charlie said.

"So where does that leave us?" Natalie asked, idly twiddling her hair.

"We need to track down this Lornor Taren bloke," Ben said. "He's the one who wrote that forrecks might have a weakness. Let's go and find him."

"It's not that simple, Ben," Natalie said. "We don't know who he is, where he is, or if he's even still alive."

"Not entirely true, actually," Charlie said, standing up suddenly, his eyes regaining some of their former energy. He hurried over to the table and started sifting through the books.

"Ah! Here it is." He grabbed a large, hardback book and hurried back over. It was called *The Hundred Most Influential Beastmasters of the 21st Century.*

Charlie started thumbing through the pages, stopping finally with another exclamation.

"Listen to this," Charlie said, and he started reading.

"The elf Lornor Taren is perhaps the oldest and certainly most controversial beastmaster still living (as of publication date, 2012). Born in the 17th century, Mr. Taren spent his first hundred years working on the great farms of Unn, before gaining employment at SpellWorks Inc., where his passion for beasts flourished. He rose swiftly through the ranks and became head of Animal Enchantments, where he lasted for several centuries, before being controversially removed for his outspoken opinion against the Royal Institute of Magic's mission to cull the forrecks for the protection of the Unseen Kingdoms. At the time of writing, he still works at SpellWorks

Inc., but his position is not clear, and SpellWorks refused to comment when approached."

"Well, he's still alive," Ben said. "We just need to find out where this SpellWorks Inc. place is."

Natalie gave Ben a surprised look. "Oh my. I completely forgot you weren't brought up here. Everyone knows about SpellWorks Inc. – they're famous. Think Google but for all things magic. They are the biggest manufacturer of spell pellets, artefacts and other magical items."

Ben and Charlie exchanged gleeful looks.

"How do we get in?" Charlie asked.

"That's the tricky part. It is strictly off limits to non-employees, unless you have a special guest pass, which are like gold dust these days."

"So what's the plan?" Ben asked.

Natalie smiled. "We sneak in."

"I like it," Ben said. Charlie looked less than thrilled with the idea.

"One thing doesn't make sense," Natalie said, her attention going back to the book Charlie had just read from. "It says the forrecks were culled. I thought they were supposed to be invincible?"

"I looked that up," Charlie said. "A mission, led by the Institute several centuries ago, hunted down the forrecks one by one with crystal dragons, which appear to be the only dragons capable of taking them down. It was slow and bloody, but by the

20th century, the forreck and the crystal dragon had basically killed each other off. Crystal dragons are now officially extinct and nobody has seen a forreck in the last two centuries."

"Wow," Ben said. "Well at least we know that, should we find a forreck, it could well be the one guarding the boots."

Charlie began tapping the book and pursed his lips. "There is one thing we haven't considered. If your parents were here, Ben, then they probably would have read these books and most likely also stumbled upon the bit about Lornor Taren. What if they have already visited him?"

Ben had the same exact thought. "As you said, we don't know if my parents were here, and even if they did find and visit Lornor Taren, we don't know what happened. We need to find out."

"Do we?"

Charlie spoke the question softly, staring thoughtfully into the lush carpet.

Ben was taken aback by the question. "What do you mean?"

When Charlie looked up, his excitement had been replaced by a mellow, almost sombre expression.

"Ben, your parents are hot on the heels of Elizabeth's Boots, a task we know is critical to stopping Suktar. I'm concerned that if we go searching for them, we might get in their way."

Ben was so shocked it held his rising anger in check. "How would we get in their way?"

Charlie kept his voice soft, aware that Ben was slowly building up steam. "Your parents are highly skilled Spellswords. What could we do to help them? They'd probably just end up babysitting us."

Ben flew off his seat and pointed a finger at Charlie, but no words came forth. He turned and stepped away, his mind swirling with anger and disbelief. He walked over and leant on the table, trying to collect his thoughts. Natalie was talking, but it was just noise, and he barely registered it. The initial shock had subsided, and the resulting anger eventually gave way to genuine confusion.

Ben turned back to Charlie. "Two years my parents have been gone. Most of that time I was led to believe they were dead. You were with me when we found out they weren't. That's why we came to the Institute in the first place, to find out what happened to them."

"A lot has changed since then," Charlie said, keeping his voice soft.

Ben slammed a fist into his palm. "Nothing has changed," he said, his voice rising. "Nothing is more important than finding my parents."

"Nothing?" Charlie's patience was starting to fray and he gripped his seat, his voice gaining some steel. "What about your parents single-handedly trying to stop a dark elf king from taking over the world?"

"Nothing!" Ben shouted, stabbing a finger towards Charlie. He stepped forwards. Charlie sprang from his chair to meet him.

"That's enough!"

Natalie's voice reverberated round the room with such force it made Ben's ears ring. In one purposeful stride she had placed herself between Charlie and Ben. Her green eyes were blazing and there was an intensity about her that cut through Ben's anger.

"Ben, you are thinking with your heart. Charlie, you are thinking with your head. It's not surprising you've come to different conclusions. It's certainly not worth fighting over. There is no right answer. Now both of you, calm down."

Ben felt like he had been splashed with icy water. He ran a hand through his hair. The red mist began to clear and that part of his mind responsible for analytical thought clicked back into gear.

"Look, I know it might not make complete sense," Ben said, with a resigned shrug. "But you only get one set of parents. I'd like to see mine again."

Charlie smiled. "As Natalie said, sometimes it's better thinking with the heart, not the head. I'm just kind of rubbish at that."

"Good!" Natalie said, clapping her hands together. "Now, can the two of you kiss and make up? I want to get out of here."

— CHAPTER NINETEEN —
Training and Trouble

Ben's hopes of visiting SpellWorks Inc. anytime soon were dashed the very next day.

"Two weeks?" Ben asked. "We can't get in any sooner?"

They were talking quietly in the corner of the common room, sipping on tea and hot chocolate to wake themselves up.

"One does not simply walk into SpellWorks," Natalie said, with a little smile. "I know someone who works there, but that's how long he thinks it will take before he can get us in. It took me all weekend just to convince him to help us."

"And we can't just wing it ourselves?"

"Not if we value our lives," Natalie said.

Charlie cleared his throat. "Two weeks it is, then."

Ben swallowed his disappointment. For the first time, they were hot on the trail of his parents, and possibly Elizabeth's Boots. He stared at his cup of tea disconsolately.

But if he thought the two-week waiting time would pass slowly, he was very wrong, as he found out the following morning at muster.

"A word, please, Mr. Greenwood and Mr. Hornberger," Dagmar said, as they were filing out with the rest of the apprentices.

Dagmar, Ben noticed, was not looking her usual imperious self. She had small bags under her eyes and they were slightly red. Even her hair, which was normally pulled back in a perfect ponytail, had a few strands out of place.

Even more astonishing than her looks was the nod of approval Dagmar gave them. "Congratulations on managing to stick to your targets. You are now on day thirty of your apprenticeship. As you know, the first grade of the apprenticeship can only last a maximum of fifty days, and the earlier you complete it, the better it reflects on you. Factoring in your current progress, I have scheduled in your first grade exam for day forty-four."

Ben and Charlie exchanged looks of alarm that Dagmar either didn't see or didn't care for.

"That gives you two weeks to finish your studies and revise, in preparation," Dagmar said. "Needless to say, failure to pass means expulsion from the apprenticeship program."

Ben and Charlie hurried over to the kitchens to begin their chores – washing dishes today; both wore worried frowns.

"I wish someone had given us more warning about this exam," Charlie said, grabbing a brush and scrubbing absently at a plate. "I don't feel like I'm ready. Do you think Dagmar will let us reschedule? Technically we could push it back five days and still be within the fifty-day requirement."

"No," Ben said firmly. "You heard what she said, the longer we take, the worse it reflects on us. We'll be ready on day forty-four."

Thoughts of SpellWorks, Elizabeth's Boots, and even his parents took a back seat for a while as Ben and Charlie spent every waking minute, barring their morning chores, trying to complete the checklists for each department. Their argument was mostly forgotten, though there was a lingering disappointment Ben couldn't quite shake off. He had been so certain he and Charlie thought alike when it came to his parents, but he had been wrong.

Progress in their studies accelerated. Charlie had breezed through the Diplomacy and Scholar checklists, and had the Warden and Trade departments under control, but he was lagging behind in Spellsword.

"I swear, these pellets are broken," Charlie said.

He and Ben were in the small practice room by themselves during lunch break. Whereas Ben had passed all five difficulty levels several weeks ago, Charlie was stuck on the last level.

"Here, give me that," Ben said. He threw the pellet almost nonchalantly at the target board, where it just missed the bull's-eye and exploded in a puff of flame.

"Oh, stop showing off," Charlie said, irritably, grabbing another pellet from the shelf.

"Willpower," Ben said, ignoring Charlie's jab. "Just believe it will explode. The trick is to make the decision with absolutely no doubts or reservations. It's a confidence thing."

"Not my strong suit," Charlie said.

"Not true. It's all in your head. You're better up there" – Ben tapped his temple – "than I am. Just raise your expectations."

Charlie nodded. He spent a good minute eyeing up the target board and juggling the pellet in his hand. Finally he nodded, eyes narrowing. Gritting his teeth, he launched the pellet with a grunt. It hit the edge of the target board and glowed red, before bouncing onto the floor.

"Did you see that!" Charlie said, pumping his fists. "It almost ignited."

"Progress," Ben said, grinning. "Let's do it again."

Ben had his own difficulties, and they happened to be in Charlie's strongest departments. Attention to detail was vital in the Department of Scholars, and Diplomacy required patience – two of Ben's weak areas.

"Okay, we're ready," Charlie said. "Give it your best shot."

They were in a small cubicle, along with Marie, one of the Diplomacy instructors, who was armed with a spellshooter.

"Let's hope you do better than last time," Marie said. "Okay, I'm firing a random diplomatic incident."

She pointed her spellshooter to the floor, and fired. A tall, gangly troll materialised before them, wearing an ill-fitting suit that looked so out of place Ben had a hard time keeping a straight face.

"Keep your manners in," Charlie said.

"Right," Ben said, swallowing his humour. He looked up at the troll and placed his fist across his chest. The troll immediately went red with fury and leapt at Ben with a deep-throated roar. The hologram disappeared just as it was about to crash into Ben.

"You raised the wrong fist in greeting," Charlie said. "Do that to a hill troll and you are just insulting them."

"Hill troll? I thought that was a mountain troll?"

"Mountain trolls have darker skin and are stockier," Charlie said. "Come on, back to the library. I want to show you a proper comparison. A mistake like that will kill you."

Ben cursed, kicked an imaginary rock and followed Charlie out the room, back to the library. And so it went, day after day, as they inched towards the finishing line.

Though they didn't get to see much of Natalie, she assured them everything was going to plan with her inside contact at SpellWorks Inc. But her research on Charlotte Rowe's family line was slightly less productive.

"I've run into some difficulties," Natalie said.

She had joined them in the library where they were researching the most efficient way of catching pixies that might have escaped the Unseen Kingdoms. Charlie's head was lost in a book, and Ben was sitting down, leaning against one of the shelves, taking a well-earned break.

"How far have you got?" Ben asked.

"I managed to follow Charlotte Rowe's family line down to the early 20th century, but then all records vanish. I have a feeling the Rowe family may have felt it safer to cut their ties with the Institute."

"Well, given what's happening to my parents, they're probably right."

Natalie nodded. "The only thing of interest I found was that Charlotte had a peculiar birthmark on her right shoulder shaped like a bird that seems to have passed down the generations. It could provide evidence of their heritage, if we ever found someone."

"That could be useful," Ben said.

Charlie slapped the book shut. "Okay, I've found it. Let's hope for our sake that we never have to track down an escaped pixie."

Ben's laughter was cut short by a familiar voice.

"What are you all doing here?"

Dagmar popped up so suddenly they all jumped. Ben's surprise turned to alarm the moment he looked up at Dagmar's face. She looked haggard, as if she hadn't slept in several days.

Ben found his voice first. "It's lunch break, Ms. Borovich. We were just doing some extra research for our studies."

Dagmar blinked, and for a moment she looked like a rabbit caught in the headlights. "What? Very well, run along," she said. Her eyes had already drifted past them and were looking intently into the library. They watched her disappear into the maze.

"What the hell is going on with her?" Charlie asked.

"I don't know, but I'm half tempted to follow her and see if we can find out. Is she spying on us or something?"

Ever since they had discovered the Guardian's common room, they had started seeing more and more of Dagmar, popping up in unexpected places. She never said anything of consequence, and behaved as though the meetings were purely incidental, but more than once Ben caught her giving them prolonged stares from the corner of his eye.

"Who knows?" Charlie said. "But we don't have time to worry about that right now. There are only five more days until the exam and I'm starting to freak out. Can we go over the trading laws for the Unseen Kingdoms again? I'm not one hundred percent confident about them."

As the day of the exam approached, even Ben started getting butterflies in his stomach. There was so much to learn, and even though they had now finished their checklists, they spent every waking moment revising, spurred on by the knowledge that failure to pass the exam meant expulsion from the Institute. To make matters worse, Joshua and his friends were taking every opportunity to taunt Ben and Charlie about the upcoming exam.

"Oh, god, here they are again," Charlie said. "Let's go somewhere else."

He was already half-standing, but Ben pulled him back down again.

"No," he said firmly. "I'm still drinking my tea and I want to finish my apple pastry."

They were in the corner of the common room, books spread out on a stool in between their chairs.

Joshua was wearing a typically fashionable open black shirt, skinny jeans and black leather shoes. His blond-highlighted hair was subtly spiked, and his blue eyes resembled a hawk's spotting its first meal of the day.

"Well, well," Joshua said. "If it isn't our two desperate apprentices. How much time left? Five days? Six?"

"Three," Ben said, knowing full-well Joshua was aware when the exam was; there was a chart posted in one of the rooms.

"Just three?" Joshua said. "I assume you've gone through all the practical steps again?"

"No," Charlie said, looking up with an expression of alarm. "Do you think we should have?"

"Oh dear," Joshua said, a hand going to his tanned face. "Of course, you have to do that. The first time through, the practical steps are easy; it's only on the second and third times where they really test you. You will definitely need that for the exam."

"We'll make do," Ben said, giving Joshua an easy smile, even as Charlie re-opened the handbook and started browsing through the various practical steps.

"Your choice, I'm just trying to help," Joshua said, with a shrug. "Personally, I never thought either of you would make it to the second grade anyway. You're not Institute material."

"What's that supposed to mean?" Ben asked softly. He could hear his blood start to pump in his ears and squeezed the armrests of his chair.

"Isn't it obvious?" Joshua said. There was now a nasty glint in his eye. "You" – he pointed to Charlie – "look so out of place I don't know whether to laugh or cry. And I would have thought you, Ben, would have the good grace to forego the Institute after everything your parents have put us through."

Ben's fist flew towards Joshua's chin as if it had a mind of its own. It connected with a satisfied crunch and Joshua reeled backwards. Ben, a keen rugby player, showed his sporting prowess by executing a perfect tackle, launching himself at Joshua's waist. Both of them hit the ground, Ben on top of Joshua. Ben had one objective – knock Joshua senseless. He aimed another punch, but his arm was caught by someone and he was hauled off Joshua by two of his crew – tall, ugly-looking boys with manic fury in their eyes. One of them aimed a clumsy punch at Ben's jaw, which he sidestepped, but he could do nothing about the other boy, who was now looming over him. He wasn't much bigger than Ben, but he was well built, with fists like bricks and an eager smile that came from confidence in brawls. Before the boy could land a blow, a scream came from behind. Charlie launched himself onto the boy's back and clung on to his neck like some mad piggy-back ride. The boy let out a low growl, melding in with Charlie's high-pitched cursing, and for a moment it was bedlam.

"I'm going to enjoy this."

Joshua had gotten to his feet and pulled out his spellshooter, which was now pointing at Ben's head.

Ben stepped back instinctively, but there was nowhere to go. From the twisted grin on Joshua's face, Ben could tell whatever spell he was about to cast wasn't going to be pleasant. He placed a hand in his pocket and felt his dad's pouch, full of spells. He never went anywhere without it, and was now grateful.

"What's your problem?" Ben asked, biding for time. How could he get the pouch out and cast the spell before Joshua pulled the trigger? "My parents were proven innocent. They never killed the elf prince. That was all a sham."

"This isn't about that," Joshua said. His finger started to depress the trigger. Ben grabbed the pouch.

"Joshua Wistletop!"

For once, the familiar voice came as a relief.

Joshua had such a crazed look in his eye that for a moment Ben thought he was going to pull the trigger anyway. But after a moment, he lowered his spellshooter.

"What on earth are you playing at?" Dagmar said, as she marched over, putting herself between Ben and Joshua. The signs of exhaustion on her face were momentarily replaced by a subtle anger, which on Dagmar spoke volumes.

"He punched me in the face," Joshua said, fingering his jaw. "I was giving him some advice on the upcoming exam and he lashed out."

"I don't care if he tried to wipe out the entire elven species," Dagmar said, her voice calm and controlled. "You do not pull a spellshooter on another apprentice. Do I make myself clear?"

Joshua looked as though he had just swallowed a lemon. "Yes, Ms. Borovich."

"Good. Now march yourself into my office."

Joshua gave one last look at Ben, before reluctantly turning and heading out of the common room.

"The rest of you, disperse," Dagmar said. "And you" – she pointed a stubby finger at Ben – "I will be speaking to you later."

The common room emptied in double quick time. Ben and Charlie headed down the stairs, and promptly ran into Natalie on her way up.

"I've been looking for you guys. I've got good news," she said brightly. Then, seeing Ben's and Charlie's looks, she frowned. "What's the matter?"

"Not here," Ben said. "Let's go to the café."

One short trip, three hot chocolates and a spell bubble later, and they were all sitting comfortably by their favourite spot in the café, next to the window. Ben quickly recapped what had happened in the common room. Only then did he notice that Charlie had a little bruise under his eye.

"It's nothing," Charlie said, waving away Natalie's hands with some embarrassment. "That scary guy I jumped on caught me with a flailing arm while I was hanging on to him."

"You saved me with that crazy move," Ben said.

Charlie seemed uncomfortable with the praise. "Did you recall what Joshua said about your parents?"

"Yes," Ben replied, stirring his hot chocolate. "He's clearly not happy with them, though I have no idea why."

"Well, it must be serious, as he really doesn't like you," Charlie said.

"I'll ask him one day," Ben said, with a shrug. Then, eager to change subjects, he turned to Natalie. "So, what's this good news?"

"I've got us a way in to SpellWorks," Natalie said, brightening. "The only catch is that it has to be done on Sunday. My inside contact insisted on that."

"Sunday?" Charlie said, sitting up and almost dropping his hot chocolate. "That's the day before our exam. That's our last chance to revise."

"The timing isn't great," Ben admitted. "How long do you think the SpellWorks trip will take?"

"Probably most of the day. It's a bit of a journey. I can re-arrange the date, but my contact said it was Sunday or next month."

"No, I don't want to wait that long," Ben said. "Sunday it is."

— CHAPTER TWENTY —
SpellWorks Inc.

Ben and Charlie spent Saturday, from morning till night, revising like maniacs. They spent a lot of time in the library, going through their handbooks, and also re-doing any practical tests they had difficulty with. Charlie was eventually able to ignite the level five pellet, and finished his Spellsword checklist. Ben finally managed to learn the proper etiquette for the ten different types of troll.

That night Ben was so exhausted he fell asleep as soon as his head hit the pillow, despite the excitement of tomorrows SpellWorks visit looming.

The next morning, Ben and Charlie met Natalie outside Taecia's Dragonway. Being the weekend, they were all more casually dressed, and Ben was again reminded of how pretty Natalie was. She wore a flowery green dress, matching her almond-like eyes, and her hair flowed over her shoulders. On her hip her spellshooter was holstered.

"So, where to?" Ben asked.

"Back onto the Dragonway."

They headed back over the station's bridge and down the stairs to platform seven. As they passed a train map, Charlie stopped and inspected their route. He looked up at Natalie with surprise.

"SpellWorks have their own station?"

"They have their own island, actually," Natalie said, smiling at Charlie's astonishment. "It's just off the coast of Italy."

The dragon arrived on time and they found themselves alone in a carriage. The journey passed quickly, despite Natalie's refusal to describe what SpellWorks looked like, claiming she couldn't do it justice. The juddering deceleration less than two hours later announced their arrival at SpellWorks station. Ben's stomach hit the seat bar and the train went into a steep incline as it headed towards the surface. They emerged into the light and the dragon coasted gently down the platform. Ben, who wasn't prone to gaping, felt his jaw open. Everything seemed to be constructed of glass or crystal, from the shiny platform floor to the gleaming columns that held up the high glass ceiling. The place was pristine and there was a pleasant fragrance in the air. Ben wasn't sure if they had entered a train station or a palace.

"Come on, guys, get out," Natalie said, nudging Ben and Charlie, who were both so busy staring they had completely forgotten to exit the carriage. Ben soon noticed another oddity:

there was no bridge connecting the platforms, and no obvious way to cross them.

"Wow – look at that!"

Charlie was pointing at a small family. They were flying serenely over the platforms, and landed safely on the other side. Ben saw another couple do the same, then several more.

"Over here," Natalie said.

She directed them to a sign, cast in glass, that said "Hand here". On the sign was a cut-out shape of a hand.

"Just think where you want to go," Natalie said, smiling at their expressions. "Watch."

Natalie pressed her slender hand onto the sign. Immediately she rose into the air and glided across the platforms.

"Seems simple enough." Ben grinned. "Do you want to go next?"

"I think I'll watch you, actually," Charlie said.

Ben spread his hand and pressed it against the sign, matching the hand imprint. He felt his stomach leave him for a second as his body started a gentle ascent. Ben gave a little whoop and kicked his legs. Upwards he went, until he envisioned the exit in his mind, at which point he started going forwards. He sailed over several platforms, easily clearing the dragons and their carriages, before landing gently at the other side of the station, next to Natalie. Ben immediately turned and saw a slightly flustered Charlie sailing through the air, his arms and legs wobbling.

"Excuse me!" he said, as he landed heavily in between Ben and Natalie. "Ow, sorry about that."

Natalie led them through a grand, intricately decorated crystal archway, and out of the station. Ben felt like he'd entered another universe. He stopped and stared, not caring that he was blocking the station's entrance, forgetting everything except the view that greeted him.

Four magnificent castles, with turrets and huge spiral towers, lined the grassy landscape in the distance. Each was tinted in a different colour – red, white, blue and green. Hovering above each one was a huge animated hologram bearing that castle's element – a burning log fire for the red castle; a cascading waterfall for the blue; a spinning tornado for the white; and a swaying tree for the green. A road led from each castle and then converged, forming one large causeway, which cut through the grassy plains and led to a fifty-foot-high crystal fence that surrounded the castles. Running around the perimeter of the fence was another road, which was just as busy as the one running to the castles.

Ben, Charlie and Natalie stood outside the station, barely fifty yards from the fence.

"That is just spectacular," Charlie said. "It looks like Disneyland times a hundred."

"Well put," Ben said. "The question is, how do we get in?"

The only break in the fence was an open gate, which led on to the road that went to the castles. But the gate was guarded.

Ben noticed two things about the people allowed through: they all wore a small shiny badge that glowed a certain colour, perhaps indicating the castle they were heading to, and very few of them were human. The majority were elves, but there were also lots of gnomes, goblins and even dwarves, as well as a few buzzing pixies and sprites.

"I never thought we'd stick out by being human," Charlie said.

"We'll be fine," Natalie said. "We just need SpellWorks security badges."

"Where can we get them? I doubt they're handing them out for free."

"Follow me," Natalie said. She checked her watch. "Seven minutes. We need to hurry."

She led them along the busy road that ran parallel to the fence. Ben was so busy looking around that he had several near collisions. It wasn't the people themselves who caught his eye, but rather what they were riding. Many of the elves rode something that resembled a Segway except it had no wheels and simply floated along. Others rode different types of animals that Ben guessed were related to the big cat family. Still more flew overhead on eagles, though Ben noticed none of them seemed able to cross the threshold of the fence even when flying above it.

Natalie set a quick pace and eventually, in the distance, they could make out a settlement.

"There are four towns, one for each castle," Natalie said. "Most SpellWorks employees live here."

"Is that where we're going?" Ben asked.

"No." She turned towards the fence and sighed with relief. "Oh good, he turned up. He's not that reliable and I feared he might not come."

On the other side of the gate, just ahead of them, was a young elf. He didn't look much older than Ben, though you could never tell with elves. With long, flowing brown hair and fine eyebrows, Ben supposed he might have been considered good-looking for their kind. But his looks were ruined slightly by the anxious expression and his frequent furtive looks around.

"Rolan," Natalie said, waving and giving him a glamorous smile. "You made it!"

It was instantly obvious to Ben that Rolan was smitten by Natalie. He softened the moment he saw her. Ben and Charlie received unfriendly glances, before he forgot all about them.

"I said I would," Rolan said, in a voice that Ben thought sounded a little feminine.

"Do you have them?"

Rolan beckoned Natalie forwards and they met at the fence. Ben saw Rolan hand Natalie something.

"I have to get them back today," he said.

"You will," Natalie assured him.

"If you get caught..."

Natalie touched Rolan's hand. "Don't worry, it won't get back to you."

Rolan seemed mollified, if not by Natalie's words, then by her touch.

"Have you thought about my offer?" he asked.

Natalie stepped back. "I'll let you know tonight." She gave him a wave. "Thanks again!"

Once they turned and headed back down the road towards the gate, Natalie shivered. "God, he's creepy."

"I thought so too," Charlie said, sounding pleased. "What was his offer?"

"It's not even worth repeating. I'm just trying to find a way to let him down gently. He doesn't take rejection lightly."

Natalie handed them each a badge and they fastened them to their shirts. They shone a dull green.

"Access to the earth castle?"

"The castle is called Gaia. And yes, it should give us access."

Ben smiled. "Rolan must be a competent little thief. I thought you said these were hard to come by."

Natalie seemed to be struggling with something. Finally she said, "He didn't steal them."

"How did he get them, then?"

"He made them. He's very good at forging things. He works in the security badges production department, and knows how they work inside and out."

Charlie slowed, his eyes narrowing. "If they are forgeries, have they been tested?"

"Not yet," Natalie said. "But Rolan is exceptionally gifted. We'll be fine."

Ben studied Natalie. "You weren't going to tell us, were you?"

"I didn't want to worry you," Natalie said, her eyes lingering a little too long on Charlie.

Charlie's face went red. He mumbled something unintelligible.

"I'm sure they'll be fine," Ben said quickly, hoping Charlie hadn't taken offence. "Let's go try them out."

To Ben's relief, both Natalie and Charlie turned their attention to the gate and the guards blocking them. There was a steady flow of people coming in and out. Ben counted four guards, but they weren't stopping people; perhaps the pin's badge was security enough. Ben saw the badges light up when they passed through.

"Will ours do that?" Charlie asked, looking down at his badge anxiously.

"They should do," Natalie said. "Rolan was supposed to replicate their functionality."

Ben smiled. "Well, he knows you'll never speak to him again if he messed up, so I'm sure they're fine. Just walk confidently through, and don't stare at the guards."

But as they approached the gate, Ben found that was easier said than done. They had to slow to a crawl, as there were people ahead of them, including a couple of dwarves riding what looked like warthogs. The mounted dwarves caught the guards' attention, which suited Ben just fine. As he passed through the gate, the pin suddenly warmed against his chest and, to his great relief, glowed green.

"That wasn't so bad," Ben said, giving them both a grin. The wide road eased the traffic congestion and Ben set a good pace towards the castles.

Charlie wiped his brow with a handkerchief. "I'm fairly sure I'm going to have heart problems when I'm older. So, what next?"

"We head to Gaia and begin our search for Mr. Lornor Taren."

"How do we know which castle he's in?"

"If he's a beastmaster, he should be in Gaia. Earth is the primary magic used to tame and train beasts," Natalie said.

"Except the book said he had been relieved of his beastmaster position," Charlie said.

"Minor details," Ben said, with a wave. "When we get into the castle, we'll find a way to track him down."

Ben's confidence wavered slightly as they neared the castle. The sheer size and splendour of it was both intimidating and awe-inspiring. The faint green turrets and towers were so tall they seemed to touch the sky.

"The doors are open. That's a good sign," Natalie said.

In actual fact, there were no doors, just a large archway for people to come and go. On top of the arch the words "SpellWorks Inc.: Gaia" were elegantly engraved.

"Maybe they don't need a door," Charlie said. "Maybe they have magic security instead."

"Ever the optimist," Ben commented.

But Charlie had a point, and Ben fiddled with his badge as they climbed the stairs towards the arched entrance.

"When we get inside," Ben said, now talking softly and quickly, "it's important that we don't look like a bunch of tourists. We will have only moments to decide where to go and what to do. Who wants to lead?"

"You," Natalie and Charlie said in unison.

"Okay, but if either of you sees something, feel free to take over. Natalie, you know this world better than us and, Charlie, you can read and observe like a wizard."

Ben couldn't help flinching as he stepped through the archway, half expecting some magical barrier to stop them in their tracks. But they walked through unopposed and entered a huge circular atrium.

"That was easy," Charlie said, looking around uncomfortably. "Am I being paranoid or does anyone else think that sneaking into one of the most magical places in the Unseen Kingdoms should be a little harder?"

"Don't be such a pessimist," Natalie whispered. "We have the security badges, remember?"

Ben couldn't help feeling Charlie had a point, but he had no time to worry about that now. He quickly took in the scene. Everything was a pristine white or made of crystal glass, reminding Ben of some futuristic space age. There were three staircases: one ahead, one left, and one right. In front of the central staircase was a signpost with a sign for each staircase. The left said "Research & Development", the middle one said "Production Labs" and the one on the right said "Enchantments & Artefacts".

Without breaking stride, Ben steered to the left staircase and started climbing.

"Good choice," Natalie said.

"What is it with stairs?" Charlie huffed. "I would have thought a place like this would have magical escalators or something."

The stairs ran deep into the left section of the castle and they emerged into a small room that was clearly located in one of the many towers, with its curved walls. There were two doors, in front and behind them. Neither were marked and both looked identical.

"Which door?" Charlie asked.

In answer, Ben led them through the front one.

Ben had told Charlie and Natalie the importance of acting like they belonged, but the moment they stepped through the door, Ben found it difficult following his own rule. The left wall was made entirely of glass, allowing unrestricted viewing into a huge open plan room that looked like a combination of a science lab and a library. There were large, chest-high tables, surrounded by stools, which were populated by elves in protective lab coats. Many were studying books, supplied from the huge shelves that were placed in the centre of the room; others were channelling magic into little pellets by touching them. They would then take the magic-infused pellet, holding it delicately in both hands, and walk it over to another section of the room that reminded Ben of the spellshooter target practice rooms at the Institute; the only difference was the grass, shrubbery and even small trees planted at the end of the room. The pellet was handed to an elf dressed in full body armour, who would then launch the spell at the planted nature at the end of the room, to wildly unpredictable results.

"Let's keep going," Natalie said, giving Ben a little nudge.

They continued to the end of the hallway, up a small staircase, and into another corridor, where exactly the same set-up was repeated, except that instead of testing the spells against nature, there were all sorts of animals, chained by magical means, contained in the huge room. Ben saw everything from squirrels to something that looked like a baby wyvern.

"We should be getting closer, if he still works here," Ben said.

"I don't want to put a dampener on things," Charlie said, "but how are we going to recognise Lornor Taren? I never saw a picture of him."

Natalie smiled. "I thought you would never ask." She delved into her pockets and pulled out two sheets, handing one to Ben and the other to Charlie. "I found this last night. It's a few years old, but it's better than nothing."

On the sheet was an illustration of the oldest elf Ben had ever seen. He had fine silver hair, absurdly long ears and a great big chin. There were faint bags beneath his eyes, and Ben thought he looked a little worse for wear.

"Perfect," Ben said. "He certainly stands out. Now we just need to stumble into him somehow."

But the castle was a maze of stairs, hallways and rooms, and they soon found themselves wandering around without having a clue where they were. To make matters worse, they had passed several elves who had given them curious looks, though so far nobody had stopped to question them.

"This is no good," Ben said, stopping at yet another t-junction. "We could go on doing this forever and not find him."

"What do you suggest?" Natalie asked.

"We need to ask someone."

"Is that a good idea?" Charlie asked nervously. "We don't want to attract attention to ourselves. What if Lornor no longer even works here? The question will sound ridiculous."

"Then we'll know we're wasting our time and leave as quickly as possible," Ben said.

"I agree that we need to change something," Natalie said. "But be careful, Ben. Do you want me to ask someone? It might not look so strange, as at least I am part-elf."

"No, I'll do it," Ben said. "It's just a matter of finding the right person."

Ben had no intention of going to one of the glass rooms and asking someone; there were far too many people watching. He needed to catch the right person alone and that opportunity came after a further ten minutes wandering the hallways. A young elf girl, wearing a small satchel, walked hurriedly towards them. She had a sweet, innocent face and fit Ben's criteria perfectly.

"Excuse me," Ben said, stepping into her path. The elf girl seemed surprised to see them, clearly intent on her destination.

"Oh, hello," she said, in a soft voice. "I'm sorry to be rude, but I'm in a bit of a rush."

"No problem," Ben said, throwing out his most charming smile. "I was just wondering, could you tell me where we might find Mr. Lornor Taren? I have an important message to give him." Ben indicated the illustration in his hand, which he had folded up.

Though he kept a calm face, Ben's heart was going a mile a minute. There was a good chance his question was ridiculous. What if Lornor Taren no longer worked here? The elf could have passed away for all they knew – he certainly looked old enough. So it was with great relief when the elf girl relaxed and pointed a finger the way she had come.

"Of course," she said. "You're not far away. Just head up the stairs, take the second door on the right, head down the corridor until you reach the turret, then take the fourth door on the left, and Mr. Taren is the second last door down that hallway."

Ben thanked her and she went on her way, now running to make up for lost time.

"There you go!" Ben said. "Simple. I knew he worked around here; animal magic is Lornor's area. One of you got those instructions, right?"

"I did," Charlie said.

"Good. Let's go pay a visit to our friend Lornor Taren."

— CHAPTER TWENTY-ONE —
Questions and Answers

"Wait!" Charlie said, tugging on Ben's arm.

Ben had been about to knock on Lornor Taren's door.

"Why?"

"What's the plan?"

"We go in, find out what this guy knows about forrecks, then leave. Pretty straightforward."

Charlie put both his hands to his head in frustration. "You think he's just going to tell us that? We're complete strangers. We can't just barge in there without some sort of story or explanation."

"Charlie is right," Natalie said. "Much as I enjoy your spontaneous plans, we should think this through."

"I have several plans," Ben said. "But I want to see what sort of person we are dealing with before I decide exactly which one to use."

"Well, we should have some sort of back story at least," Charlie said.

"Fine. What do you suggest?"

Charlie seemed taken aback. "Me? Well, I'm not sure."

"Maybe we're messengers, requesting information for our seniors," Natalie suggested. "Or we could be researchers, asking for information."

"Let's do the researchers ploy," Ben said. He had no intention of using any such back story, and was starting to get impatient.

Ben knocked firmly on the door. There was a moments silence, then a surprisingly deep voice spoke.

"Come in."

Ben turned the handle. The door opened and they entered a luxurious office that was in serious need of a clean. There were shelves everywhere, filled with books in a manner that suggested someone enjoyed taking them out but wasn't particularly bothered how they went back in. At the back of the room was a grand desk, filled with more books, and on top of those books, a black cat slept. Ben did a double take; with magic permeating every inch of this place, the last thing he expected was an ordinary pet cat. Behind the desk, on a leather chair every bit as grand as the desk, was Mr. Lornor Taren.

Ben had hoped to shape his plan around a kindly, doting old elf, but the reality was quite the opposite. Lornor stared at them with bulbous brown eyes that looked too big for his head. His skin was creased with age and drooped at the cheeks and chin, and he had thinning silver hair. His right hand stroked the cat slowly, which was about the only affectionate thing Ben could detect in this elf. Lornor gave them each a long, calculating stare.

"Institute apprentices," Lornor said, with undisguised disdain. "Ones or Twos, by the looks of you."

Lornor's thinly disguised hostility almost threw Ben. "Charlie and I, Ben Greenwood, are Ones. Natalie is a Two. How did you know?"

Lornor gave a sniff. "I can always smell Institute members. They give off this unhealthy odour of arrogance and righteousness."

Ben kept a straight face, but underneath he felt a growing alarm. The strength of emotion that Lornor spoke of the Institute with was frightening and had Ben struggling to work out how to open the conversation without enticing more animosity. Lornor saved him from having to.

"You may be wondering why I arranged this meeting," Lornor said. His right hand never stopped stroking the cat, and the left one scratched his chin with long, skeletal fingers.

"Arranged?" Ben said, for the first time unable to mask his surprise.

Lornor gave a cold smile. "Do you really think you could wander into SpellWorks? Maybe in the Institute you allow such security lapses, but not here."

Ben resisted the urge to finger his security badge, but Lornor must have spotted Charlie or Natalie doing it.

"Those fake security badges gave you away the moment you passed through the gates," Lornor said, giving another hint of a smile. "It also, incidentally, cost your friend his job."

Ben could just see the stunned faces of Charlie and Natalie from his peripheral vision, but he refused to give Lornor the satisfaction of having all three of them looking like rabbits caught in the headlights.

"So why did you want to see us?" Ben said. "It's clear you have about as much love for the Institute as I do for cucumber sandwiches."

"That's exactly why I wanted to see you," Lornor said. "For over two hundred years, the Institute and I have not been on speaking terms, since their horrific culling of the forreck. Now, in the last two weeks, I suddenly get two separate visits. I am curious."

"Two visits?"

Ben's question was chorused by Natalie and Charlie.

"Ah, you did not know," Lornor said. "Further confirmation of the Institute's inept management."

Ben's throat suddenly felt dry. "Who else came here?"

This time, Lornor had eyes only for Ben. "You know, already, I think."

"My parents," Ben whispered, barely able to get the words out. "What did they want?"

Lornor gave a humourless chuckle. "Information on forrecks. Isn't it ironic? The Institute are responsible for the eradication of one of the most incredible animals in the Unseen Kingdoms, and now suddenly they are interested in them."

"What did you tell my parents?" Ben asked, the question coming out before he realised how presumptuous it was. But Lornor seemed to be enjoying himself.

"I gave them little titbits," Lornor said, giving his cat an even firmer stroke. "Enough to whet their appetites, taunting them with information while withholding any truly important data. They wanted to know if there were any forrecks left; I told them there may be one, though I didn't tell them where. They asked if I knew of any potential forreck weakness. I told them I did, but refused to disclose what it was. As you can imagine, your parents became rather frustrated."

Lornor gave another little smile that Ben was starting to find increasingly annoying, and he had to resist an urge to step forwards and throttle the old elf.

"I know what you are thinking, young Greenwood," Lornor said, his voice soft. "You are wondering how you might extract the information your parents tried so hard to obtain." Lornor made a tutting noise. "I'm afraid that, just like your parents, you will fail."

Ben bit his lip in frustration, and felt blood on his tongue. He turned to Natalie and Charlie – both were shooting dagger-like stares at Lornor, but neither made any move to do anything.

Ben thought fast. They could not leave this room without getting that information.

"As pleasurable as thwarting the Institute is, I must be getting back to work," Lornor said. "Which means it's time for you to go."

Lornor looked pointedly at their chests.

Their security badges started flashing and making small beeping noises.

"Ah, right on time," Lornor said, with another smile. He massaged his hand, before resuming his cat-stroking. "Security should be here any moment. As much as I despised your parents, young Greenwood, their escape did impress me. However, I am quite certain you will not be as lucky."

"We should go," Charlie said, looking at the door anxiously.

"No," Ben said. An idea was forming. A desperate one.

Ben moved quickly, and yanked Natalie's spellshooter from her holster. In three quick steps, he approached Lornor, who shrank back, more in surprise than fear. But Ben wasn't going for the elf. He yanked the cat off the desk and took a step back. He pointed the spellshooter at the cat's head, so the tip entered its ear.

"Start talking or the cat gets it," Ben said, with a savageness and brutality that surprised even him.

To his surprise and delight, Lornor's confidence showed its first crack, a small flicker of fear, quickly hidden by a stone-faced stare.

"You think you can blackmail me with the cat?" Lornor laughed, but Ben could tell it was forced.

"Let's see, shall we?" Ben said, with a nasty smile. "Let's see how pussy responds to being engulfed in flames."

Lornor's hard face cracked again, but to Ben's frustration, he kept his mouth firmly shut. There was only one thing for it. Ben focused, and summoned forth the spell. He watched as the red pellet made its way down the orb, towards the barrel.

"Ben, don't!" Natalie said, rushing forwards and grabbing his arm.

He nearly lost focus of the spell, and it retreated back up the orb slightly before he could command it down again. He glanced again at Lornor and saw that he too was watching the pellet, his eyes widening as it floated back towards the barrel.

Natalie tugged on his arm again. Ben wanted to shrug her off, but doing so would cost him valuable seconds – seconds they didn't have. Security would be here any moment. Ben thought he could hear footsteps outside the door, but it was hard to tell with the blood pounding in his ears.

Charlie stepped forwards suddenly, and pulled Natalie back.

"Do it, Ben," he said, with relish, his eyes alight. "Light the cat up. Let's see if it survives longer than our experiment with Rusty the dog."

Lornor's fear turned to incredulity, and he extended a hand out before he could stop himself.

"Stop!" he said. "What is it you want?"

Ben felt like hugging Charlie; his acting skills really were top notch. He gave Lornor a grim smile, but didn't release the cat. "First, I want you to write down the location of any surviving forrecks."

Lornor gave Ben a look of pure hatred. "There is only one that I know of, and it has only survived due to extraordinary circumstance. It was owned by someone with very close ties to the Institute. Her name was Charlotte Rowe."

Ben felt his heart leap from his chest to his throat. Beside him, he saw Charlie and Natalie stiffen.

"Where can we find this forreck?" Ben asked.

"If he still survives, he probably resides where he always has: in the cavern beneath the Institute."

"I didn't know there was a cavern beneath the Institute."

"Not many people do. It was sealed off many years ago. You won't find it easy to get to. Forrecks like being underground, so he will most likely be at the deepest level of the cavern. I have heard the cavern beneath the Institute is one of the deepest in the Unseen Kingdoms."

Ben swallowed his elation. More noise erupted from behind the door, but thankfully nobody seemed intent on entering the room, yet.

"We need to get going," Charlie said, once more looking anxiously at the door.

"You won't escape," Lornor said, regaining a fraction of his confidence. "And when they catch you, I am going to make sure you suffer."

"A bit like your cat, if you don't answer my next question," Ben said. "What weakness does the forreck have that you hint at in your books?"

Lornor took an age to reply, and for a moment Ben thought he was going to have to take drastic action.

"Solar eclipse," Lornor said, eventually, the words coming reluctantly from his lips. "For some reason, the blocking of the sun affects the forreck. There is one next Friday, as it happens, not that it matters to you, as you won't be leaving here for a long time."

"A solar eclipse doesn't last long, though," Charlie said, ignoring Lornor's taunting.

"No, but I suspect that the forreck is affected at least an hour before and after the incident," Lornor said. "As I said, I haven't accumulated sufficient evidence to support this theory. Nor do I know how debilitating the effect will be on the forreck."

Ben could sense Lornor had finished talking, and that he wasn't going to learn anything more, cat or no cat. Ben quickly placed the cat back onto the desk, and whispered an apology into her ear.

Lornor glared at him, and grabbed his cat with both hands.

"Let's get out of here," Ben said, handing Natalie back her spellshooter.

A sudden pounding on the door made Ben jump, and a commanding voice spoke. "Open up and relinquish your weapons! This is SpellWorks security. You have ten seconds."

— Chapter Twenty-Two —

Desperate Escape

Lornor's smile turned into a grin. "Ah, there we are, right on time. I'm going to enjoy this."

Ben, Charlie and Natalie turned and stared at the door as if it had just grown tentacles.

"We're trapped!" Charlie said, his hands going to his forehead.

"At least the door seems to be locked," Natalie said.

Lornor coughed. "Oh, not for long." He waved a hand, and the top bolt snapped open. Another wave and the middle one did likewise.

Ben dipped his hand into his pocket, curling around his dad's pouch. He took a deep breath and concentrated, pushing aside the fact that they had seconds before they were caught and searching for a spell that might help them.

Bingo.

The bottom and final bolt started to open, but it seemed to happen in slow motion, as if Lornor was trying to draw out their agony.

"Natalie, when the door opens, fire something at them," Ben said.

"Like what?" Natalie said. To her credit she kept the incredulity from her voice, but not the desperation. "I don't have anything strong enough to harm these people."

"Doesn't matter," Ben said. "Just make sure it's obvious; some sort of fireball or ice blast would be good." He turned to include Charlie. "As soon as the spell has been fired, I want both of you to hit the floor and cover your heads. You got that?"

"I get that you're babbling nonsense, yes," Charlie said, wiping his sweaty forehead. "What are you planning?"

Ben didn't have time to answer. The bottom bolt snapped to the right and the door burst inwards, almost coming off its hinges.

Through the door came two uniformed, identical-looking elves. They wore suits of silver armour that looked so supple they could almost be leather. Over the armour were elaborate blue and white jackets that came down to their knees. On their heads were tall, shiny helmets, increasing their already impressive height. Both elves were armed with short swords, and their free hands were glowing with a pale white energy.

"Now!" Ben said, turning urgently to Natalie.

Natalie's spellshooter was shaking slightly, but she grimaced, eyes narrowing, and pulled the trigger. A burning, sizzling star-shaped object spun its way towards the two security guards, crackling and hissing as it cut through the air.

Both security guards stared at the fiery object with a flicker of surprise. One of them raised a hand in the most subtle of movements, but Ben didn't wait to see how he snuffed out the spell. For a second at least, they were both distracted by Natalie's attack.

Ben called forth the spell from his dad's pouch and felt it touch his fingers. The power of it made him gasp. Would he be able to cast something this strong? No time to worry about that now. Ben plucked the spell from the pouch and threw it as hard as he could, with every ounce of intention and willpower he could muster, piling everything he had learnt during his spellshooter lessons into one throw. Ben just had time to see the pellet hit the floor between the two security guards before he hit the deck, covering his head.

The explosion was deafening. The blast of air was so intense Ben was almost lifted off the floor. He felt objects flying and heard books knocked off the shelves, followed by several large thumps. It was all over in seconds. Ben lifted his head. There were books everywhere; you could barely see the floor. The security guards were no longer standing by the door, but had been thrown against one of the book shelves, which had collapsed on them.

"What was that?" Charlie asked, after they had all picked themselves up.

"A twister," Ben said. "Huge blasts of swirling air. I have to admit, I didn't expect such spectacular results. I wish I could have seen it."

"Where did you get such a powerful spell?" Charlie asked.

"And how were you able to cast it?" Natalie added, looking even more astonished than Charlie.

"I'll explain later. Let's get going before reinforcements arrive."

They re-emerged into the hallway and Ben checked both ways, searching for trouble. All three of them had removed their security badges and left them on the desk of the stupefied Lornor.

"Where to now?" Charlie asked. "Surely the entrance will be blocked?"

"Yes, the entrance is out of the question," Ben said. He started walking down the passageway, followed quickly by Charlie and Natalie.

"Where else can we go?" Natalie said.

They quickly came to a fork in the passageway, and Ben scrutinised both options, before choosing the steeper of the two.

"We go up," Ben said.

To Ben's surprise, neither Charlie nor Natalie questioned his decision. He suspected they might have guessed his plan, but neither had anything better to offer.

Ben searched out every staircase he could find, and slowly they started ascending the castle. Charlie stiffened every time they passed someone, though that became increasingly less frequent and most paid them no heed. In fact, many didn't even make eye contact with them, which Ben started to find troubling, though he didn't mention it to the other two, preferring not to worry them.

"Guards!" Charlie hissed, as a couple of elves, dressed identically to those they had met in Lornor's room, appeared round the corner.

Ben spotted a door just ahead of them and quickly rammed it open. They bundled into a darkened room. Ben's eyes quickly adjusted and he was relieved to find that they were in a small storage facility. The only noise came from their breathing, which was so loud Ben thought it might give them away. But after a slow count to sixty, it was clear the guards hadn't spotted them, and they continued on their way.

Twice more they had to take detours or scramble to find a place to hide, as security guards passed them by. Ben was just starting to wonder if they would ever make it to the top, when he saw a steep spiral staircase that led up to a large circular hole in the ceiling. Through the hole Ben could see clear blue sky.

"Here we are!" Ben said, rubbing his hands.

"I think I know where this is going, and I don't like it," Charlie said, as he followed Ben up the staircase.

"Well, feel free to suggest an alternate plan," Ben said. The stairs were so steep he had to use hands and feet to climb them.

"Politely giving ourselves up comes to mind," Charlie muttered. "I mean, we're just kids. Are they really going to imprison us?"

"Yes," Natalie said firmly. "SpellWorks can be ruthless. I know a guy who tried to steal a prototype of some invisible armour. SpellWorks locked him away for two years."

"Wow," Charlie said. "That's just what I needed to hear moments before our inevitable capture."

"A little optimism wouldn't go amiss," Ben said.

He reached the top of the stairs and poked his head through. A pleasant breeze greeted him and he took a deep breath, relishing the open air and potential freedom.

Just like the Royal Institute of Magic, the roof of SpellWorks Inc. consisted of paddocks. These ones were smaller than the Institute's, but at the same time more spacious and infinitely nicer. There was no smell of pooh, and the grass intersecting the paddocks was perfectly cut. There were sprawling trees at regular intervals, creating an almost park-like feel.

Ben stood up and surveyed the scene, while Charlie and Natalie scrambled up through the hole. The paddocks were primarily filled with pegasi. Their white coats and gold wings gave them a majestic, almost regal look.

"Can you fly one of those?" Ben asked Natalie. She was staring at them with a half-open mouth, and had a peculiar starry look in her eyes.

"I've always wanted to fly an Egyptian Pegasus. Yes, I can ride them." She seemed so eager that she almost started walking without them.

"I know I'm going to sound like a pessimist again, but isn't this a bit easy?" Charlie said. "You really think they're just going to let us walk up to one of those things and fly away?"

Ben didn't answer. He had been wondering the same thing. Other than the animals, the place was completely deserted. His skin started to get tingly; something didn't feel right.

"Come on," Natalie said, grabbing both Ben's and Charlie's arms. There was a wondrous look in her eyes that was clearly blinding any danger she might have sensed. "Let's go and saddle up. I want to see if the wings are as soft as I've read."

They took one step forwards.

The security guards materialised from nowhere. One moment the path to freedom was clear; the next, they found themselves surrounded by five fully armoured elves. The one directly in front of them stepped forwards. He looked identical to the others, except for a long, blue feather protruding from his helmet.

"We have been expecting you," the guard spoke, in a calm, measured voice. "It will be easier if you come quietly, but, of course, that is up to you."

"I say we go quietly," Charlie whispered, trying to limit his mouth movement.

"I bet we could make it back down the hole," Natalie said.

"No," Ben said firmly. "There's no way out that way."

His hand went into his pouch and he started feeling for the spells. There weren't many defensive spells left, and his options were limited.

"When I give the go-ahead, we run to that pegasus on the left," Ben said.

He had hoped the security guards would come towards them, creating a scene of disorganisation, but these guards were a cool bunch, and stayed their distance. Ben cursed. He was going to have to make the first move.

"Ready?" he said softly. The little pellet in the pouch touched his fingertips and he rubbed it gently.

"Of course not," Charlie said, with a hint of anger. "Ready for what?"

"To run," Ben said. He took out the pellet and threw it on the floor in front of them. Immediately a silky, ethereal net surrounded them, hovering inches above the ground.

"Now!" Ben shouted.

Ben started running, Natalie and Charlie right behind him. The net warped to encapsulate all three of them as they ran. From the corner of Ben's eye he saw two small missiles, cutting through the air and leaving a smoky trail. They cannoned into the field and exploded. The net saved them, but the vibrations nearly threw Ben from his feet. He barely had time to recover when two more hit the net, and Ben saw its fibres start to weaken.

They were less than fifty feet from the pegasus.

"Guard!" Natalie cried.

Dead ahead a security guard blocked their path. His hand was glowing, forming another missile.

Ben thrust his hand down into the pouch. He barely had time to demand an appropriate spell, and just picked the first pellet his hands fell upon. With a quick throw, he launched it at the guard. They were too close for the guard to mount a proper defence, and it hit him in the stomach. His eyes widened, and all of a sudden the guard started floating away.

For a minute, Ben thought they were going to make it.

He didn't spot the half a dozen missiles until it was too late. These ones were bigger, stronger and the net field was already starting to wobble.

The impact threw Ben from his feet. He saw Charlie and Natalie cartwheel through the air. With a grunt, Ben landed heavily on his arm, the air forced from his lungs. His vision blurred, but with superhuman effort he attempted to get back up. He made it onto one knee, before witnessing a sight far more damaging than the impact from the missiles: both Natalie and Charlie were down, unmoving. Ben stared at them, so horror-struck that he didn't spot the final missile. The protective net was history. Ben heard a crack, a flash of light, and then everything went black.

— CHAPTER TWENTY-THREE —
The Power of the Institute

Ben woke to a splitting headache, lying on a firm bed, staring up at a pristine white ceiling. His vision was blurry and just about every part of his body ached. The idea of moving made him wince. His memory was foggy and he couldn't recall exactly where he was or how he got here. Slowly it started coming back.

SpellWorks. Forrecks. Lornor. The failed escape.

Ben's eyes shot open and he sat up – or tried to. He groaned in agony the moment he moved.

"Thank god, you're awake!" Natalie said. She rushed over to sit on the corner of his bed. She seemed anxious to tend to him, but her hands were poised uncertainly, unsure where to start. Natalie had a gash just above her eyebrow, but, other than that, didn't appear too worse for wear.

"I'm fine," Ben said, forcing himself to sit up.

They were in a small room, empty except for three beds, which were really nothing more than mattresses resting on thin pieces of wood. In the middle of the room was a small table with a pitcher of water. There were no windows and only one door, which Ben knew would be locked.

"This place isn't too bad for a prison," Ben said.

"We're not in prison," Charlie said. He had several dark red patches on his shirt and trousers. "This is a temporary holding room while they decide what to do with us."

"Ah. How long have I been out?"

"Three hours," Natalie said. "It's almost dinner time."

Charlie had his legs crossed on the bed with his chin resting on his hand, staring despondently at the bed. It took Ben a moment to realise why Charlie was so down.

"The exam," Ben said, with a sudden urgency that belied his physical state.

"Exactly," Charlie said, looking up. "We can say goodbye to the Royal Institute of Magic. We'll never get back in time for tomorrow."

The thought of failing to make the exam gave Ben a shot of energy. He hauled himself to his feet, ignoring his protesting body.

"We have to make it back," Ben said.

He hobbled over to the door and started pounding on it, shouting for assistance. He kept it up until his voice was hoarse and the skin on his fist was raw.

"We tried that already," Charlie said. "If anyone is there, they're clearly not interested in us."

"They will come when they are ready," Natalie said. "Until we are convicted, they will treat us okay, which means someone will come and give us some dinner to eat."

"I've got no intention of getting convicted," Ben said, slamming his hand on the door one more time.

"I'm not sure it's entirely up to us," Charlie said. "And even if by some miracle we made it back for tomorrow's exam, would they even let us take it after everything we've done?"

Charlie had a point, but Ben didn't care about that right now. If they got out, they could at least plead their case to the Institute. Ben put his hand in his pocket, but his pouch was no longer there.

"Those spells were the first thing they took when they brought us in," Natalie said. "Where did you get them from?"

Ben sighed and slumped back down on his bed. "I got them from the Guardians' common room. They are my dad's."

"Well, that helps explain why you could cast such powerful spells," Natalie said. "The family connection can make it easier, though I still can't believe how powerful they were."

"Not powerful enough, though," Ben said, feeling quite bitter.

A sullen silence fell between the three of them. For Ben, the magnitude of what they had done was starting to sink in. He felt like being swallowed up by the ground.

"I owe you an apology, Ben."

Ben looked up in surprise and saw Charlie looking at him. "Why?"

"I questioned the logic of coming here. If we hadn't, we would never have found out that your parents went to Lornor and failed to learn anything."

Ben smiled ruefully. "That's true. On the other hand, if we had followed your logic, we wouldn't be in this mess."

"I guess that makes us even," Charlie said, looking a little more like his old self.

"Good, can we move on now?" Natalie asked. Her voice was impatient, but Ben thought she was suppressing a smile. "Let's talk about what we learned from Lornor."

Charlie stuck a thumb out, and started itemising. "We know Ben's parents were looking for forrecks and any potential weakness they might have, but went away none the wiser."

Natalie nodded. "Right. We also know that the last remaining forreck was owned by Charlotte Rowe, and may still be living beneath the Institute. That forreck may be protecting Elizabeth's Boots, which were entrusted to Charlotte Rowe."

Ben roused himself from his morbid state. "According to Lornor, the forreck's only weakness may be a solar eclipse, which happens to occur next week." He grabbed the thin sheet on his bed and squeezed it in frustration. "Given that my parents failed to find out anything from Lornor, we are the only ones with any chance of getting those boots."

"Our chances aren't much better than theirs while we're stuck in here," Charlie said.

There was little else they could do but wait for dinner and hope someone turned up. Ben spent the time thinking up plans for escape, each one wilder than the next. Charlie tried to rest, his body clearly still hurting, while Natalie sat on her bed, fiddling with her hair, lost in thought.

By the time six o'clock came, Ben's body had recovered a great deal, but his stomach was rumbling with hunger pains.

"They should be here soon," Natalie said, glancing at her watch. "SpellWorks is known for its punctuality, even when it comes to serving prisoners."

Sure enough, the moment six o'clock struck, Ben heard the faint sound of voices, followed by footsteps. For a second, Ben had visions of another mad escape, but he cast it from his mind, cursing himself for an idiot; would he ever learn? Probably not.

"I hope they serve good food here," Charlie said, patting his stomach.

The voices became louder, and it soon became obvious there was an argument going on. One voice was an incoherent rant, while the other was calm and collected.

"That's Lornor," Charlie said of the angry voice, perking up suddenly.

"So it is," Ben said. "He's probably angry because they haven't sent any cleaners to tidy up his room."

"I don't think that's the reason," Natalie said, with a sudden smile. Her elf ears were sharper than Ben's and Charlie's. "Listen!"

The voices and footsteps were almost at the door by the time Ben could clearly make out what was being said.

"I demand to know who has such authority!" Lornor said.

"You may demand all you like," the calm voice replied.

"A trial! They must sit through a trial; our law demands it. I will stand witness and testify!"

"Not necessary, I'm afraid," the same voice said, with equal measure.

Ben felt a rush of hope, mirrored in Charlie's and Natalie's eyes. Before they could say a word, the door opened, and two very contrasting elves stood in the doorway.

Lornor was in a dishevelled state, his thinning hair a mess, his eyes red with fury. The other elf was small and as relaxed as Lornor was fired up. He wore a fine green coat, embellished with emeralds, that flowed down to his ankles.

"Follow me, please," the elf said, in a voice that was gentle yet firm.

Ignoring his pains and strains, Ben jumped out of bed, quickly followed by Charlie and Natalie. Lornor gave them looks of pure hatred, baring his teeth, before following hard on their heels.

"I will take this to the chairman himself," Lornor said. "He still has my ear. He will hear reason."

"Do as you please," the elf said, without offering any defence.

Ben hadn't a clue what was going on, but the fact that Lornor was in a rage was clearly a good thing. They didn't seem to be going to prison yet – were they heading to another temporary holding room? Hope threatened to swell his chest, but he forced it down, unwilling to draw conclusions until he knew exactly what was going on.

The elf led them through the maze of passageways and series of steps, until they were walking down one of the three main staircases, with the open arched entrance in clear view. Ben glanced back at Natalie and Charlie, who were now both smiling, unable or unwilling to hide their own expectations.

The elf stopped them by the entrance, and handed Ben back his pouch of spells, before giving them each a long stare. "Let me be clear that SpellWorks frowns heavily upon your actions, and you will not be welcome back here until you have made sufficient amends. Our laws state that you should go to trial and face the consequences. However, it appears you have some very powerful friends who have argued your case at the highest level. You are free to go, but please understand that, should you return, you will face the punishment you have managed to avoid." The elf turned and directed his gaze to a figure just outside the entrance. "They are all yours, Ms. Walker."

Ben almost fell over in surprise. On the top of the steps stood Wren. Her long silvery hair, piled on her head, was unmistakable, as were her sparkling grey eyes and peculiar agelessness. The five green diamonds floating above her shoulder were getting looks from everyone who passed.

"Thank you, Lindell," Wren said. "Please convey my thanks once again to your chairman."

Lindell gave her a little bow, and turned to go. Lornor stood there for a moment, his hands extended, as if he wanted to strangle the lot of them.

"Come now, Lornor," the elf said. "Let's get back to work."

For a minute, Lornor looked as if he was going to launch himself at them – not helped by Ben's insolent grin and wave. But, eventually, he disappeared back into the SpellWorks castle, leaving Ben, Charlie and Natalie alone at the entrance with Wren.

"Let's go, before they change their minds, shall we?" Wren said, with the merest hint of a smile.

As soon as they made it to the bottom, Ben felt a beautiful surge of freedom that made him want to dance. Wren, however, did not share his delight.

"I think you owe me an explanation. Needless to say, the Institute is very unhappy. We are, among other things, peace keepers and even law makers; we do not expect our apprentices to fly in the face of the very things we stand for," Wren said.

The tone in Wren's voice brought Ben back to earth with a thud. He glanced at Charlie and Natalie; both looked dumbfounded and were clearly unable to come up with a convincing story. Ben thought fast. How much could he say without giving the game away? He still remembered Queen Elizabeth's orders to his great ancestor, Michael Greenwood: the Institute were not to know about the Armour. But they were in so much trouble, he had to say something to justify their actions.

"We were looking for my parents," Ben said slowly, careful to keep his voice measured and to look Wren right in the eye.

"At SpellWorks?" Wren said, raising her eyebrows.

Ben nodded. Now for the tricky part. The trick to a good lie was to keep it as close to the truth as possible.

"We found some books, and this pouch" – Ben held the pouch up for a moment – "in my grandma's attic. The books were all from an author called Lornor Taren. We knew it was a long shot, but we thought to track him down, in case my parents might have done the same, because they were obviously quite interested in him."

"And had they?"

Ben paused, just for a moment. Lying could seriously backfire if Wren managed to extract the truth from Lornor, though he very much doubted that mad old elf would tell the Institute anything.

"Yes, they had."

It was the first time Ben had seen Wren truly surprised. "What did they want with Lornor?"

"I'm not sure," Ben said, planting his next lie carefully. "It turns out Lornor isn't very fond of the Institute."

"A slight understatement," Wren said. She was silent for a moment, staring ahead thoughtfully. Ben dared not glance at Charlie or Natalie, in case they let something slip. He could feel his body shaking slightly, whether from the day's ordeal or from nerves, he couldn't tell, but he clenched his fists hard to try to stop it. The next words Wren uttered could decide their fate. He went over his story in his head, but could see no way he could have improved it without putting them in more trouble.

"At some point, Ben, you are going to have to trust us," Wren said, giving him a kindly look. "If not the Institute, then at least me."

Ben nodded, but didn't trust himself to speak.

"Your story has enough truth that I believe I can convince the executive council not to expel you," Wren said. "I only ask one thing. When the time comes and the odds are stacked against you too heavily, come to me, as a friend and ally, not an Institute Director. You have a remarkable talent for survival, Ben Greenwood, but I fear your luck may run out."

"I will do that," Ben said, and he was surprised to find that he meant it.

Wren smiled, her eyes lighting up in the way that always made Ben feel a little better.

"Good! Now, I want all of you to take the Dragonway straight home. You look like you all need some rest. I don't want to put any pressure on you, but, believe me, you will need to be at your best for the exam tomorrow."

— CHAPTER TWENTY-FOUR —
First Grade Exam

The morning of the exam was another bright, sunny day, but Ben barely noticed the weather. While waiting for Charlie by his house, Ben started reciting a complicated trade formula when dealing with dwarves that he had learnt just last night. His body had mostly recovered from the physical battering it had taken yesterday, thanks to some powerful healing spells from Wren, but he now felt a little sick, and his stomach did unpleasant somersaults every time he thought of the exam. Ben had taken plenty of tests at school, but he had never felt like this. The difference was that he cared about this one; he really cared. The thought of failing and being dumped out of the Institute was too awful to think about.

But as bad as Ben felt, it was nothing compared to Charlie, who looked absolutely miserable.

"I don't know what you're worried about," Ben said, as they started walking. "You're an exam master."

"School exams," Charlie said, staring forlornly at the pavement. "And only because you know what to expect. You sit down, and answer questions from stuff you've studied in a book. This is completely different. We have absolutely no clue what it entails."

They spent most of the journey to the Institute discussing what they might encounter and quizzing each other on each department in a final flurry of revision.

Before they knew it, they were back in Taecia, climbing the hill to the Institute. As they passed the Institute's walls and approached the entrance, Ben felt a flutter of nerves, unconnected with the forthcoming exam.

"Do you think Wren managed to convince the executive council to let us stay?" Charlie asked, voicing the exact question that was on Ben's mind.

"I think so," Ben said. "I can't imagine the guards letting us through the gates otherwise."

Nevertheless, Ben passed through the Institute entrance with a feeling of trepidation, which lasted until Natalie met them inside, with a big smile.

"We're off the hook!" she said, raising her hand so they could both give her a high five. "Wren worked her magic, as usual. The only thing we have to do is forty hours of community service."

"I'll take that," Ben said, feeling a weight lift from his shoulders. He had been so focused on the exam he hadn't realised how much his uncertainty about his future at the Institute had been affecting him.

"How are you guys doing? Are you feeling confident?"

"We'd be feeling more confident if you told us a bit about the exam," Ben said, flashing her a cheeky smile.

"You know I can't," Natalie said, giving Ben a stern frown. "The only thing I can tell you is that it's different for each person. But you'll both be absolutely fine, trust me."

They headed up the stairs together.

"Were you confident when you took the exam?" Charlie asked.

"No," Natalie admitted. "I was a bundle of nerves, far worse than both of you. But I think you two are better prepared than I was."

"Let's hope you're right."

Muster proceeded as normal, though Ben was thinking so much about the exam Dagmar had to repeat his name three times before he answered. As everyone began filing out, Dagmar instructed them to stay. Natalie caught their eyes and gave them a thumbs up, before disappearing with the rest, leaving Ben and Charlie alone.

Dagmar looked even wearier than normal, but Ben didn't have time to think about that right now. His attention was on only one thing: the exam.

"Follow me," Dagmar said.

She led them out of the muster room and along the hallway, stopping at a series of doors Ben hadn't paid much attention to before. They were labelled "Exam Room #1", "Exam Room #2", and so on. Dagmar stopped in between rooms four and five. From her pocket she pulled out two small purple envelopes. One had Ben's name written on it; the other Charlie's.

"Do not open these until you are inside the exam room," she said, handing them the envelopes. "This is not like your ordinary exam you take at school. There are no questions; no right or wrong answers. You will be given a task, and it is up to you how you complete it. The more you can display what you have learnt in each department, the better your marks will be. You have until six o'clock to complete the exam, though the quicker you complete it, the higher you will score. Your final grade will be comprised of individual scores for each department. Failure to complete the exam, or complete it with a score too low, and you will not be invited to continue to the next grade of the apprenticeship. Your performance will be closely monitored by an Institute examiner, though you will not see him, and he will not intervene unless it is a matter of life or death. Any questions?"

Ben knew he'd have some the moment he entered the exam room, but his mind had gone temporarily blank. Charlie looked incapable of speech.

"Very well. You may start the exam." She gave them the merest flicker of a smile, which was all the encouragement they were going to get from her. "Good luck."

She walked away, leaving Ben and Charlie alone, staring at their envelopes.

"Good luck, Charlie," Ben said.

Charlie nodded, returned the sentiment, and walked numbly into room number five. Ben watched him go, and then, preparing himself for anything, pushed open the door to room number four.

The room was bare except for a long table, covered with an expensive-looking tablecloth. On it was a peculiar array of items. There was a file, with several sheets of paper inside. On the cover were the words "Grignak Bronny. Street goblin. ID NO: JK677751". Next to the file was a plain silver necklace, with a tag that read "JK677751". Ben recognised the necklace instantly; it was a tracker and could be used to locate a designated Unseen, in this instance, Grignak Bronny. The only other item on the table was money – two hundred pounds, in twenty-pound notes.

Ben made certain there was nothing else on the table, even searching underneath the table cloth. Satisfied there wasn't, he finally took out the envelope that Dagmar had given him, and began reading.

"EXAM: *APPRENTICESHIP, FIRST GRADE. BEN GREENWOOD.*

Mission Goal:

Find and return Grignak Bronny to the Institute.

Mission Details:

Street goblin Grignak has violated his Institute Travel Card by leaving London and fleeing to the village of Lampton Green. Reason unknown. You are to return Grignak to the Institute in a safe and secure manner. Should the target become hostile, use force as necessary, maintaining discretion at all times."

Ben read the mission three times, making sure he'd gleaned the significance of every single word. The Institute Travel Card was a legal okay to visit, or even live in, certain parts of the United Kingdom – in Grignak's case, London. It was a way to make sure the population of Unseens remained properly controlled. Violating the terms of your Institute Travel Card was a criminal offence.

Ben folded the message up neatly and tucked it in his pocket, then stared at the file. Inside was a detailed profile of Grignak, the knowledge of which could be crucial when he confronted the goblin. Dagmar's words came floating back to him. *"The more you can display what you have learnt in each department, the better your marks will be."* This was clearly an opportunity to demonstrate his Scholar knowledge.

Ben pocketed the money and the necklace, and tucked the file under his arm, before leaving the room. The moment he stepped outside, he noticed that the diamond on his right shoulder was flashing. The Institute members and apprentices he passed made it clear they would not talk or interrupt anything he was doing.

Ben hurried up the main staircase and went straight to the library. He found an empty table, sat down, and opened the file. He started reading, slowly and methodically, about the sorry and often illegal story of Grignak Bronny. There was a wealth of information on Grignak's past employment, his family, and even the various crimes he had committed. When he was done, he put the file down. Now what? There were plenty of other potential avenues he could explore, but Ben wasn't sure how much they would help. He checked his watch. It was almost 10am. No, there simply wasn't enough time to sit here and do research all day. However, there was one thing he did need to find out about.

Ben hit the library shelves, searching for anything he could find on street goblins, which turned out to be frustratingly difficult. He eventually found a book titled *101 Goblins and Where to Find Them* in the children's section. Inside, Ben found a helpful description of the street goblin.

"Hundreds of years of city dwelling has turned these goblins into street-smart, survival experts. They are smaller than your typical goblin and often scrawny in appearance, with a hooked nose and intelligent, scheming eyes. They are ferocious fighters, and particularly resistant to Earth magic and most mind spells. Many street goblins now live within the UK, having migrated from the Unseen Kingdoms to London, Birmingham and Leeds. Those that manage to avoid petty

crime normally work in the food industry. Due to their physical prowess, some have managed to find employment in the sporting world, most notably, Bolgop Grimp, who plays League 1 football for Crawley Town."

Ben spent a further twenty minutes gleaning what information he could from other books, but he made slow progress, and the time factor was starting to weigh heavily on him. After a fruitless search through *Goblins: A Political History,* Ben had had enough. It was now coming up to 11am. Ben felt a tiny quiver of panic, which he quelled instantly. There was still time, but he couldn't hang around here any longer.

Ben took a few pieces of the file on Grignak that he felt he might need and tucked them in his pocket. He then left the Institute at a jog.

The next step in his mission had become obvious as soon as he had read the task and seen the money. There was no way Ben could defeat a street goblin without some assistance. He needed spells.

Ben headed to Taecia Square, following a series of winding lanes, which eventually led to a large, well-trodden path filled with people with shopping on their minds. A mighty arch soon came into view, towering above the buildings. On the front it read "Queen Elizabeth's Taecia".

As soon as he passed underneath, the pavement opened up to a square surrounded on all sides by timber-framed shops. In the middle was a throng of people, many walking with shopping bags, others basking in the sun while sipping on cool drinks. The relaxed sound of chatter was a stark contrast to the pressure Ben felt under.

Ben headed to the "W" store, which, as usual, had a crowd of people waiting to get in. Ben briefly admired the elegant shop signage – a wizard's hat, cast in silver with the letter "W" imprinted on it – remembering the first time he'd set eyes upon the store. He felt the cash in his pocket. Ben wouldn't be able to buy many spells, as the place was so expensive, but it would be quick, easy and the choice was incredible.

Ben thought back to the exam, and quickly realised buying spells from the "W" store would be a big mistake. This was the perfect opportunity to demonstrate his ability in the Department of Trade. Ben immediately dismissed the "W" store from his mind. He knew exactly where he needed to go.

There were many alleyways leading off Taecia Square, and Ben took one of the more popular ones, which had a steady stream of people going in both directions. He set a quick pace and it wasn't long before he came upon exactly what he was looking for. The road opened up and stalls started appearing either side. Up ahead, a banner floated above the road, which read "Chief Biglot's Magic Market: Deals Guaranteed!"

Ben smiled. When they said "deals guaranteed", they generally meant for the seller, who would do all in his considerable power to extract as much money from the hapless buyer as possible. Chief Biglot was a prominent dwarf lord, and this was his market. Dwarves were the best hagglers, bargain hunters and salesmen in the Unseen Kingdoms, and Chief Biglot hired a hundred of the best to sell his wares. Striking a deal with one of his salesmen was like going into battle. There were deals to be had, but you had to be good – very good.

Ben had never been here himself but had read a lot about it when studying in Trade. He knew a few friends who had come here and somehow spent all their money with nothing to show for it. But if Ben could get a few good spells and avoid getting completely ripped off, he was sure he would score well with the Department of Trade. On the other hand, if he ended up spending more on a spell than at the "W" store, things could go sour very quickly.

Ben walked slowly, watching the masters in action. The sound of dwarves advertising their wares in deep, throaty voices, coupled with the frequent, often argumentative haggling, filled the air like a wall of noise.

"Staffs of Levitation, 50% off until 3pm today! Only five left!"

"Heat-proof spell pouches, three for the price of two."

"Largest variety of air spells here!"

Ben pulled out a list of spells he figured he'd need, arranged in order of importance. Could he get everything for just two hundred pounds? Ben glanced at his watch. It was 11:30am. He would give himself an hour, no more, to get everything.

Ben rubbed his hands together and, like a fighter going into battle, joined the fray.

Last year, Ben ran a national half-marathon in the heat of summer and finished in the top ten for his age group. That, it turns out, was a walk in the park compared to the hour he spent buying spells. If it wasn't for his training in the Department of Trade, he would have lost all his money in the first ten minutes. But he had studied dwarf salesmen extensively and knew many of their tricks and how to deal with them. *Never show any sign of fear or fragility; don't be afraid to walk away; never accept their first three offers; ask to see proof of any claims they make; never tell them how much you have to spend.* There were many other rules, but those were the ones that saved Ben this morning. After an hour of intense bargaining and sweating, he emerged with almost everything he had on his list, with twenty pounds still in hand.

Ben stumbled back to Taecia Square with his purchases and allowed himself a fifteen-minute break at a café while he downed some lunch and got his breath back. He tucked into a chicken baguette, surveying the crowded square. Somewhere here was an Institute examiner, watching and assessing his every move, most likely invisible. Ben considered his work so far. It was just past midday and he had demonstrated his ability in the Trade and Scholar departments. That still left Spellsword, Warden and Diplomacy.

Once more feeling the time constraint, Ben finished up his lunch and headed on his way. His next destination was the Dragonway. Ben stood impatiently on the platform, and was glad when his dragon turned up after just five minutes. The journey took a little longer than normal, for instead of stopping at Croydon, he was heading into London. Ben spent the time studying the sheets of paper he had taken from Grignak's file, gleaning every last bit of information he could.

It felt strange not getting off when the dragon stopped at Croydon and, when they continued into the tunnel, Ben felt a little buzz of excitement, going into the unknown. After another fifteen minutes, the dragon arrived in London. Despite having been to the Croydon station every day for the past several weeks, the London station took his breath away. There were five platforms, instead of just one. The ceiling was impossibly high and had a faint curve, creating a dome-like effect. Thousands of twinkling lights shone down on a station that was both more modern and yet vastly older and grander than the Croydon one he was used to. Amid the smoke and roars from the dragons was the chatter of voices, hurried footsteps and occasional whistle from the conductors. The majority of people were human, but there was a fair proportion of dwarves, elves and smaller creatures. Ben felt like a tourist all over again as he stepped off the carriage and meandered his way along the platform. He saw two signs: one directing him to the Institute's London headquarters; the other to London Victoria Underground

Station. As tempted as Ben was to visit the Institute's headquarters in London, Ben, like many others, followed the sign to the Underground.

The security was both larger and more streamlined than Croydon's slightly archaic system. As Ben was an Institute apprentice, they let him keep his spell pouches, though he was instructed to "turn off" the flashing diamond above his shoulder – something he had completely forgotten about. Soon he was walking among a group of people down a torch-lit passageway, which led all the way to the lift. Unlike the one in Croydon, this lift contained no seats. Ben quickly grabbed onto a handle bar, but he needn't have held on so tightly, as the lift accelerated far more smoothly than the Croydon one. They travelled from what seemed like the Earth's core until the lift finally slowed and came to a gentle stop. With a ding, the doors opened, and everyone started filing out.

Ben couldn't help staring. They were bang in the middle of the London Victoria Underground station, right near the escalators that went up to the main train station. Regular people passed the lift by without giving it a second glance. Ben remembered passing this exact lift several times himself, but he could never be bothered to take it, as it always seemed quicker and easier to take the escalator. With a smile and a shake of the head, Ben joined the London throng and headed up to the main train station.

Ben weaved through the crowd until he arrived at the huge train timetable that hung from the ceiling, just in front of the platforms. There it was: platform nineteen – Lampton Green, leaving in three minutes. He made the train by the skin of his teeth and searched for the emptiest carriage he could find. Being early afternoon, most of the commuters had already gone to work, so there were plenty of empty seats. After the train was safely on its way, Ben took a surreptitious look around, and took out the necklace. It was an elegant thing, though perhaps suited more to a girl's taste, and not something he would ordinarily wear, but fashion was the last thing on his mind right now. He needed the necklace to track down Grignak. He put the necklace on and tucked it underneath his top so it wouldn't show.

He felt a presence immediately, albeit a minuscule one, right at the edge of his mind. Ben closed his eyes and focused. Relaxing was key, he remembered from his Warden training. Let the perceptions come. A blurred image flashed before him of a young boy wearing rough clothes, walking past an old library. The picture made Ben jerk and he immediately lost it. Taking a calming breath, he relaxed again, but it still took several minutes before the image returned. Ben studied the boy: greasy hair; hooked nose; crooked teeth; ragged jeans. He was scrawny but walked with a confidence that suggested a wiry strength beneath his rags.

Sight was the easiest perception to obtain through the necklace, but what he really needed was distance and orientation. How far away was the target? Where exactly in Lampton Green was he? Ben took another calming breath, swallowing his impatience.

But the journey was not a long one and Ben was still trying to get the goblin's exact destination by the time he reached Lampton Green station. Ben disembarked and walked slowly down the platform, concentrating so hard on the necklace he nearly ran into an elderly couple, and then received a dirty look from a mum as he almost knocked her child over.

This was no good. Clearly walking and concentrating on the necklace was a step too far. He hated to waste time, but there was nothing for it – he needed to sit down. Ben found a small coffee shop within the station. He bought a water, picked up a free newspaper and sat down. While pretending to read the paper, he re-doubled his efforts to pinpoint the location of Grignak. He got a couple of peculiar looks, and realised his face had become rigid and his tongue was sticking out, but he didn't care. He was getting closer, he could feel it. The pictures were now coming through crystal clear. He saw the boy walking past a bank, heading up a hill. Ben re-doubled his efforts and felt a small bead of sweat trickle down his forehead.

It came to him in a flash of knowingness. Grignak was one and a half miles northeast. Ben jumped up so quickly the old lady sitting next to him almost spilt her coffee. With a quick apology, he left the train station and headed up a small road that led into the heart of the village. Ben glanced at his watch. It had just passed two o'clock. He quickened his pace, winding his way past the occasional shopper and the more frequent parent pushing their buggy, hogging the pavement. He stopped briefly as the road converged with the main village road that lay on a hill. Ben focused again on the necklace; this time the directions came easily. The goblin was now less than a mile away.

Ben set off up the hill. Every minute he re-focused on the necklace and found that he was slowly gaining on his target. The village centre was little more than a half-mile strip and it soon gave way to a surprisingly large park, complete with woods and a small duck-filled lake. There were paths, winding their way through the park, populated by the occasional walker, jogger, or mum pushing their buggy.

Ben stopped to get his breath back and re-check his proximity to his target. The necklace pulsed suddenly, giving off a warmth that tingled his neck. The pulsing continued, slowly, rhythmically.

He was close. Really close.

Ben squinted, recalling the goblin's disguise.

There! A small ice-cream parlour stood less than a hundred yards away, busy serving mums and kids. Off to the side was a scrawny boy, devouring a large Häagen-Dazs tub of ice-cream none too elegantly. Ben was surprised at how young he looked, no more than fourteen or fifteen.

Now that he was this close, Ben suddenly felt himself hesitate. He needed a plan. Normally he had plans coming out of his ears, but this was different. One false move and he could blow the whole exam. Ben needed to come up with something while Grignak the boy/goblin was pre-occupied eating his ice-cream. At the rate he was eating, he would be done soon, and when he was finished, he would undoubtedly move on, making things more difficult.

Ben thought quickly, trying to ignore the time crunch. In an ideal world, he would simply go up to the goblin, inform him that he had broken the law by leaving London, and order him back to the Institute. He was fairly confident that with his spells, he could deal with any retaliation from the goblin, though things would get more complicated if he made a scene. But if Ben went down that route, he would fail miserably in the Department of Diplomacy. That left only one option: he would have to try to talk the goblin into turning himself in.

Taking a deep, calming breath, Ben walked casually over to the ice-cream stand, careful to avoid eye contact with Grignak. He stopped just yards from the goblin, but forced attention onto the list of ice-creams.

"What can I get you?" the ice-cream man asked in a friendly voice.

"I'll have the Orange Fruitie," Ben said, going for the cheapest option out of habit.

Ben ordered the lolly in part to create a relaxed, non-threatening atmosphere. *Street goblins are suspicious by nature and, unless you handle them carefully, are likely to bolt.* Ben had learned that by heart.

Grignak had a long finger in the tub and was scraping up the last vestiges of ice-cream when Ben approached him. Though he looked calm, Ben's heart was thumping. *Here we go.*

— Chapter Twenty-five —
Troublesome Street Goblins

"Hello, Grignak," Ben said, in a casual, almost friendly tone.

Grignak looked up sharply, his finger stopping halfway to his mouth.

"Who are you?" Grignak asked, in an unfriendly voice that was softened by the fact that his disguise was a boy yet to hit puberty.

"My name is Ben Greenwood. I work for the Royal Institute of Magic."

Ben instantly regretted the words "Royal Institute of Magic"; they made Grignak flinch.

"I ain't done nothing wrong," Grignak said, glancing around nervously. Surely he wasn't preparing to bolt already? Ben tensed himself, just in case.

"Nothing serious," Ben agreed. *Keep your voice mild.* "However, as you are no doubt aware, you were supposed to stay in London."

"Says who?" Grignak challenged.

Ben was prepared for Grignak's constant back-lashing, having read that street goblins had a penchant for it.

"Say the laws of the Unseen Kingdoms, including Prith, your home country. You even signed such an agreement when you entered London, I believe."

Grignak had no immediate response to that. Instead, he threw his ice-cream in the bin, the little spoon missing and falling onto the floor.

"Couldn't stay in London," Grignak muttered. "Weren't safe no more."

"Why not?"

"Work became dangerous; too much risk for Grignak."

Ben struggled to recall what Grignak did for work. It was all in the file, but he must have read that part a little too quickly.

"If you were in danger, you should have contacted your Institute liaison officer," Ben said.

"Him?" Grignak said, spitting on the floor. "I did. He's useless. Didn't believe a word I said. Called me a liar."

"Why don't you try me?" Ben suggested. "I promise to listen to you fairly."

"Bit late for that now, innit?" Grignak said. "I've broken the law."

"Not necessarily," Ben said. "If you can provide us with evidence of another crime, we may be able to waive yours." Ben had no idea if this was true, and wished he had paid closer attention to the laws when studying Diplomacy. But the offer seemed to do the trick. Grignak became thoughtful.

"I got nowhere to go if I went home," Grignak said.

"Your brother," Ben said immediately, remembering Grignak's file again. "He would be happy to take you in."

"Hmm," Grignak said.

He was definitely thinking about it. Ben maintained a casual air, but inside he was praying the goblin took the bait. He didn't have many more cards to play.

"What if I refuse your offer?" Grignak asked. "What if I choose to remain here?"

"Then you will be arrested by the Institute," Ben said, his calm momentarily giving way to frustration. "Either way, you will be returning to the Unseen Kingdoms, peacefully or otherwise."

As soon as the words left his mouth, Ben knew he had made a terrible mistake. *Never threaten a street goblin during negotiations except when all else has failed.*

Grignak gave Ben a cruel smile, more reminiscent of a goblin than a human. "You think you can take me in by yourself? 'Cause I don't see any *real* Institute members around – know what I mean?"

"Let's not get ahead of ourselves," Ben said, desperately trying to backtrack.

Too late. Grignak spat at his feet, then turned, and bolted.

Ben cursed. He threw his ice-cream in the bin and gave chase.

Stupid. Stupid. Stupid! Ben cursed himself repeatedly as he ran. One wrong move in the negotiations and he had blown it, all because he had become impatient. How was that going to affect his Diplomacy score? No time to worry about that now; he had to catch that goblin before things got any worse.

Grignak was quick, but his legs were small, and Ben was able to slowly reel him in. The path wound through the centre of the park towards a cluster of trees, just big enough to constitute a small wood. If the goblin made it in there, Ben was in trouble. Street goblins, despite their name, were just as at home in the woods and could climb trees like monkeys. Straining his legs and lungs, Ben accelerated, until he was right on Grignak's heels. He took a running leap and tackled Grignak at the waist. They both hit the ground hard, rolling several times before coming to a painful halt on the tarmac.

Grignak's arms snaked out and tried to encircle Ben's neck. Grignak was strong for his size, but Ben was almost a head taller and, though the boy kicked and bucked, Ben slowly pinned him down.

"Stop moving!" Ben ordered. Grignak spat at him in response.

Ben reached into his pocket in search of a spell.

In that instance, Grignak's appearance suddenly melted. His form blurred and rippled; the clothes became tight as muscles formed, his skin turned green, and his face transformed into a teeth-gnashing, angry goblin. With a snarl, Grignak threw Ben and sent him sailing into the air. Ben managed to land smoothly and got quickly to his feet.

"That feels better!" Grignak said, in a typically nasal goblin-like voice. He stood, arms and legs apart, looking a completely different proposition from the scrawny boy Ben had tracked down. Ben eyed the goblin warily, but before he could decide what to do, the goblin turned and fled again, heading into the woods.

Ben was about to give chase when the sound of a cough and a strangled gasp came from his right. He turned, with a feeling of mounting dread. Just off the path were a couple of young boys with open mouths and expressions of such astonishment that they might have looked amusing in any other circumstance.

"That was insane," one of them said.

"Beyond insane," the other agreed. "How did that boy do that?"

"You can get incredible costumes these days," Ben said, giving them both a genuine smile. His hand went into his pocket and he extracted two spells, glad now that he had bought them. He threw one at each boy. They barely noticed, both still staring into the woods where the goblin had bolted. The moment the pellets hit them their eyes glazed over. They blinked, shook their heads, and then continued walking, as if the last minute's action had never happened. Ben took a quick look around, searching for anyone else who might have witnessed the scene, but thankfully there was nobody about. He tried not to think about what that little fiasco would do to his Warden score, and quickly discarded it from his mind.

Ben approached the woods warily. There was no point rushing in now that he had lost sight of the goblin. Grignak would be waiting at a place of his choosing, and would see Ben coming no matter what.

Sunlight filtered through the sparsely placed trees. The woods were alive with singing birds, flowers in bloom and leaves gently swaying in the wind, creating an atmosphere in stark contrast to Ben's tautly wound body. He had one hand in his pouch while he scanned the tree tops, which he figured was the most likely place Grignak would hide. The deeper into the woods he went, the more concerned he became that Grignak might jump him from behind, and several times he did a full circle, but he saw no sign of the goblin.

"I can smell your fear from here, Greenwood."

The voice came from above. There was a thump, and Grignak jumped down from the tree, landing dead ahead of him. He was smiling, if you could call it that, baring his sharp green teeth. In his right hand was a branch that Grignak had shaped into a club, complete with a large knotted head.

"Nope, that's the roses," Ben said, pointing to a bed of red flowers. "Nice, aren't they?"

Grignak adjusted his grip on the wooden club and narrowed his green eyes to slits. Ben stood, legs apart, spell at the ready. His hand was shaking a little inside his pocket. Ben had faced several simulated combat scenarios, but this was his first real life experience. No amount of training could have prepared him for the sweat-inducing, heart-shaking adrenaline rush that he was going through now.

Grignak charged with a roar. His speed and acceleration were frightening, but Ben was ready. He flung a spell into Grignak's chest. Grignak ducked, rolled, and then with incredible dexterity, continued running without losing momentum. An explosion came as the missed spell smashed into a tree, but Ben barely noticed it. He had another spell ready and threw it at Grignak, who was now so close Ben could smell him. He was too close to miss. The spell hit Grignak straight on the chest, stopping him in his tracks. Tendrils of ice started snaking round Grignak's body, creating a shell. Grignak roared with anger and the shell of ice cracked and shattered before it could fully form.

These spells weren't strong enough, Ben realised.

Grignak charged again. Ben played his last card. He threw another pellet at the goblin's face, and then jumped to the side to avoid the flailing club as it sailed past his head.

Ben watched, heart in mouth. The energy-sapping spell should render its victim lethargic and as easy to manipulate as putty, according to the dwarf who sold it to him. Grignak did look visibly weaker; his shoulders sagged, his eyes became slightly droopy, and the club seemed a little looser in his hand. But he certainly didn't look like soft putty, and when his eyes refocused, Ben saw plenty of determination left in there.

Grignak lifted his club and started forwards.

Ben pulled one of his few remaining pellets from his pouch, and squeezed it into the palm of his hand. A short sword materialised within his grip. As far as swords go, it was only marginally better than a stick of wood and would struggle to poke a hole through a piece of paper. But it was light, it was durable and, more importantly, it could take significant impact – perfect when faced with a goblin bearing a large wooden club.

Grignak came forwards with a blow to the head, which Ben parried, the impact jarring his hands. He managed to keep hold of his sword and followed it up with another block, before narrowly dodging a strike that would have sucked the air from his lungs.

Grignak came again, and Ben had to be at his most alert to place his sword in the right place to avoid his head getting pummelled. Again and again the goblin attacked, with Ben venturing only the occasional response. Though Ben was tempted to launch something more ambitious, Grignak was an experienced fighter and Ben was fairly certain any such move would end in disaster. Instead, he stuck to his initial strategy. With each attack Grignak made, he became that bit weaker, thanks to the effects of the energy-sapping spell. Soon Grignak was huffing and puffing, and was able to launch attacks only with a grimace of defiance.

Ben waited until he was sure the timing was right. Grignak came forwards, barely able to lift his club. Ben parried it easily and then went on the attack, launching a series of lightning strikes. Grignak, despite being exhausted, managed to parry and dodge the first two, before being caught cleanly on the temple by the third. The goblin went down on his knees and dropped his club, though he continued to stare up at Ben with a look of defiance and hatred.

Ben moved in and grabbed Grignak's wrists, meeting only weak resistance that he overcame easily. He put them behind the goblin's back and brought out another spell, which he pressed against the goblin's hands. Instantly handcuffs formed, chaining Grignak's wrists. Ben did the same with the goblin's ankles.

Grignak tried to bite Ben's arm, and he had to take a quick step back. The goblin stood up slowly, and made a motion to attack again, but Ben saw the fight go out of him. He had done it! Ben wiped his brow, which was wet with sweat and blood. Elation swelled his chest, but he forced it down. It wasn't over yet.

"I'm going to escort you back to the Institute," Ben said. "Should you cooperate, I will do what I can to make your punishment as lenient as possible. Try to escape, and I'll make your life hell. Am I clear?"

Grignak gave him another evil look, but nodded without argument.

"Good. Now, change back into your human disguise," Ben ordered.

Grignak's appearance faded and transformed. Within moments, the ugly, rough-clothed boy was back, looking a little worse for wear, still chained by the spell.

It was only when Ben marched Grignak through the village, back to the train station, that he realised how battered and bruised he felt. He was aching in all sorts of places; he was pretty sure he'd sprained his wrist, blocking Grignak's blows, and there were several mysterious patches of blood on his clothes. As quickly as he wanted to return to the Institute, he was almost glad when the still lethargic Grignak set a slow pace, for Ben doubted he could go much faster.

They attracted one or two looks, mainly because of their weary state rather than anything else. Ben had double-checked with the dwarf salesman who had sold him the handcuff spell that they would be invisible to the human eye.

Ben allowed Grignak to return to his natural goblin state when they reached the London Dragonway, and he proved no trouble on the journey back to Taecia. Ben checked his watch upon arrival. It was now 4:45pm, an hour and fifteen minutes before the exam's deadline. He noticed Grignak was sitting straighter, which meant the energy-sapping spell was finally wearing off. Ben focused as they stepped off the carriage and exited the station.

"Remember what I said," Ben said. "If you come peacefully, I'll do what I can to help. If not, it won't be pleasant."

"I've done that, haven't I?" Grignak said, with an accusing look.

"Almost, yes," Ben agreed, keeping his voice mild. He was careful not to show any weakness, but the truth was that if Grignak ran now, Ben wasn't sure if he'd have the energy to chase him.

They marched slowly up the hill. Several times Ben thought he saw Grignak twitch and Ben had to resist the urge to reach out and grab him. The great walls surrounding the Institute came into view, and Ben's mind started drifting to the common room, a nice comfy chair and a cup of tea. He shook himself. Stay focused!

They passed through the Institute's wall, and Ben put every last bit of energy focusing on Grignak, to make sure there were no last-second shenanigans. As he entered the front door he felt like a triathlon runner crossing the line, with a mixture of pure elation and utter exhaustion.

"Seven hours twenty-seven minutes," Dagmar said.

Ben hadn't even noticed the Master of Apprentices standing there. She tapped her watch and then took Grignak from him.

"You have completed the first grade exam," Dagmar continued. "The examiners will meet tonight and your results shall be given a week from now."

Ben nodded, too tired to care about the results at the moment. He just wanted to lie down. But before he could head up the stairs to the common room, he realised he had forgotten about his best friend.

"Any sign of Charlie?" Ben asked.

"Not yet."

Ben knew that Dagmar would know exactly where Charlie was and how he was doing, thanks to the examiners, but the chances of her sharing that information with him were beyond insignificant.

"You made it!"

Ben turned just in time to see Natalie running down the stairs. She flung her arms around him, and he almost collapsed.

"Oh my, I'm sorry," Natalie said, taking a step back, her hand going to her mouth. Her anxiety only increased the longer she looked at him. "Let's get you to the healing room."

Ben shook his head. "I want to wait for Charlie."

"Of course," Natalie said, as if it should have occurred to her. "Well, at least let me get you a cup of tea."

"And one of those custard buns," Ben said, with a tired smile.

Ben positioned himself at the end of the bottom step on the grand staircase, cup of tea and bun in hand, with a good view of the front entrance. Natalie sat with him most of the time, but Ben didn't feel like talking; he barely had enough energy to use his vocal cords.

Every ten minutes Ben checked his watch, and when 5:30pm came, that turned into every five. He noticed Dagmar, who had been waiting patiently by the entrance, was also now glancing at her watch. Was there a hint of concern in her expression? Ben hadn't thought about it much, and it only now occurred to him that she would want her apprentices to pass. If nothing else, her pride was at stake.

"He's cutting it tight, isn't he?" Natalie said, giving Ben an anxious look. It was now 5:45pm.

"He'll make it," Ben said, not entirely sure where his optimism was coming from. "Charlie would never fail an exam."

But at 5:50pm Ben wasn't so sure. He stood up and started pacing the reception area, his eyes constantly flicking to the entrance. *Come on, Charlie.* Ben had never thought about the prospect of continuing at the Institute without his friend. Natalie was great, but Charlie was Charlie. They did the commute together; they went home together; they confided in each other about everything; and there was an inherent bond and trust that he simply did not have with anyone else, except his parents.

"Where the hell are you, Charlie?" Ben muttered, an unexplainable anger surfacing.

"Patience, Mr. Greenwood," Dagmar said.

"Patience?" Ben said, glancing at his watch. "Unless my watch has sped up, he's only got two minutes left. It's 5:58pm."

"And here he is," Dagmar said, with a little smile.

Charlie staggered through the entrance in such a state that it made Ben look impeccably clean. His clothes were torn, his trousers were shredded, and there were strands of hay stuck to his body and hair. His skin looked tender and bruised and Ben spotted several open wounds. In his hand he held a large bird cage, and in that cage was a small pixie, buzzing around furiously, but clearly unable to escape.

"It's 5:59pm," Dagmar said, taking the bird cage and inspecting her watch. "You should give yourself a little more leeway in the future, Mr. Hornberger."

Charlie managed a flicker of a smile. "I like to live on the edge."

Then he collapsed in a heap on the floor.

— CHAPTER TWENTY-SIX —
The Secret Search

Charlie spent the night in the healing room and by the following morning he was back on his feet, though he still looked battered and bruised, with a nasty scar that ran across his right cheek.

The three of them were sitting in the common room, having just had muster. Most apprentices had either left for their morning chores or else to study. Ben and Charlie had the luxury of being excused from both until their exam results came in, next Monday. They could more or less do as they pleased until then, which was perfect timing, as they needed every last moment to search for the caves beneath the Institute. It was Tuesday and the solar eclipse was on Friday.

"You know what the ironic thing is?" Charlie said, sipping his tea. "I was actually doing quite well. My mission was to capture this lunatic, mentally unstable pixie that was causing mischief in London. I spent a lot of time researching this pixie and her life, as well as their culture, so that I would have the best chance possible of capturing her peacefully."

"I'm guessing it didn't go to plan?" Ben said.

"Actually, it did. I tracked the pixie and we had a good chat. It took about half an hour, but I managed to get her to willingly go into the cage. Everything was going swimmingly."

"So what happened?" Natalie asked.

"Well, everything had gone so well that I hadn't needed to use any force, so I hadn't been tested in the Department of Spellswords. To rectify that, the examiner threw a hungry imp my way. You know how well imps and pixies get along."

"Not great, I'm guessing," Ben said.

"Think elves and dwarves, then multiply their animosity by a hundred," Charlie said. "Anyway, I bumped into this imp on my way back to London Victoria station. I'm sure one of the examiners placed him there to test me. That's when all hell broke loose. The spells I purchased in Taecia Square were useless. I couldn't afford any good ones, and my attempt to bargain with the chap selling the spells was shot down. Of the ones I purchased, I only got a couple to actually work. In the end, it turned into a massive three-way brawl – me and the pixie against the imp. It wasn't pleasant."

Ben couldn't help laughing. "I wish someone had recorded that. You could have been an internet sensation."

"Very funny," Charlie said. "Just to make matters worse, I spotted at least half a dozen people who may have seen the imp in plain view and I didn't have enough spells to blank their memories."

"The Institute will clean that up," Natalie said.

"I'm sure they will, but it doesn't exactly bode well for my Warden score, does it?"

Neither Ben nor Natalie had a suitable reply.

"Let's talk about the cavern," Ben said, when Jake and Alan, a couple of Fours, left the common room, leaving them alone. "Where should we start? I've never seen anything below the ground floor."

"There are old dungeons beneath the Institute," Natalie said. "They are no longer used now, but they were housed in the basement."

"That's a start," Ben said, brightening. "How do we get there?"

"I've never been down there, but I think you access them from another entrance round the back of the Institute. Obviously that door is now locked and barred."

"Obviously," Charlie said. "Otherwise it would be too easy."

"Well, shall we check it out?" Ben said.

They had to wait until lunch as Natalie had to complete her morning chores. Ben and Charlie spent the remaining time in the library, looking for any mention of a cavern beneath the Institute.

"Any joy?" Natalie asked, when they told her what they'd been up to.

"Lots of interesting stuff, but nothing useful," Charlie said, and he proceeded to give Natalie a brief history lesson on the Institute dungeons, listing all the famous people they had housed and a lengthy explanation on why they were no longer used. Natalie did a good job of listening and an even better one of seeming interested, Ben thought, as she led them outside and round the back of the Institute. A small outbuilding, no more than a shed with an arched roof, was attached to the back of the grand Institute building, looking rather out of place.

"There it is," Natalie said.

The little building had no door. Inside was a staircase that led down to the basement and, presumably, the dungeon. Blocking the entrance to the dungeon was a stone door.

In front of that door stood Dagmar.

"Back!" Ben hissed, the moment he saw the Master of Apprentices.

They quickly hid behind the walls of the outbuilding. Ben poked his head around so he could see down the stairs.

"What on earth is she doing here?" Charlie whispered.

Very little, it seemed. Dagmar stood in front of the door, her hand feeling the stone and the bolts fastened across it. She turned suddenly, without warning, and Ben moved his head away just in time.

"We need to hide," Ben said, urgently. He spotted a large oak tree less than ten paces away and darted behind it. The trunk was so large that when Charlie and Natalie followed suit, there was enough space for all three of them.

Ben did a slow count to twenty before poking his head round the tree. Dagmar had gone. She must have walked the other way round the Institute. Nevertheless, they approached the stairs cautiously, and relaxed only when they verified she was truly gone.

The stairs were sturdy but well worn, and they descended them carefully, stopping at the bottom when they reached the bolted door. Ben tested his strength against it; the door didn't budge.

"Is there no other way in?" Ben asked.

"There may be, but I don't know about it," Natalie said.

"Well, we'll need to find one, because short of shooting some serious spells at this door, it's not going to budge."

"Do you think Dagmar was trying to get in?"

"I don't know, but I wish I did," Ben said.

Over the next few days, they had little time to think about Dagmar, instead focusing their energy searching for the cavern. It was tricky at times because they believed the cavern entrance would most likely be on the ground floor, which was always busy. There were plenty of doors that led off from the ground floor, but it was difficult to explore them without arousing suspicion. Ben managed it a couple of times, but he got caught by an Institute member who accused him of trying to sneak his way to the magic lifts, which were restricted to senior Institute members.

Tuesday became Wednesday and Ben started taking even greater risks, searching areas of the Institute he shouldn't be setting foot in for several years. On another day, he would have been mesmerised by what he saw, but right now he felt only a growing desperation. There was simply no passage or stairway that showed any sign of leading to the cavern. Ben became obsessed with finding it, and every waking minute was spent either searching or discussing where it could be.

By the time Thursday rolled round, Ben was certain he had searched everywhere he could physically gain access to, with no joy.

"I don't want to state the obvious, but we're running out of time," Charlie said.

The three of them were returning from Taecia Square, where Natalie had been instructed to pick up a new spellshooter from the "W" store on behalf of a prominent Institute member.

"We must be missing something," Ben said, slamming a fist into an open hand. "There has to be a passageway or a hidden door somewhere. We just have to keep looking."

Ben was fully aware how desperate he sounded, but he didn't care. If they couldn't find the forreck tomorrow, they would lose their one chance to get Elizabeth's Boots. The next solar eclipse didn't happen for six months. The dark elves could have launched a full-scale war by then.

"We'll find it," Natalie said, injecting her voice with a determination and certainty that lifted Ben's gloom. "Why don't Charlie and I head back to the library to see if we can discover anything more, while you keep searching?"

Ben couldn't think of anywhere to search that he'd not already looked, but he agreed with the plan; the alternative was to accept defeat, which was out of the question.

Charlie and Natalie headed up to the library, already chatting about some obscure reference to a book that might help. Ben watched them head up the stairs, and then surveyed the ground floor, hands on hips, for what felt like the millionth time. He mentally ran through each doorway and visualised what lay beyond. This was no good. He'd been everywhere, many places more than once. He had looked everywhere inside. What did that leave?

Outside.

Ben wandered outside the Institute, and decided to circle round the building again. He must have done it three dozen times in the last couple of days, yet he still felt a glimmer of irrational hope that maybe this time he would spot something.

The sky was blue and the sun's rays lightened his mood a little. He did a couple of circles around the Institute, looking for a sign of an opening, a crevice, a false stone – anything that might look suspicious. Again, he found nothing, and ended up by the little outbuilding.

Ben thought again of Dagmar. What had she been doing? Taking a quick glance around to make sure nobody was in sight, Ben descended the stairs again, stopping at the door. He placed a hand on the stone and slapped it. It was as solid as it looked. Ben bit his lip in frustration. They had tried a dozen different ways to open the door in the last few days without success. Had Dagmar been trying to work out how to open it as well? He recalled her staring at the door; she certainly hadn't been resorting to force.

Ben placed a hand on the stone, feeling its hard texture. It was the first time Ben had actually touched the door without the intention of breaking the thing down, and he was surprised by how cool it felt.

Something touched the edge of Ben's mind, making him jump. A faint consciousness. Ben gave a sudden intake of breath. It was the door; it felt *alive*. Ben thought of the lockers in the Institute, but this was different. The lockers were a magical race inhabiting the lockers. This door was a consciousness unto itself.

Ben ran his hand over each stone, touching softly, with a tenderness normally reserved for a pet. The further down the door he went, the stronger the consciousness became, until the door felt like a real person. Ben was on his hands and knees now, touching the stone at the base of the door, focusing on the consciousness, hoping for a sign or a signal.

Then he saw it.

An outline of a door within the door, so faint that unless he focused he lost sight of it. The inner door was no more than three feet high and fit underneath the bolt. Ben began searching for a handle of some sort, his face just inches from the door. It took him a moment; the handle was so well camouflaged it was something he could only feel, not see. Holding his breath, Ben turned the handle. There was a faint click, and the tiny door opened.

Darkness lay beyond, but just enough sunlight crept through to make out stairs. Lots of stairs.

— CHAPTER TWENTY-SEVEN —
Beneath the Institute

"A living door? Even by today's standards that's weird," Charlie said.

Ben had rushed into the library and practically dragged Charlie and Natalie outside, before revealing his discovery.

They were now loitering in the front courtyard with great impatience, waiting for an opportune moment to circle the Institute without being noticed. Draven and a couple of his Wardens were talking by the water fountain.

"Doesn't he have anything better to do?" Ben asked, tapping his foot impatiently.

Five painful minutes later, Draven finally walked – stomped might be a better word – back into the Institute and for a moment, at least, the courtyard was empty.

They walked quickly round to the back of the Institute and hurried to the little outbuilding. After a quick look around to make sure nobody was watching, they went down the steps and stopped at the stone door.

"Now what?" Charlie said.

Ben pressed a gentle hand against the stone. He felt the door's presence immediately, almost like touching a tree brimming with life.

"Touch there," Ben said, retreating his own hand.

Charlie did so, his face a mixture of curiosity and trepidation. After a moment he retreated his hand and shook his head.

"I don't feel anything," he said.

"Really? How's that possible? You're more sensitive than I am to these things."

Natalie extended her slender arm. "Let me try."

Her hand stayed on the door for even less time than Charlie's.

"Nothing for me either," she said.

Ben felt a moment of alarm. He touched it again himself, and once again felt its life pulsing through him, if anything, stronger than before.

"It's still there," Ben said, with a sigh of relief. "I don't understand how you're not feeling it."

"Maybe it's a Guardian thing," Natalie suggested.

Ben hadn't thought of that. Charlie clearly thought Natalie might be on to something, for his face lit up.

"That would make sense," Charlie said. "Maybe this is another one of those passages that only Guardians can access, just like the one that led to the common room."

"Well, let's see if I can still get it open," Ben said.

His hand went slowly down the door, feeling the texture of the stone, just like last time. And just like last time, the door's consciousness became more significant the further down he went. He got onto his hands and knees, feeling the stone, looking for the edges of the little door.

This time he saw it clearly. Even the handle, which he could previously detect only by touch, was visible. Ben turned it carefully. The door clicked, and opened. Ben turned round and grinned at Natalie and Charlie, whose excitement mirrored his own.

Inside was a set of stairs that descended steeply into an inky blackness. Ben crawled through the doorway and clambered onto the stairs. He stood up and grazed his head on the ceiling. The passageway was so narrow he could reach out and touch both walls with his hands. The air felt stale and it was cold enough to make him shiver. He went down a couple of steps, giving Charlie and Natalie enough room to squeeze in. Charlie shut the little door behind them and they were instantly plunged into darkness. Ben put his hand on the wall for fear of losing his balance.

"Sorry," Charlie said, his voice echoing from behind. "I don't suppose anyone brought a torch?"

"I did actually," Natalie said. She fired her spellshooter and a beam of light shone forth. The darkness was so intense that the light only penetrated a couple of steps, but it was enough for Ben to make his way slowly down. The stairs led them to a long, wide passageway with old torch lamps hanging from the walls, giving the place a dim, gloomy ambience.

"The dungeon," Charlie said softly.

At regular intervals along the passageway were prison cells, their doors ajar. Ben walked slowly, inspecting each cell. They were uniformly empty, save for one, which contained a pile of old bones. At the end of the passageway was a set of keys hanging from the wall; they looked like they were for the cell doors.

"Twenty cells," Natalie said. "Most in need of a good spring clean."

Ben surveyed the dungeon, hands on hips. "There's nothing here."

"I wouldn't expect there to be," Charlie said. "Lornor said the boots and the forreck were in a cavern, not a dungeon."

"So now what?"

"If there is a cavern underneath the Institute, there's a good chance it's connected to this dungeon. We just have to find it."

They spent the next hour inspecting every inch of the dungeon, searching for clues. Each cell looked as though it had been cleaned out before it had been abandoned. Ben even took to inspecting the walls of each cell, searching for a possible secret entrance to the cavern. Finally, the three of them sank down against the wall, exhausted.

"I was sure we'd find the cavern entrance here," Natalie said.

So had Ben. He had been so sure, he hadn't even considered that they might make it underneath the Institute and still fail. He wanted to get up and search the place again, but he knew it would be pointless.

Charlie's thoughtful face was in contrast to Ben's and Natalie's dejected ones. He was tapping a chubby finger against his lip.

"I think we're doing this wrong," Charlie said. "We've been stuck like this before and you, Ben, have always managed to get us through because of your unique position."

"That's right," Natalie said, sitting up straighter. "I completely forgot about that. As a Guardian, you're able to access hidden parts of the Institute."

Ben felt a glimmer of hope, but it didn't quite match Natalie's sudden exuberance. "Normally that happens when we hit a barrier or a wall that we can't get past. How would that work here? I can't go around feeling every inch of surface – we'd be here all week."

"Who says you always need a wall?" Charlie said. "Why don't you try it now and see what happens?"

"Try what?"

Charlie gave a vague wave. "You know, your Guardian thing, whatever it is you do that results in suddenly finding a hidden passageway."

"Right. Well, normally I spin around, tap my head three times and sacrifice a goat to Fortuna, the god of luck."

Charlie made a show of looking around. "We might have an issue with the goat."

"Guys, come on," Natalie said. "Really, Ben, is there nothing you can do? I know it's different from other times, but we're kind of desperate. In case you've forgotten, the solar eclipse is tomorrow."

"I haven't forgotten," Ben said. He got to his feet, and started pacing the dungeon slowly. Joking aside, the Guardian aspect was a good idea; it was how they got into the dungeon in the first place. Ben took a deep breath and closed his eyes. Where hadn't they looked? The answer came to him so suddenly his eyes jolted open.

The floor.

"What are you doing?" Charlie asked.

"Shh, let him concentrate."

Ben had got onto his hands and knees. He knew immediately he had done the right thing. A subtle vibration ran up his limbs, into his chest, making his hairs stand on end. He crawled forwards. The vibrations increased. He crawled a bit further, and they receded. Left? No. Right? Yes, the vibrations increased further. He crawled forwards again. It was slow, painstaking progress, but gradually he homed in on the floor slabs producing the greatest vibrations. It was here, somewhere – though he still wasn't sure what he was looking for. He was dimly aware that Charlie and Natalie were staring at him, but he blanked them out. Ben's eyes locked on the slabs – some were no bigger than a brick; others could have held a car. They were solid, unmoving, built by a master craftsman many centuries ago.

Ben wasn't sure how he spotted it, but he knew when his eyes ran over a small, perfectly square slab that this one was special. He put his hand on the centre of it, and gently pressed down.

There was a loud click, followed by the rumble of cogs moving.

Natalie screamed.

A giant slab was moving, creating a large black hole in the ground. Natalie was on that slab. She leapt to safety, landing next to a stunned Charlie.

Ben got up and hurried over to the hole, and the three of them peered into it. Blackness, total and complete. Natalie pointed her spellshooter into the hole, but the light was too weak to penetrate.

"You did it," Charlie said. "Now, any volunteers to jump into the black, bottomless pit?"

"I'll do it," Ben said.

"What a surprise."

"Be careful, Ben," Natalie said. "You have absolutely no idea how far the drop is."

Ben was very aware of that. Just looking into the blackness made his stomach do unpleasant things.

"This is obviously a way in," Ben said, trying to convince himself as much as anyone. "I can't see how they would make a drop that would kill someone."

Ben sat down so that his legs were dangling over the edge. It really was black down there; he felt like he was jumping into space. Several times he tried dropping down, but his body's natural desire to survive kept holding him back.

"Do you want me to push you?" Charlie asked, with a perfectly straight face.

"No, I'm fine."

Ben counted down in his head. Five. Four. Three. Two. One.

With a cry, he leapt off the edge, into the black hole. He extended his arms and bent his legs. The fall seemed to take forever, but it was only seconds before Ben saw the ground rise to meet him. He landed painfully and rolled, his knees absorbing most of the fall. The rock was hard beneath his body, scratching and bruising his exposed skin. He lay there for a moment, heart hammering, until his ragged breathing slowed. Then he stood up and dusted himself down. The fall had been less than ten feet. He could see the faces of Charlie and Natalie peering down, but from their anxious faces it was clear they couldn't see him.

"I'm fine!" he shouted up to them. Their expressions didn't alter; so they couldn't hear him either. Ben cursed. He would have to be quick, in order not to worry them. He appeared to be on some sort of ledge. There was a dim light that permeated the place, though Ben couldn't identify its source. Ben walked tentatively to the edge. The sight that greeted him took his breath away. It was a cavern so vast that it looked like an underground mountain range. Cliffs, rocks and caves descended as far as the eye could see. There were small plateaus at various points, providing brief breaks for anyone trying to climb down. Ben loved climbing. He used to seek out the biggest trees he could find and even belonged to a rock climbing club. But this was something else; this was a hundred times bigger than anything he'd ever encountered.

A sudden thump and a curse broke Ben's hypnotic gaze. He turned and saw Charlie lying flat on his back.

"Oh, that hurt!" he said, sitting up and rubbing his backside.

"What are you doing down here?" Ben asked, with surprise.

Charlie gave him an angry look. "I didn't have a choice, did I? You vanished, and you weren't responding to our calls. We had no idea what had happened to you."

Ben felt a sudden rush of gratitude towards Charlie, knowing just how dangerous that jump was. For all he knew, Ben had jumped to his death, and yet Charlie had still followed him.

"I'm sorry," Ben said. "I could hear you, but you couldn't hear me."

"That's inconvenient," Charlie said, standing up.

Ben realised the danger they were in. The opening above was too high to reach without assistance. If Natalie joined them, they would be in deep trouble.

"We need to get back up, quick," Ben said, urgently.

Too late. Natalie jumped, and landed with a good deal more grace than either Ben or Charlie.

"Oh, that wasn't too bad," she said, dusting her hands off. Then she spotted Ben's and Charlie's horrified looks. "What is it?"

"We can't get back up," Charlie said, his voice numb.

Natalie paled and looked up at the hole above her. She jumped with surprising height, but her hands were still a good two feet short of the ledge. She got her spellshooter out, and fired a pellet into her chest. Nothing happened. Magic, it seemed, didn't work down here.

"What's that?"

Charlie was pointing to a dark spot at the other end of the ledge. Whatever it was, it seemed to deflect light, and they couldn't make it out until they were almost upon it.

It was a rope, neatly curled. Ben picked it up. It felt soft in his hands, almost silk-like.

"Useful if we're going down, but not for going up," Ben said ruefully.

But Natalie snatched the rope from him with excitement.

"That might not be true," she said. She ran over to the hole, and threw one end of the rope upwards. The rope gained purchase from somewhere. To Ben's astonishment, when Natalie tugged it, the rope became taut, instead of falling back down.

"I knew it!" she said. "This is a magical rope. Someone must have left the rope down here, so they could get back up again."

"I wonder who," Ben mused.

Charlie tested the rope. "Who knows? Can we get out of here? I don't trust this rope."

As he was climbing up, Ben took one last glance back at the abyss. They would be back tomorrow.

— CHAPTER TWENTY-EIGHT —
Going Alone

Ben found sleep difficult that night; his mind clearly had no intention of taking a break. But, knowing how important rest could be, Ben forced himself to stay in bed as long as possible the following morning.

Breakfast too was important. Though he didn't feel like eating, he didn't know when his next meal would come and he needed the energy for the long climb down the cavern. His grandma had eaten all the eggs (though she had kindly left the shells scattered across the kitchen top), so Ben settled for a big bowl of corn flakes. He dipped his hand into his money box and was dismayed to find that he was down to his last twenty-pound note. Was he really that low? The Institute had been giving him a small weekly wage, but somehow he seemed to spend it all. Ben was starting to suspect that his grandma had found his hiding spot again. He would have to find another place for it.

Charlie was surprisingly lacking in his usual gear when Ben met him on the road outside the house.

"No backpack and sleeping bag?" Ben asked, with a playful nudge on the shoulder.

"I thought about it, but I have a feeling we'll either be in and out in short order, or we'll be dead."

"Full of optimism as always," Ben said, as they headed towards the Croydon headquarters.

Neither of them talked a great deal on their journey to the Institute. Partly because they didn't want to be overheard, and partly because they had already ironed out all the details yesterday. The solar eclipse would occur at 12:17pm and would last for roughly nine minutes. Their best chance of getting round the forreck would be in that time frame, but according to Lornor there was a two-hour window where the forreck would theoretically be weakened. Because they didn't know how long it would take to find the boots, their plan was to get into the cavern as early as possible.

It was one of those rare days where Ben barely noticed their arrival into Taecia or their walk up to the Institute. His legs were on automatic, his mind engrossed in every possibility that might befall them when they entered the cavern. He came back into the real world only when he heard Natalie's voice. They had passed the Institute walls and were approaching the water fountain. Natalie was talking to a couple of Threes, whose names Ben had forgotten. Both were guys and they were clearly trying to chat her up. Ben watched with amusement, Charlie less so, as Natalie eventually managed to excuse herself.

"Sorry about that," Natalie said, looking a little embarrassed and also slightly concerned, Ben was surprised to see. "I hope they don't report me."

"What do you mean?"

"I'm going to be skipping the morning's chores, and may also miss this afternoon's study period," Natalie said. "My plan had been to say that I wasn't feeling well, but they've just seen me looking perfectly healthy."

"They won't tell," Ben assured her. "That would ruin their chances of going out with you."

Natalie had the good grace to blush, but Ben knew she wasn't ignorant of her beauty and that he was probably right.

"Shall we get going?" Charlie asked, a little stiffly, clearly uncomfortable with the topic of conversation.

They had to wait twenty minutes for an opportune moment to sneak round the back of the Institute. Ben found the door within the door easily this time. They crawled through and walked silently down the stairs until they reached the dungeon. Ben took a little longer to locate the stone that triggered the trap door, for it was no longer in the same place. Despite knowing exactly how far down the jump was into the hole, Ben still felt a shot of adrenaline when he dropped off the ledge into the darkness. He landed hard, but managed to stay on his feet this time. Charlie landed with a bump and a roll, whereas Natalie landed smoothly.

Ben walked to the edge and stared down at the mighty cavern, dimly lit by a faint glow that came from somewhere above. There were rocks, crags and stalactites everywhere. Ben's trained eye picked the best place to start their descent.

"Climbing isn't my strong point," Charlie said, joining Ben at the edge.

"Natalie and I will help you," Ben said. He was starting to suspect that Natalie was a better climber than he was.

"What's our plan?" Charlie asked. "And please don't give me some simplistic answer. We're about to encounter an animal that can take down a dragon."

"According to Lornor, the forreck is most comfortable at the deepest level of the cavern," Ben said. "So we go down, until we can't go down any further."

"And then what?" Natalie asked.

"Once we are fairly certain we know where the forreck is, we wait for the solar eclipse, at 12:17pm. Then we approach with extreme caution."

"And if the forreck is still alive and kicking?"

"Then we retreat," Ben said reluctantly. "Let's hope that's not the case, otherwise we can say goodbye to Elizabeth's Boots."

"I like the plan," Natalie said. "It's 9:30am now, so that gives us nearly three hours to get down there."

Ben rubbed his hands together. "Let's get going."

Ben considered himself a good climber, but, as he had suspected, Natalie turned out to be even better. Ben could reach for unlikely holds and take reckless risks, but Natalie's balance was phenomenal and she could jump like a gazelle, leaping from one precipice to the next, while Ben and Charlie stared on in astonishment. Charlie tried gamely to keep up, but Ben and Natalie would often have to wait or help by pointing out holds. Ben was glad they had allocated so much time, because it was slow going, and the cavern seemed to have no end. Thoughts of the forreck and Elizabeth's Boots receded; all effort was focused on reaching the bottom of the cavern. A glance up and Ben was reminded how far they had come; their entrance point was no longer visible. Ben wasn't even sure if he remembered how to get back.

"What's that?"

They were taking a brief rest on a small ledge, and Charlie had wandered to the edge. He was pointing at something down below.

Ben and Natalie joined him, and instantly saw what he was talking about. A strange blue fog covered a plateau less than twenty feet below them

"Uh oh," Natalie said.

"I don't suppose that's a good 'uh oh'," Charlie said. "As in, uh oh, that weird blue fog will levitate us serenely to the bottom of this endless cavern."

"Not quite," Natalie said. "That blue fog is a spell cloud. They are used to defend an area because they can stay put for years without disappearing. When we enter that fog, we will trigger a spell."

"What's it doing here?" Ben asked.

"My guess is that Charlotte Rowe set up various defensive measures to stop people getting down to the bottom."

"What sort of spell do you think is in the spell cloud?" Charlie asked.

Natalie shrugged. "The possibilities are endless."

"Well, let's find out," Ben said. He picked up a stone, and threw it into the fog. A fireball, no bigger than a tennis ball, formed from nowhere and flew right into the stone, turning it into a black mess.

The three of them watched in stunned silence.

"Time to look for an alternate way down," Charlie said.

But after five minutes of searching, they saw no way round without losing a substantial amount of time.

"Better we lose time than our skin, surely?" Charlie said.

"I'd rather not lose either," Ben said. He bent down and picked up several stones. "I wonder what would happen if I did this."

He threw three stones, a fraction of a second between them. The first one attracted a fireball, but the moment the second stone entered the fog, the fireball diverted its path and hit the second stone, leaving the first one untouched. The third stone was hit by another fireball.

"See that!" Ben said, pointing with excitement at the blue fog.

"I saw two of the three stones get burnt to a crisp," Charlie said.

"That's right," Ben said, grinning. "The first one didn't get hit." He started searching for more stones and picking them up. "We can use these like submarines use counter-measures, to divert the fireballs away from us."

"That might work," Natalie said, and she joined Ben searching for stones.

"It's fraught with risk and has little chance of success," Charlie said. "Which means it's a typical Ben plan." He sighed and joined in the hunt for stones.

When their pockets were full, they started down the small cliff, approaching the blue fog slowly. Ben, who was the furthest down, stopped just a foot from the fog.

"The plateau is small," Ben said. "We should be able to run through it in a matter of seconds. Then there is the jump – do you think you can make it, Charlie?"

The jump in question was a five-foot gap at the end of the foggy plateau, which led to another huge rock and safety.

"I should be okay," Charlie said, his voice a little shaky. "So who goes first?"

"We go together," Ben said, staring grimly at the blue fog. "That will confuse it more, and I doubt it can produce enough fire balls to stop all of us. I will lead, as I think the person in front will attract the most. Are you both ready?"

"No," Charlie said, at the same time as Natalie said, "Yes."

"On three," Ben said. "One, two... three!"

Ben leapt off the cliff and dropped right into the blue fog. He hit the ground running. From the corner of his eye he saw the first fireball materialise and speed towards him, tinted blue from the fog. Ben threw a stone to the side of him. The fireball swerved, leaving a trail of smoke, and engulfed the stone. Even as it exploded, another fireball formed, but its target was elsewhere – Charlie or Natalie, Ben couldn't see who. The edge of the plateau was fast approaching, and Ben could see another fireball coming his way, but he didn't have time to divert it. He planted his foot firmly on the edge of the cliff and leapt. Something hot scorched his trailing leg and he gave a cry of pain. He lost momentum and only just cleared the gap, rolling and sliding on the new rock. He sat up, and was promptly knocked down again as Charlie rolled into him. He looked frazzled and wide-eyed, but unhurt.

"That wasn't so bad," Natalie said.

Ben hadn't seen her jump the gap, but from the looks of it she had sailed across serenely, and looked unharmed.

"Yes, let's do it again, shall we?" Charlie said, getting to his feet.

Ben rubbed his left thigh as he rose. His trousers were singed and the skin was red and tender.

"Ben, are you okay?" Natalie asked, with alarm.

"I'm fine," Ben said, grimacing. It stung badly, but he didn't want to make a scene. "Let's keep going. It's just passed 10:30am, which means we have less than two hours left."

Ben had a nasty feeling they would be seeing more spell clouds, and less than twenty minutes later his fear was realised. With time starting to become pressing, Ben was reluctant to let the spell clouds divert their course, but occasionally it was unavoidable, as it was when they encountered a pale yellow fog that instantly turned a thrown stone to ice, or the red fog that caused another stone to explode. Despite that, they made steady progress, climbing ever downwards, until they encountered the black fog. It floated within a small passage that was squeezed between two huge rocks.

"It looks thicker than the others," Charlie commented.

Ben threw a stone into the mist. Nothing happened.

"Doesn't seem too bad," Ben commented.

Natalie, however, was frowning. "If it's not doing anything, it must be a mind spell."

"What sort of mind spell?" Charlie asked.

"It could be anything that controls your emotions, thoughts or feelings."

"That doesn't sound pleasant," Charlie said.

"Makes a nice change to being blasted a thousand different ways, though," Ben said, throwing another stone into the fog just to make sure. Again, nothing happened. "You guys ready?"

It was hard to determine exactly how long the fog went on for within the passageway, but to Ben it didn't look like more than thirty feet – a quick sprint and they would be through in a matter of seconds. The passageway was too narrow for them to walk abreast, so Ben lined up first, followed by Charlie and then Natalie.

Ben wouldn't admit it to the others, but as he looked into the black fog, he was more concerned by it than any of the previous fogs they had encountered. Ben hated not being in control. The idea that a spell could affect him mentally gave him the shivers.

"Having second thoughts?" Charlie asked hopefully from behind, after Ben hadn't moved.

"No," Ben said. He took a deep breath, and stepped into the fog. The moment he did so, the fog shifted and swirled. Ben saw a shape form. The figure came forwards, and before Ben could react it collided with him. There was a sudden pressure in his head, and Ben felt a presence enter his mind – at least it tried to. It stopped on the threshold of his consciousness and stayed there, a floating malice, until Ben made it through the fog, whereupon it retreated and disappeared.

"Well, that wasn't too bad, though a little unpleasant," Ben said. He turned around.

Charlie and Natalie had yet to enter the fog.

"What's the hold up?" Ben asked. They weren't far away and his voice carried easily.

"How did you get through?" Charlie called back.

"What do you mean?" Ben asked, frowning. "Barely anything happened."

"Clearly not for you," Natalie said. "But the moment Charlie and I entered the fog, we suddenly had the strongest desire to turn around. Before we knew it, we ended up back here."

"Why did it not affect me? I'm not mentally stronger than you guys."

"I bet it's your Guardian status again," Charlie mused. "All these spells were set up by Charlotte Rowe. I reckon the only people she intended to enter were other Guardians."

Ben measured the distance. It really wasn't far. "Have you tried running? Maybe you'll get over here before the spell has time to kick in."

"Worth a go," Charlie said. He took a step back, and then charged into the mist at full pelt. He had taken no more than three steps into it when he suddenly did an about turn and ran back to Natalie as fast as he had entered.

"Nope," Charlie said, panting, hands on knees.

"It's really bizarre," Natalie added. "The moment I enter the fog, I suddenly think how terrible it would be if I made it across, and that it would be far better to stay on this side. I lose control of my mind, and since my mind controls my body, I'm totally helpless."

Ben ran a hand through his hair with an air of frustration. "There's no way after everything we've gone through that we're going to stop here."

Ben walked back through the fog, experiencing no more effects than his first time through, until he was with Charlie and Natalie again.

"Right. You might not want to get across, but you won't have much choice if I drag you with me," Ben said, a devilish smile on his lips.

"That might work," Natalie said.

"Unless it drives us insane," Charlie added.

"I think it would take a lot more to break a mind," Ben said. "As long as I can get you across promptly, you'll be fine."

"I didn't realise you had a degree in psychology."

"I think Ben's right," Natalie said, pursing her lips. "The key will be getting us over there quickly."

"Don't worry about that," Ben said, going through the motions of limbering up. "Right, who's first?"

"Me," Charlie said, somewhat reluctantly.

Ben placed his hands on Charlie's shoulders. "Let's go."

They managed a couple of steps into the mist before Charlie's eyes suddenly took on a distant, disorientated look. He slowed, and then stopped. Ben urged him forwards, but Charlie resisted. Ben changed his grip into a bear hug, and yanked Charlie forwards. Charlie instantly became a dead weight and fell to the floor, breathing softly, but clearly unconscious. With a curse about Charlie's weight, Ben grabbed him under the arms and pulled him through the fog. The distance seemed far greater when it involved dragging a body, especially one as rounded as Charlie's. Ben was breathing heavily by the time he exited the fog, and collapsed on the floor next to Charlie.

"Did we do it?" Charlie asked, sitting up suddenly. The dazed look had vanished and he appeared perfectly normal again.

"Just about," Ben said, hauling himself to his feet. "Now it's Natalie's turn."

Ben repeated the drill with Natalie. Though she was several inches taller than Charlie, she had a delicate, almost elf-like frame, and Ben was able to haul her through the mist with little difficulty.

"Let's hope there aren't too many more mind spells to contend with," Ben said, as he dusted himself off while Natalie recovered.

But to Ben's dismay, the mind spell clouds became increasingly frequent. One or two were nearly always in sight, and some of them were unavoidable. To make matters worse, the spells became increasingly powerful. Instead of falling unconscious while walking through the mist, Ben and Natalie were now actively trying to escape Ben's clutches by any means possible. When they reached the other side, they would apologise profusely (especially Natalie), but that didn't stop Ben gradually accumulating cuts, bruises and scratches as he battled with the oblivious Charlie and Natalie.

It was becoming exhausting, and not just for Ben. Despite Charlie and Natalie being completely unaware of their regular battles, they also felt the physical effects afterwards. Struggling for your life every five or ten minutes was tiring.

The other problem was time. Each fog they went through slowed their progress and, before Ben knew it, eleven o'clock had come and gone.

"This one looks nasty," Charlie said.

They had stopped in front of a steep tunnel that ran under a fallen rock. The black fog within the tunnel was so thick they could barely see its end.

"Looks like a hundred feet, at least," Ben said. "That's our biggest yet."

Ben prepared himself for yet another battle. "Okay, which of you extremely annoying people is first?"

Charlie was examining the fog closely. "This one seems different. Do you see the small particles floating in the mist?"

"I see them," Natalie said immediately.

It took Ben a moment, but he soon saw what Charlie was talking about – small specks of silver floating within the fog.

"What do you think that means?" Ben asked.

"I think it's bad news," Charlie said. "The mind spell clouds have become harder the deeper we travel. I bet this one is at a whole new level."

"How much worse can it get? You're already practically ripping my head off trying to escape."

"I don't know, but I think I should try it out to get a feel for it," Charlie said.

"Are you sure?" Natalie asked, frowning with worry.

Charlie nodded. "I think so. Ben, can you be close by in case you need to drag me out?"

Ben immediately stood by Charlie's side, close enough to reach him if needed.

Charlie puffed out his cheeks. "Okay, here goes."

Charlie stepped into the fog. For a moment, Ben thought nothing was going to happen. Charlie didn't turn into a crazed maniac with glazed eyes, intent on retreating back to safety. But just as Ben began to relax, Charlie's face scrunched up and he gave a cry of pain. He took another step forwards, and suddenly the cry of pain became one of agony. His hands went to his head, his eyes squeezed shut. Incredibly, Charlie took another step forwards. Blood started leaking from his ears, and Charlie fell to his knees. Ben grabbed him and hauled him out of the fog. Charlie collapsed on the floor, writhing around in pain, still screaming. Ben and Natalie watched helplessly. It was a full minute before Charlie's screams turned to groans, and the blood stopped flowing. Several more minutes passed before Charlie sat up, panting, his brow caked with sweat.

"Are you okay?" Natalie asked. She was bent down next to Charlie, her eyes full of worry.

"Give me a minute," Charlie said, in a strained voice. They waited patiently, and finally Charlie gave a sigh of relief and slowly got to his feet.

"What happened?" Ben asked.

"Pain," Charlie replied, staring at the fog. "Pain like I've not experienced before. Not mental pain – real physical pain. My head felt like it was going to explode. Had you not pulled me out, I think it would have."

Ben didn't respond. There was nothing to say. He knew from Charlie's demoralised face that his friend would not be able to face that pain again.

The problem was there was no way round.

Ben knew this might happen. The spell clouds were getting increasingly difficult to overcome and time was starting to worry him. There was only one solution, and it wasn't a pleasant one.

"I will go alone," Ben said.

The announcement caused a predictable uproar. Charlie's protests were half-hearted, but Natalie, who hadn't yet experienced the fog, was adamant.

"We're not leaving you," Natalie said. "Right, Charlie? Not when we're this close."

"Right," Charlie said, after a little pause, which caused Natalie to frown with surprise.

"Getting you both through the spell clouds is taking too long," Ben said, "and they are getting increasingly powerful.

Even if I got you both through this one, the next one could be even more difficult."

Natalie turned to Charlie. "Was it really that bad?"

Charlie looked beaten. "Yes. The pain – I could not face that again."

"We could double back. I saw another way down about ten minutes ago," Natalie said.

"We don't have the time, and we would still end up encountering increasingly powerful mind spell clouds like this one."

Natalie bit her lip. "I don't like it. We're a team."

"Normally," Ben said, his voice gentle, "but not in this instance."

Natalie looked ready to argue, but another look at Charlie and she changed her mind.

"We will wait for you here," Natalie said.

"I won't be long," Ben said. "We must be near the bottom by now."

"Good luck," Natalie said, coming forwards and giving him a hug. To Ben's surprise, Charlie did the same.

Ben turned and walked into the black fog, alone.

— CHAPTER TWENTY-NINE —
Revelations

It was strange being alone in this vast cavern. Ben hadn't appreciated the comfort and reassurance of friends until now. Between the three of them someone was nearly always talking, but now the only sound was that of his footsteps and slightly laboured breathing, as he descended as fast as he dared. Progress was far quicker now that he didn't have to drag Charlie and Natalie through each passing fog, and soon he had left his two friends far behind.

He checked his watch every fifteen minutes and resisted the urge to speed up when 11:30am came and went. He had already almost lost his grip several times and couldn't afford to be any more reckless.

Ben heard the noise as he was jumping onto yet another slab of rock. It was a faint echo from somewhere below. He paused. Had he imagined it? No, there it was again. A voice perhaps? It was too soft to tell.

Ben continued his downward climb, so intent on listening that he had several near accidents. Gradually the noise became louder and more distinct. Definitely a voice. Two voices even. Then a crashing noise – the sound of rock crashing against rock.

Curiosity overpowered his anxiety. Who could possibly be down here? Could it be another spell cloud, designed to scare him off? Ben could think of no other explanation.

He squeezed through a small gap in between a couple of stalagmites, and the noise suddenly exploded into full volume. There was a fight going on, Ben was sure of it, and it was happening right below him. Ben instinctively hit the ground. A sudden sickening feeling hit him. What if it was the forreck down there fighting someone? What if Lornor was wrong, or lying, and the forreck was unaffected by the eclipse?

Ben dragged himself forwards using his elbows until he reached the edge of the rock. He peered over and received the shock of his life.

Thirty feet below, at the very base of the cavern, were two combatants. One was a Shadowseeker, sword drawn, hand pulsing with energy, trying to get into a tunnel that cut into one of the walls. But a woman stood in front of the tunnel, spellshooter drawn, blocking his path.

It was Dagmar.

Ben's face paled, his mouth slowly opened, and for a moment he forgot to breathe. Questions threatened to explode out of his mouth, but they evaporated the moment the

Shadowseeker fired a purple bolt of energy at Dagmar; she deflected it with a shield that materialised from her spellshooter. The Shadowseeker leapt forwards, sword slicing through the air. Ben made a choking noise that was drowned out by a defiant growl from Dagmar. She shot a spell into her hand and a shining white sword materialised, which she used to block the Shadowseeker's blade. The Shadowseeker launched a series of blistering attacks, which incredibly Dagmar managed to parry, though Ben could tell from the strain on her face that she wouldn't last long.

Ben needed to act. Now. The thought that he might be ineffectual only briefly flitted through his mind. He flew down the cliff, ignoring the scrapes and cuts on the way, and jumped the last ten feet. Dagmar and the Shadowseeker were so engaged in combat they didn't notice his heavy landing. He dipped into his pocket, feeling for the last few remaining spells from his dad's pouch. The choice was limited, but he didn't need anything spectacular. He pulled out a white pellet, closed his eyes, and threw it hard onto the stone floor.

The flash of light was so powerful it made his eyes hurt even when shut. He heard Dagmar and the Shadowseeker cry out. Ben knew he had only seconds. He opened his eyes just a fraction and ran past the Shadowseeker so that he was standing side by side with Dagmar, the two of them now blocking the tunnel. He made it just in time; both Dagmar and the Shadowseeker were already recovering.

The Shadowseeker looked similar to the one he'd seen at Croydon HQ, but somehow darker, deadlier and bigger. He was bald and his face was filled with gold piercings. His eyes glowed purple.

"Ben Greenwood," the Shadowseeker said, in a deep, resonant voice that instantly reminded Ben of someone, though he couldn't think who. "I was wondering when you would turn up."

"Greenwood?" Dagmar, by contrast, clearly hadn't expected to see him. Her eyebrows threatened to jump off her head, and her haggard look was momentarily replaced with complete astonishment.

"Ms. Borovich, what are you doing here?" Ben asked, his eyes trained on the Shadowseeker.

"Never mind that. What are *you* doing here?" Dagmar asked. She seemed unable to compute that Ben was really standing next to her. "You need to leave, now. I will distract him."

"Oh, nobody is going anywhere," the Shadowseeker said, in an almost casual tone. There was something really familiar about his arrogance, and calm, confident voice.

"Have we met before?" Ben asked. He wasn't expecting an answer, but it gave him time to think. It must be twelve o'clock now, just minutes from the perfect time to approach the forreck.

"Your powers of observation are marginally better than most humans," the Shadowseeker said. He seemed in no hurry – was he also waiting to get past the forreck?

"We have met several times, most recently at the Floating Prison, when I was trying to capture your parents. I failed and was summarily punished so severely that my previous body was no longer fit for living. But His Royal Highness, the prince, was kind enough to give me another chance, and here I am, in a functional, if somewhat inferior body to my last one."

Ben felt the blood drain from his face. "Elessar?"

"Good," Elessar said. "Now, as you are probably aware, time is pressing. It is almost time to pick up what I came for, which means I need you out the way."

"Move!" Dagmar ordered, but Ben ignored her.

Elessar raised a hand and fired a bolt of purple fire. Dagmar returned the fire and the two balls of energy met and exploded in mid-air. Elessar immediately fired another, this one a swirling boomerang-like object, and again Dagmar blocked, with a similar spell. This continued faster than Ben could track, with Elessar firing and Dagmar blocking. Each time, Elessar's spell managed to get closer to Dagmar before being repelled, and her face looked increasingly strained. Ben watched helplessly and fumbled in his pocket for a spell. But before he could begin to decide what to use, Elessar unleashed a diamond-like bullet that Dagmar couldn't get to in time. It hit her square in the chest and knocked her back into the stone wall. She slumped to the ground, groaning.

"Your turn, Ben Greenwood," Elessar said, with an oily smile that looked terrifying with his glowing purple eyes. "Don't worry, I remember how you deflected my spells in the past. We'll go for the more traditional method."

Elessar raised his sword and advanced, almost casually.

Ben knew without checking his pouch that there was only one spell that could help him. It was a spell he had been saving for just this sort of occasion. He pulled it from his pouch and squeezed the pellet against his hand. A blue-tinted sword materialised in his hand. This was no useless wooden stick like the spell he had cast on his exam. Ben could feel the perfectly balanced weight in his hands, and the edges gleamed with a sharpness that could probably cut the air. The moment his hand squeezed the hilt, Ben felt a powerful, almost pleasurable jolt in his mind and then throughout his body. Memories from his dad suddenly became accessible – memories about swordsmanship – tactics; technique; knowledge; experience. The sword, a foreigner just a moment ago, suddenly felt like an extension of his arm.

"Run, fool boy."

Ben glanced back. Dagmar had managed to sit up, her back to the wall, but she was in no state to do anything. Her spellshooter hung down in her limp hand, and her shirt was torn at the shoulder, revealing a strange birthmark that looked remarkably like a bird.

Ben frowned. That was significant, but he couldn't remember why. Natalie's voice came to him, almost unbidden.

"The only thing of interest I found was that Charlotte had a peculiar birthmark on her right shoulder shaped like a bird that seems to have passed down the generations. It could provide evidence of their heritage, if we ever found someone."

The shock of the revelation nearly cost Ben his life. Elessar came forwards and attacked. Ben brought his sword up just in time to deflect the strike. Elessar appeared in no hurry to end the fight; he was content to prod and probe, which was just as well, because Ben was having trouble focusing on the fight.

Dagmar was Charlotte Rowe's descendant.

Dagmar was a Guardian.

Suddenly, Dagmar's behaviour in the last couple of weeks started to make sense.

"I have been looking forward to this moment," Elessar said. "Ever since you embarrassed me at the Floating Prison, I have been thinking about how best I could gain retribution. Then I remembered how much you cared for your parents, and how hard you tried to find them."

Ben didn't reply, but his body stiffened. Elessar seemed more intent on talking than fighting, which suited Ben perfectly, as he was more intent on listening than blocking.

"As you know, we put considerable time and effort into capturing your parents," Elessar said. "Well, I am happy to report that two weeks ago, we finally caught up with your dear mother."

"No." Ben's voice was a choked whisper.

"Needless to say, there was much we wanted to know about Elizabeth's Armour," Elessar said, continuing in a conversational, almost jovial manner. "We have some of the finest torturers in the Unseen Kingdoms, and it wasn't long before your mother was singing to our tune."

Ben felt sick. His world spun and it took great effort to keep his sword aloft.

"She told us about Elizabeth's Boots, how they are protected by a forreck, and how they tried seeking help from Lornor Taren. As it turns out, we are a big client of his, and he was most obliging. He told us of the solar eclipse and that the last remaining forreck was likely beneath your Institute. It was just a matter of working out how to get down here, which, I admit, took a bit of work, as most passages were meant only for Guardians. Dagmar made things difficult. I think she knew what I was up to. I guessed she was a Guardian, and I knew all about you, of course, from your parents."

Ben was having difficulty taking everything in. Pictures of his mum being tortured kept floating before him.

"You didn't mention my dad," Ben said.

"Ah, yes. Your dad. His attempt at rescuing your mother was doomed from the start." Elessar's expression became slightly irritated. "Through some extreme good fortune, your father managed to penetrate King Suktar's palace and reach your mother. Of course, it was a suicidal mission. Once you are inside, there is no escaping. Your father decided to delay the inevitable by casting himself and your mother into the void. We wait for their return so we can finish the interrogation. It won't be long."

"The void?"

Elessar shook his head. "My apologies. With all this talking, I've lost track of time. I must be off."

And with that, Elessar attacked in earnest.

— CHAPTER THIRTY —

Elizabeth's Boots

If Ben hadn't gained his dad's knowledge through the spell, he would have been dead within seconds. Elessar's sword was a blur, but Ben blocked, parried and read Elessar's feints. The two of them danced all over the cavern floor. Occasionally Dagmar came into view, and Ben saw her watching in astonishment.

Elessar was no longer smiling; there was even a look of anger in those purple eyes. But Ben's sword arm was starting to tire, and his parries were starting to slow, some deflecting Elessar's blow by inches. Elessar could sense he was close and attacked with renewed ferocity.

Ben ducked another blow and felt the sword slice a few strands of hair. If he didn't change something rapidly, Ben knew he would be dead within minutes. He had one option left – an option that he knew his dad used rarely because of its risk.

Stepping inside Elessar's latest strike, Ben attacked. He gave it everything, his own sword cutting and slicing. Elessar retreated in surprise. Ben pressed forwards and with a flurry of moves his dad tried only in emergencies, he penetrated Elessar's defence and nicked the elf's slanted ear.

Elessar gave a cry of pain and annoyance. Ben tried to push home his advantage, but the pain seemed to energise Elessar, and he blocked everything Ben threw at him. After a moment of frenzied fighting, they both retreated a couple of steps, panting.

"You're almost spent," Elessar said, twirling his sword slowly, a triumphant smile playing across his lips.

Ben didn't answer; talking would only expend unnecessary energy. But beneath his grim, determined exterior was a growing desperation. Elessar was right. Ben was having trouble lifting his sword. How much longer could he go on? Three minutes? Five at the most? He glanced at Dagmar; she was sitting up, looking on with quiet desperation, clearly unable to help. Ben thought about running, but he couldn't abandon Dagmar or leave the boots at the mercy of Elessar. Even if he wanted to, he wouldn't be able to climb the rocks before Elessar caught him. There were the spells in his pouch, but there was nothing that would be of any use to him now.

"Goodbye, Ben Greenwood," Elessar said, and he came forwards again.

The sound of soft footsteps made Elessar pause. They were coming from the tunnel Dagmar had been trying to block. Charlie and Natalie? No, that wasn't possible.

Elessar was no longer focusing on Ben. His purple eyes were trained on the tunnel, his mouth open slightly, his empty hand glowing with energy.

The forreck emerged from the passageway and stopped, surveying the scene that greeted him with almost human-like intelligence.

"No," Elessar whispered, the blood draining from his face. He raised a hand, as if silently praying for the forreck to stop. Such was Elessar's shock that Ben was momentarily forgotten.

Ben took his sword and made one last attack. It was a last desperate attempt that he fully expected Elessar to block, even though he wasn't looking. But the sword reached Elessar's belly unopposed and sank deep into the elf's flesh.

Elessar groaned, and stared down at the sword, his hands gripping it feebly, too late realising his fatal mistake. Ben removed the sword and stepped back. Elessar fell to his knees, what life there was in those evil purple eyes slowly fading, and collapsed in a pool of his own blood.

Ben was breathing hard. His hands were sweaty, his heart thumping against his chest. He had just killed someone. A flurry of emotions washed through him – horror; regret; dread – but these all passed quickly. Killing an enemy, one as evil as Elessar, was no crime – quite the opposite, he kept telling himself.

"Ben. Do not move."

It was Dagmar's voice. He turned, and found that she had struggled to her feet and was staring hard at the forreck. The forreck, however, did not return her gaze. It was staring right at Ben.

Ben forgot all about Elessar.

The forreck was a thing of terrifying beauty. It was the size of a tiger, with the blackest fur Ben had ever seen that contrasted with the white stripe that zigzagged down its back and covered its tail. Its eyes were green and impossibly large. Though the forreck was standing still, Ben could feel the strength and power emanating from its limbs and in its poise.

With impeccable timing, Ben's sword spell disappeared with a blink, as did the vast knowledge on swordsmanship he had borrowed from his dad. Moments ago he knew twenty different types of ripostes; now he barely knew how to hold a sword. But that didn't concern him. Even with the sword and his dad's vast array of knowledge, Ben knew he would be ineffectual against a forreck.

The forreck still hadn't moved; it was surveying him, studying him. Ben wasn't sure whether to look it in the eye or to turn his gaze away in an act of submission.

His heart was hammering worse than at any time during the duel with Elessar. He wanted to wipe the sweat from his brow, but was afraid that any sudden movement might trigger the forreck into action.

"What should I do?" Ben asked, with forced calm.

"Don't move," Dagmar said. "Even if it comes towards you."

Even as Dagmar spoke, the forreck started a slow walk towards Ben. Its expression had changed, its green eyes narrowed.

"Uh oh," Ben said, resisting the overwhelming urge to run. "You want me to stand here while this killing machine eats me?"

"If it wants to eat you, running won't help," Dagmar said, her voice characteristically calm.

"So what can I do?"

"Nothing. You can do nothing against a forreck. Just stay still."

The forreck walked like a natural hunter, confident and unhurried. With every step it took, Ben's panic grew, until the forreck was almost within spitting distance.

"I'm not going to stand here while it bloody eats me," he said, his voice rising. Whatever Dagmar said, if the forreck attacked, Ben was going to run like hell.

"George!"

Dagmar's voice rang out with its accustomed authority, and Ben immediately looked around for the newcomer, but there was nobody about.

"George," Dagmar said again. "This is your master speaking. Come to me."

Ben could feel the forreck's breath on his face. He stood so still he was fairly certain even his heart had stopped. The forreck turned, almost lazily, towards Dagmar. For a full minute it kept flicking its gaze between the two of them. If Ben didn't know better, he would say the forreck was thinking, weighing his options. Eventually the forreck seemed to come to a decision and walked slowly over to Dagmar. Ben almost collapsed with relief, but his respite was temporary, as Dagmar was now in danger. The forreck stopped right in front of Dagmar, who Ben noticed was shaking just a fraction.

"I am your rightful owner," Dagmar said, somehow keeping her voice level despite the proximity of the forreck. "I am the descendent of the Lady Charlotte Rowe. You are in the company of allies, not enemies. Be at rest."

There was an eerie silence, as Dagmar and George, the forreck, faced off. The forreck gave a nod so subtle Ben might have imagined it, before curling himself up by Dagmar's feet. Dagmar reached out a hand and stroked George's forehead. He responded with a deep purring noise that sounded like a Ferrari in neutral.

"We're safe," Dagmar announced. She looked visibly shaken, but recovered quickly, a feat made all the more impressive given her physical state.

Ben walked slowly to the forreck. He wanted to pat George but had a change of heart when George turned his green eyes Ben's way.

"So much for Lornor's data about the solar eclipse."

"Actually, he was right," Dagmar said, her hand still on the forreck's forehead. "Had it not been a solar eclipse, George would have killed us before I had time to call him to heel." She motioned to Ben. "Come on, let's finish this."

Ben was still full of questions, but he followed Dagmar through the small tunnel. It was dark, but not long and they soon emerged into a magnificent cave that even rendered Dagmar speechless. It was domed, with a spectacular ceiling painted with an intricacy worthy of a grand church. The walls were incredibly smooth and looked as though they were made of marble, and the floor had been lovingly cobbled. In the centre of the room was a pedestal, and on top of it were Elizabeth's Boots. Crafted of silver, they looked as if they had just come from the forge and not as though they had been sitting underground for the past five hundred years.

Ben and Dagmar both stared at the boots, lost in wonder.

"Now what?" Ben asked in a soft voice.

"The boots are no longer safe here. I will need to move them elsewhere."

Ben got the feeling she had somewhere in mind, but felt now wasn't the time to ask. "Do you think George will be okay with that?"

Dagmar glanced at the forreck, who had followed them in.

"Yes, he has accepted me. I can feel it."

Dagmar walked slowly up to the pedestal and almost reverentially picked the boots up. George watched with interest, but made no move to intervene.

"They are both light and yet feel stronger than steel," Dagmar said. She stared at the boots, deep in thought. "I've put this off for too long."

Ben watched in surprise as Dagmar took her own shoes off and put the boots on. At first glance they looked a poor fit for Dagmar's huge feet, but she put them on without difficulty.

Dagmar closed her eyes and took a deep breath. "Such power. It's almost too much to bear.

"What sort of power do you feel?"

Dagmar opened her eyes, and properly scrutinised him for the first time since they had surprised each other in the cave. Ben could almost see the cogs turning inside her head, throwing out old conclusions and drawing new ones.

"How much do you know about Elizabeth's Armour?" Dagmar asked.

It wasn't an answer to Ben's question, but at least the conversation was finally going in the right direction.

"I know Queen Elizabeth entrusted a piece to each original director and that when Suktar comes back to power, the descendants entrusted with the Armour should re-unite to take him down."

"What piece was your family entrusted with?" Dagmar asked.

"The sword."

If Ben didn't know better, he would have thought Dagmar gave him an almost sympathetic look.

"Are you aware that Queen Elizabeth tasked you with re-uniting the Armour?"

"I am," Ben said. He frowned. "Though my parents are doing that. I am just trying to help."

"Your parents." Dagmar nodded. "That makes sense now. I always had a feeling they might have been Guardians, but I was confused because of you."

"What do you mean?"

"Only the youngest member of each family line is a true Guardian. The moment you were born, your parents relinquished that role."

"No," Ben said immediately. "That doesn't make sense. They have been searching for Elizabeth's Armour for the last two years. I know because they left me."

Dagmar started stroking George absently. "I know you are young, Ben, but I'm going to be up front with you because I believe you can handle it. Your parents, I believe, were searching for Elizabeth's Armour because they didn't want to burden you with the task."

"My parents," Ben said, with a sudden urgency. Elessar's words came floating back to him, making his blood freeze. "Elessar said they have been captured and have escaped into the void. Do you know what he was talking about?"

The word "void" produced a rare look of surprise and dismay in Dagmar, her lips pursing. "That... that is not good news. The void is a sort of underworld, filled with terrible monsters and daemons. It can only be accessed through the very strongest spells, which transport your mind there, while your body remains. Your mind forms a physical representation of your body in the void, enabling them to touch, see and feel. If they die in the void, they will not return to their bodies in the real world."

"Why would my parents go there?" Ben asked in horror.

"They must have been desperate. While in the void, their bodies here cannot be harmed."

"How can they get back?"

"I'm not entirely sure," Dagmar said. "Very little is known about the void because it is such a dangerous journey. We do have a few Scholars who have researched the topic. I will ask them as soon as we return to the Institute."

The more Ben thought about it, the sicker he felt. "Why would they even want to come back? They would just return to their bodies in Suktar's palace."

"That is correct."

Ben turned away, suddenly concerned that his emotions might get the better of him. He squeezed his eyes shut and had to take several deep breaths before he could face looking at Dagmar again.

"I am sorry," Dagmar said. Her expression couldn't be described as soft, but certainly it wasn't as stern as usual.

Ben nodded. He needed to change the subject. "Those times we saw you in the Institute, what were you doing?"

"Searching for the Shadowseeker. Once I realised he wasn't after you, I figured he must be after the boots. I tried to flush him out. We met a couple of times, but he always managed to slip away. Eventually I realised I couldn't risk the boots anymore and would have to move them. I waited for the solar eclipse, but so, it seems, did the Shadowseeker."

It was all coming together, but Ben's attention went back to Dagmar's words moments earlier, which suddenly seemed difficult to take in.

"So it's down to me to find the remaining pieces of Elizabeth's Armour and re-unite everyone?"

"It is," Dagmar said. "Do your parents have the sword?"

"I think so, but I don't know where it is, and I can't exactly ask them right now." He felt a sense of hopelessness engulf him. "Even if by some miracle I found all the Guardians and the pieces of the Armour, what do I do then?"

"We search out and destroy Suktar," Dagmar said.

"We?"

"You will not be alone. But as the bearer of the sword, your job will be to strike the blow that ends his life."

Ben ran a hand through his hair. "Great. So I have to kill him. What does everyone else do?"

"Each person will have a certain role, though I don't know what they are."

"What is your role?" Ben asked.

Dagmar glanced down at her boots. "My job is to get us to Suktar. He will not be easy to find."

Ben attempted to make sense of it all – his parents in some sort of underworld hell; finding Elizabeth's Armour; taking down Suktar. It was too much, even for him. Ben sat down on the floor. To his surprise, Dagmar sat down next to him, legs crossed, and George joined in, lying across the two of them, purring.

They sat there for some time, lost in their thoughts. Dagmar made no attempt to talk and Ben was content to let his mind drift for a while. Eventually, Ben started to relax and his mind cleared, bringing forth a new set of questions into view.

"You don't look like Charlotte," Ben said.

There were some similarities, such as Dagmar's diminutive size and flawless pale skin, but Charlotte was slender and petite, whereas Dagmar most certainly wasn't.

"How do you know what Charlotte looked like?" Dagmar asked.

"I saw her in an old memory spell my parents left me."

Ben expected his answer to prompt a dozen more questions from Dagmar, but she merely nodded, accepting his response as if it were perfectly reasonable.

"At some point down the family tree, one of Rowe's descendants married an Unseen. I have some dwarf blood in me," Dagmar said.

"Oh right. Well, that makes more sense," Ben said.

Dagmar stood up, pushing George off their laps. For a moment Ben thought his talk of her appearance might have caused offence, but her impassive face suggested otherwise.

"We should get going," Dagmar said, glancing towards the tunnel. "I presume Mr. Hornberger and Ms. Dyer came with you but got stuck somewhere?"

Ben leapt up. "Oh my god. Charlie and Natalie! They must still be waiting for me."

Dagmar had a silent word with George. Ben couldn't hear what was said, but the forreck sat himself back down and appeared content to remain behind. Ben and Dagmar began the journey back up the cavern. Dagmar proved a surprisingly able climber, despite her short, stocky build, and the two of them made good progress. The climb proved a welcome distraction, and both were content to limit the conversation to the climb.

It took less than half an hour before Ben recognised the thick black fog mist in the narrow tunnel that had foiled Charlie and Natalie. Ben found them sitting with their backs to the wall, talking quietly to each other. The looks on their faces when they saw him and Dagmar lightened Ben's mood.

"Ms. Borovich!" Natalie said, standing up, her hand covering her gaping mouth.

Charlie scratched his head. "How is this possible?"

Ben gave a tired smile. "I'll explain on the way up."

The climb was arduous, but the time passed quickly, with Ben giving a blow-by-blow account of everything that had happened.

"I wonder what the dark elves will do now," Charlie mused, as he looked for a hand grip.

"They will continue with their invasion plans," Dagmar said. "But I also think they will double their effort to find Elizabeth's Armour."

"Why, though?" Ben asked. He had reached the top of a large rock and was sitting down, waiting for the others. "If the Guardians are the only ones who can wield it properly, why doesn't he just kill us off? Surely that would be easier, knowing that the Armour is the only thing that threatens his immortality."

"There will be a reason," Dagmar said. "Suktar is a dark elf of incredible intelligence and cunning, as well as supreme power."

They kept talking (except Dagmar, who just listened) for the rest of the journey until they reached the little door and crawled through, back into the outside world. They had to shield their eyes as they emerged from the small outbuilding, the sunlight a stark contrast to the perpetual gloom they had experienced for the last few hours.

"It's 3:30pm," Charlie said, glancing at his watch. "Not bad timing. I don't know about you guys, but I could murder some food."

"I must get to work," Dagmar said. "People will be asking about me." She gave a nod to the three of them. "I will see you all Monday morning. Ben and Charlie, I will have your exam results then."

Ben slapped his forehead. "I completely forgot about them."

Dagmar raised an eyebrow. "Let's hope you have passed, otherwise you will have some difficulty fulfilling the task given to you by Her Majesty, Queen Elizabeth I."

Dagmar turned and left, her little legs striding so quickly it almost looked comical.

"Was she serious?" Ben asked, as he watched her go.

"She can't have been, though I didn't think she was capable of a joke."

"She wasn't serious," Natalie said, without a great deal of confidence. "Come on, let's go stuff our faces."

— CHAPTER THIRTY-ONE —
Unexpected Help

The weekend was possibly the slowest in history and Ben was genuinely concerned that Monday might not ever arrive. When he wasn't thinking of his parents, he was worrying over his exam results. Ben wasn't used to worrying, especially when it came to exams, but there was so much riding on this one. Surely Dagmar, a fellow Guardian, wouldn't stop him searching out the rest of Elizabeth's Armour? But knowing her, anything was possible.

To pass the time, Ben re-connected with some friends and spent most of the weekend playing football and video games. He was constantly texting Charlie, but their conversation was limited as Charlie was with his parents.

Sunday night seemed to contain a dozen extra hours, most of which Ben spent in bed, trying to get to sleep.

"Looks like you slept about as well as me," Charlie said with a yawn, when they met on the way to the Institute the following morning. "I've lost count of the number of times I've gone over the exam in my head, thinking about all the things I did wrong. I just hope my Diplomacy and Scholar scores counter my pathetic Trade and Spellsword performances."

"There's no point worrying about it now," Ben said, "We'll find out soon enough."

But Ben found it impossible to take his own advice and spent most of the journey evaluating and re-evaluating his own exam and trying to work out what his score might be.

It was business as usual at the Royal Institute of Magic. The ground floor was a hive of activity despite the early hour and as usual the lively atmosphere gave Ben a lift. Thankfully there was no indication that anyone knew what they had got up to last Friday.

"There's Draven," Charlie whispered, as they approached the stairs. He came down the staircase and passed them by, glancing their way for a second, before continuing his conversation with another Warden. To a stranger it might have sounded like he was arguing something, but Ben knew that was his default tone of voice.

"Did you see that?" Charlie said, looking back as Draven strode out of the Institute. "I didn't like the way he looked at us. That's bad news. He must know our exam results. We've failed for sure."

"Oh, put a sock in it," Ben said, without malice. "Let's get to muster and get this over with. The suspense is killing me."

Dagmar looked back to her old self, even down to the baton she held underneath her arm. The weariness had vanished and she stood with her back so straight it seemed to add a few valuable inches to her frame. She looked calm and unflustered, as if yesterday, or indeed the events of the last two weeks, had never happened. Her revitalised appearance did not go unnoticed by the apprentices, but Ben could understand why nobody saw fit to comment on it.

Muster proceeded with customary military speed. Ben, who normally listened to Dagmar's morning announcements with interest, found himself unable to concentrate and was relieved when Dagmar dismissed the apprentices for the morning.

"Mr. Greenwood, Mr. Hornberger," Dagmar said. "Come with me, please."

Ben and Charlie exchanged glances before following Dagmar, as she clomped her way down the hall, until they reached a door marked "Master of Apprentices". Dagmar opened it and beckoned Ben and Charlie through.

Ben wasn't surprised to find Dagmar's office a modest, functional one. On her desk were baskets, neatly stacked with papers. There were several large shelves lining both sides of the wall, filled with books and files that Ben was fairly certain were perfectly organised. Dagmar's only concession to extravagance was a large portrait of a pretty woman with steely brown eyes, with the Royal Institute of Magic in the background.

"Charlotte Rowe," Charlie whispered, glancing up at the portrait.

"That is correct," Dagmar said. She stood in front of her desk, facing them, and showed no sign that she was going to sit down. Ben wasn't sure he had ever seen Dagmar sit on a chair.

"I have your exam results," she said, with an abruptness that caught Ben off-guard. From her pocket she pulled out two small envelopes. She handed one to each of them. Ben took it, trying to read Dagmar's expression, but it was like trying to read a rock.

The envelope was written in flowing script and simply read "Ben Greenwood: Exam Results, First Grade". Ben broke the elaborate seal with a shaky finger and pulled forth a small piece of paper. He read the contents.

Name: Ben Greenwood
Exam: First Grade
Department Results:
Diplomacy: D
Scholar: C
Spellsword: A
Trade: A
Warden: B
Overall: B (pass)

Ben grinned and pumped his fist in a manner normally reserved for a last-minute victory in football. Relief and joy swept through him and he felt a weight lift from his shoulders.

"I passed!" Charlie said, staring at his paper in genuine disbelief. "I can't believe it, I was *sure* I had failed."

"Congratulations to you both," Dagmar said. Ben thought he saw a flicker of a smile, but it was gone in a flash. "I expect you to put in extra time and effort on those departments where you scored poorly."

"Of course," Ben said.

"You are permitted a break of up to two weeks before starting the second grade, but should you turn up any later, you will not be starting at all."

Dagmar's typically direct warning did little to quash Ben's or Charlie's elation.

"Now, on to other matters." Dagmar paused for a moment, her gaze going to the door, to make sure they were truly alone. "Elizabeth's Armour. Guardians. Your parents." She paused again, and Ben had a feeling that for once she wasn't quite sure what to say. "As the youngest member of the Greenwood family, it is your duty to find the other Guardians and re-unite everyone, bringing Elizabeth's Armour back together. There are five pieces. The boots we have; the sword we must hope your parents have safely hidden. Beyond that, you have three pieces, and their guardians, to find. Not an easy task, especially for one so young."

"I wouldn't say no to some help," Ben said. His flippant remark would normally have received a stern look, but not this time.

"I wish I could. However, as you know, Queen Elizabeth was very specific in not involving the Institute, and with good reason. There are a few important members who might become corrupt with the knowledge of Elizabeth's Armour, and I am too closely connected to those people."

"I understand," Ben said.

"I'm not finished," Dagmar said, raising an eyebrow. "While I cannot actively help you, that doesn't mean I can't provide advice and assistance. I have experience and resources within the Institute and the Unseen Kingdoms that you will need to have any chance of success."

"Thank you," Ben said. "What about my parents?"

"I suspect they will attempt to return from the void only once their bodies are safe," Dagmar said.

"Which is slightly tricky, given that they're in Suktar's palace. When will they be safe in there?"

"Once we rescue them, which we will do when we find Suktar. To do that, we need to have all the Guardians with their pieces of the Armour."

Ben's face creased with worry. "Will they survive in the void until then?"

"If it had been anyone other than your parents, I would have said no. But your father is an extremely resourceful man, and your mother is an exceptional Spellsword."

Dagmar's reassurance alleviated his concern, but brought forth another, more immediate problem.

"What is your plan for locating the next piece of the Armour and its Guardian?" Dagmar asked, reading Ben's mind.

"I don't have one, yet," Ben said, exchanging a look with Charlie. "But I will."

"No doubt," Dagmar said. "However, you may want to take this. I believe it will help."

Dagmar held out a photo, which Ben took, full of curiosity. "What is it?"

"That is your lead to the next Guardian, entrusted with Elizabeth's Helm."

"This?" Ben took another look at the photo. From anyone else Ben would have assumed this a joke, but not Dagmar.

"Let me see," Charlie said, grabbing the photo. His eyes widened to saucers. "Oh, you've got to be kidding."

"I do not kid, Mr. Hornberger," Dagmar said.

"No, of course not, sorry."

Ben took another look at the photo and smiled. This was going to be interesting.

THE END

FROM THE AUTHOR

Thank you for reading Royal Institute of Magic: The Shadowseeker - I hope you enjoyed it. I am busy working on book 3!

If you would like to stay in touch, please visit my website at **www.royalinstituteofmagic.com** where you can also sign up to the newsletter in order to receive information on upcoming releases, exclusive content, and free giveaways!

If you feel so inclined, I would also greatly appreciate it if you could write a little review on **Amazon.** It only takes a few minutes and gives other potential readers a better idea of what the book is like.

Writing can be a pretty lonely business, so it's always nice to hear from readers. Please feel free to get in touch at **victor@royalinstituteofmagic.com** and I'll reply within 24 hours - promise!

I look forward to hearing from you.

Regards,
- Victor

ABOUT THE AUTHOR

Victor Kloss was born in 1980 and lived his first five years in London, before moving to a small town in West Sussex. By day he builds websites, by night he writes (or tries to).

His love for Children's Fantasy stems from Enid Blyton, Tolkien, and recently, JK Rowling. His hobbies include football, golf, reading and taking walks with his wife and daughter.

Visit Victor's website at www.royalinstituteofmagic.com or contact him at victor@royalinstituteofmagic.com.

ALSO BY

Elizabeth's Legacy (Royal Institute of Magic, Book 1)
The Shadowseeker (Royal Institute of Magic, Book 2)

CPSIA information can be obtained
at www.ICGtesting.com
Printed in the USA
LVOW11s1750261117
557619LV00001B/123/P